Harvey laughed to himself in a sad way and rubbed his eyes. "You want me to help you with a list of things you won't disclose to me." He leaned forward and bit the skin around his thumb. "Classic."

"I would tell you on a need-to-know basis."

"This isn't going to be, like, riding-a-horse-bareback-down-the-beach, is it?"

I smiled and leaned in to him, only a few breaths between us. "No," I said. "No, it's not." Cancer would take away plenty. My hair, my body, my life. What I'd never realized, though, was that there was one privilege to dying: the right to live without consequence.

"I'm in." He said it like it was inevitable, like he could say no, but it wouldn't matter.

"You won't regret it."

"You have a plan, though, right?"

"I'm still working on the logistics."

"But—"

"Harvey," I said, my voice low. "Trust me."

I knew what this looked like. It looked like I was using Harvey. But here was the reality of the situation: the minute my life went from semipermanent to most likely temporary, I decided to latch on to everything in my world that had always been permanent, and for me, Harvey was so permanent he was concrete.

side effects may vary

Julie Murphy

Balzer + Bray
An Imprint of HarperCollins*Publishers*

To Mom for giving me this beautiful life,
and to Ian for sharing it with me

Balzer + Bray is an imprint of HarperCollins Publishers.

Side Effects May Vary
Copyright © 2014 by Julie Murphy

Library of Congress Cataloging-in-Publication Data
Murphy, Julie, date.
    Side effects may vary / Julie Murphy.
        p.   cm
    Summary: "Alice is ready to go out in a blaze of glory,
but then she discovers she's in remission from cancer and she
must deal with all of the mistakes she's made and the people
she's hurt"— Provided by publisher.
        ISBN 978-0-06-224537-3
        [1.   Leukemia—Fiction.   2.   Revenge—Fiction.
3. Interpersonal   relations—Fiction.   4.   Love—Fiction.
5. Friendship—Fiction.]   I. Title.
PZ7.M95352 Si   2014   2013009981
[Fic]—dc23   CIP
                                                        AC

Typography by Alison Klapthor
15 16 17 18 19   CG/RRDH   10 9 8 7 6 5 4 3 2 1
❖

First paperback edition, 2015

Alice.

Then

If ever my parents gave me a religion, it was the gospel of honesty. Babies don't come from storks, and my mom never dared to tell me that a flu shot would hurt her more than it would me. But even though we lived by the truth, there were some things I would never know how to say out loud. What I hadn't said for the last year was: *I miss Harvey.* I couldn't say it out loud, but that didn't stop it from being true. In the collection of my memories there was no specific moment that I was most fond of, a moment that defined this whisper of loss. Still, every time I thought of simple things like eating pizza on Friday night, Harvey was there. And now, he was not.

"Let's get out of here," someone whispered in my ear, tickling the hair at my neck. For the briefest moment, I wondered if it was Harvey.

I didn't turn, but flicked my eyes up to see the corner of Luke's lips in the reflection of the magnetic mirror on my locker door.

"I've got bio," I said, answering his silent question.

"I've got an idea."

I smiled and his arms twisted around my waist, like he'd

won me. I shook my head. "It's our first test review of the year. I can't miss it."

Luke pulled me to face him and slammed my locker door shut. "This weekend's our one year. I'm going to be out of town with the team, so I thought we could do something today. Please," he begged, his grin widening. It was true. One month into my sophomore year marked one year with Luke. Dropping his chin down into my shoulder, his lips pressed against my hair, he said, "Come on, Alice. Don't be like this. I said I was sorry. Laurel's trying to get to you. You know it's not true."

Laurel, a senior and Luke's ex-girlfriend, had cornered me in the bathroom three days ago. *He's a cheater,* she said. *If you're not sleeping with him, I can guarantee you that other girls are.* I'd skipped gym to ask Luke about it. He looked at me like he was about to cry; I couldn't tell if it was because he was scared of losing me or of getting caught. I wanted to believe him.

Luke was a junior and a year older than me. There were a lot of reasons why we'd started dating. I liked the way he nibbled on his knuckles when he was thinking and how he trimmed his hair every week—a blond fuzz that felt good against the tips of my fingers. He was funny, but only when he didn't mean to be. He didn't lie, not even when he'd gotten my birthday confused. My mom didn't like him. And Celeste—who was more enemy than friend and always foolish enough to want anything of mine—had a thing for him.

Tracing circles on the small of my back, he said, "You know homecoming's in a few weeks, right?"

Luke was one of the junior class representatives for homecoming court, and I'd teased him about it relentlessly. "Yeah, my mom was going to take me to buy a dress this weekend. Unless you decided to go with some other girl."

He sighed. "Let me know what color dress you get. I'll pick up a tie to match."

I nodded, smiling into his shoulder.

My mom never thought Luke was smart enough to date her daughter, and she wasn't too appreciative of his popular-jock status either. Actually, at home, my parents simply referred to him as "bro." Really, neither of them was a fan of any boys who weren't Harvey. But when I'd told Mom about homecoming, she'd immediately volunteered to drive me to the designer outlet mall on the way to Alton—the best shopping in a thirty-mile radius.

I watched the crowd of students brush past as Luke stayed there with his lips on my neck, trying to arouse something, but all I felt was the ache for Harvey whirring in my chest.

He almost didn't see me. His head bobbed above most of the crowd, his brown hair curling at his neck, long overdue for a haircut. Every time I saw Harvey, he was taller and broader than I'd remembered. Still, though, I saw the little boy with eyes too big for his face who I'd bossed around since I could string together enough words to make a sentence. Our moms had always been best friends in a way that felt more like family. We'd grown up together because we didn't have much of a choice in the matter. There was never that horrible getting-to-know-you phase most everyone had to go through.

Then we'd drifted. High school did that to you, turned you into pieces of driftwood. And the parts of you that you'd tried to keep in one piece became the property of the wind and the water, sending those dear pieces everywhere you were not. He'd gone right; I'd gone left.

"Cut the PDA!" called Coach Wolfen as he jogged past us through the door of the teachers' lounge.

Harvey turned back and saw me there, pressed up against Luke. I couldn't be sure—but his shoulders seemed to fall a little before he headed in the other direction. There was this part of me that liked seeing that.

Luke groaned. "Yeah, yeah."

My eyes searched past Luke, but Harvey was already gone. "Let's go."

Once we'd cleared the school parking lot, Luke asked, "Cool if we go to your place?"

"Yeah." Both my parents were at work.

As he drove along my street, Luke turned down the music. "You go in," he said. "I'll leave the car around the corner and meet you back here." He slid the gearshift into park.

I unbuckled my seat belt, but before I opened the car door, he reached for my hand, his grip loose at first, then tightening. He leaned over and studied my face, his brow wrinkled like he wanted to see every detail of me, like he might find some kind of answer he'd been searching for. Luke touched his hand to my cheek and kissed me. I leaned into him, his hands traveling a familiar path through my hair.

"I brought condoms," he whispered. "Maybe we could go to your room?"

My back stiffened a little. I wasn't the type of girl who wanted to plan out her first time with candles and rose petals or any of that. But, I don't know. I didn't expect it to happen right that moment, on a Tuesday afternoon while my parents were at work. It was weird to think about having sex in my bedroom, the room that still had the floral border I'd begged my parents for in second grade.

I closed my eyes for a moment, unable to concentrate, like focusing on anything would make me pass out.

"Are you okay?"

"Yeah. Yeah, I'm fine," I said. "Just got dizzy for a second."

He pulled my hands in, holding them inside of his. "Don't be nervous."

I nodded. "I'll wait for you by the front door."

On the porch, I patted my pockets. My keys. They were in my backpack, in Luke's car. He'd already driven off. I walked around the side of the house and through the gate to the backyard. The patio door might be unlocked. My mom was weird about leaving spare keys out. She'd rather me go to a neighbor's house or call Harvey's mom, Natalie, but my dad was horrible about locking the door.

Out of the corner of my eye, I saw something move from behind the blinds of my parents' bedroom.

Maybe it was instinct or whatever, but I hit the ground.

Rising into a squat, I peeked over the bushes. I waited for the figure to pass again. There hadn't been any cars in the driveway. My heart slapped against my chest and my breath quickened.

He wore a button-up shirt and boxers and dress socks. I covered my mouth, so as not to make a sound. What kind of pervert breaks into other people's homes and gets undressed? I reached for my cell phone, but it was in Luke's car with my keys.

Then I saw my mom. She pulled the duvet cover at the end of the bed, straightening the edges. She wore the same navy blue pencil skirt I'd seen her in that morning and her bra, which was a total mom bra: beige with a floral pattern and no padding. The man. He looked a little bit younger than her, but I could see his light brown hair fading into gray at his temples.

I'd heard in class once that our society has become so accustomed to violence that when we actually do witness real gore and brutality, we're unable to differentiate between what's real and what's not. This was how that moment felt for me. Truth and fiction were one big blur. I'd seen infidelity on television and in movies. I'd seen it so many times. This exact scenario. Daytime affair while the other spouse was at work, a working relationship gone too far. My breaths came fast and hitched, unable to catch their rhythm. I curled my fingers into fists to stop them from trembling.

Who was this man? Maybe he had a family. He and my mom might work together. Or he could be her client. This could be a one-time thing. Or it might not. This might be the beginning. She could be leaving us for him. Anger slipped through my veins.

He held my mom's hips and kissed her shoulder before zipping up the back of her skirt. The pale stretch marks across her belly shone against her skin. She had a little pooch, but it didn't look like she was bothered by it even though it always made her groan in fitting rooms.

She looked happy.

I wanted to be angry. But I was sad. Sad that she couldn't feel that way with us—me and Dad. It was like she was cheating on *both* of us inside *our* home. I wish I had better, smarter words, but all I wanted was to throw a rock through the window and scream *Fuck you, Mom*.

The fence creaked.

"Hey," said Luke. "What's going on?" He was trying to be nice, but I could see that he was anxious. Like a little boy whose baseball game was about to get rained out. He craned his neck. "Is someone in your house? Is that your . . . wait, that's not your dad, is—"

I stood and pushed back on his shoulders. I wouldn't let him know about this. No one could know about this. "It's no one. Just some cleaning people that come once a month. Let's go. What about your house?"

"My mom doesn't work, remember?" He dug his car keys out of his front pocket. "What about Craven's Park?"

I felt sick, like physically sick. "Can you take me back to school?"

He sighed. "Fine. Let's go."

I followed Luke down the sidewalk back to his car,

maintaining the distance between us. I wanted to feel bad for leading him on and letting him think that we might finally do it. But now, all I could think of was my mom smiling, happy. Broken families were such a commonality, almost to the point of being cliché. I think I went to school with more kids who had stepmoms and stepdads than I did with kids whose biological parents were still married. Infidelity. Divorce. That was the new normal. But just because it was normal didn't make the cut any less deep.

Luke stopped a few steps ahead of me. "Are you okay?" he asked. "Did something happen back there?"

"I'm good. Just can't get in without my key." I stood at his passenger side door. "Let's go park somewhere."

"It's fine," he said. "We don't have to."

In a way, he seemed almost relieved.

"You're sure you're okay?"

"Yeah," I said. "Come on. But I'm not doing it with you in the back of your car, just so you know."

I expected him to laugh, but he didn't.

There was no way I could go back to school and sit in a goddamn classroom, not while this silent avalanche slid down on my world. In the back of Luke's car, I closed my eyes and let his hands roam as I wished for a problem—a distraction—so big it would blanket me and my parents and everyone I loved most in an all-consuming darkness.

About a month later, I got the big distraction I'd hoped for. I was diagnosed with acute lymphocytic leukemia. Cancer. I had fucking cancer.

Harvey.

Now

"Why can't we watch one of those reality shows about cat-hoarding old ladies?" mumbled Alice.

I laughed. "You've never even seen this movie and it's only the opening credits. Give it a chance, Al."

She lay next to me on her bed with her head propped up on a mountain of pillows. Her eyes were closed, her skin warm and clammy, but still her lips smiled a little.

Tonight we decided to watch *A Christmas Story*, the movie with the leg lamp and the Christmas dinner at a Chinese food restaurant—the movie that everyone else in the world, except Alice, had seen a million times. I didn't know how that was even possible since it played on TV every Christmas for twenty-four hours straight. Christmas wasn't for another two weeks, and if there was one thing Alice wasn't guaranteed, it was another two weeks. It'd been a little over a year since she'd been diagnosed. I didn't know what I expected one year later to look like, but it wasn't this. It wasn't Alice lying in her bed, waiting for the cancer to eat up whatever was left, while I half-assed my way through eleventh grade, trying to pretend that stupid things like homework and my lame minimum-wage job mattered.

She hadn't been able to leave the house much for the last couple of weeks, so we started working our way through my best friend Dennis's collection of must-see movies. Dennis loved movies, pop culture, and video games, but he was smart too, like future Rhodes Scholar smart. His whole family was like that. His twin sister, Debora, was this political mastermind. When we were kids, she used to make us play Congress. It was miserable.

A Christmas Story had been at the top of Dennis's list, and we'd tried to watch it a few times, but Al always said she hated Christmas stuff. Really, I thought Alice got off on hating all the things others were so quick to love.

In fifth grade, she came with me and Mom to pick out a small Christmas tree for the apartment. It was a warm Christmas, but it snowed a little that night. I followed the tree guy up and down the aisles with my mom behind me and Alice behind her. I found the perfect tree. I was sure I had. Alice didn't say so, but I knew she thought so too because as I circled the tree, pretending to inspect every limb, she swayed a little and hummed to herself as *Noel* played over the crackling loudspeakers and the snow melted on her cheeks.

Other than the glow of the television, her whole room was dark. We were quiet for a few minutes, so I watched the movie as Alice's breathing evened out and her body slumped against mine. She sounded sicker than normal, like she had a respiratory infection or something. When people like her—people with cancer—got sick like this, a common cold could be the thing that ended it all. It didn't seem fair. *She had cancer, but it was the flu that did her in.*

I tried not to think about that because this moment felt perfect. Her lying here, next to me, her body curving into mine. It was perfect except that she was dying and I was living and I didn't know how we could do both at the same time.

She had these good days every once in a while, and those were bold-faced lies that I fell for every time. Last week she had three good days and two the week before. The closer we got to what Alice affectionately referred to as her "expiration date" the more I was fooled into believing all of this wasn't real.

I knew that I should have left so she could turn the TV off and get some rest, but I was selfish. I wanted every moment. When Alice was gone, she was going to take a giant Alice-shaped chunk out of me and it would go with her, wherever it was that she was going. I was scared to think what might be inside that chunk of me. Whatever it was—our past, our present, our never-going-to-come-true future—would die with her. Everything about the situation made me manic. But when the girl you loved was dying, it was hard not to let yourself go with her.

I shut out Alice's wheezing breaths and pretended that she was 98.6 degrees and healthy. I watched the movie all the way through the end of the credits and well on into the copyright info. Finally, the TV stereo began to buzz and I knew it was time to go home. Normally, I would have turned off the TV and snuck out of her room. Instead, I sat there next to her in her little twin bed. Her hipbones protruded through the blanket while her chest rose and fell with each jagged breath. Medicine on her nightstand was stacked high like a fortified city. The huge box of tissues too. For a little while Alice was getting these insane nosebleeds, and she would sit around for hours with a tissue stuffed up each nostril. But those had petered out and tonight she was just congested, I guessed. Or maybe this was the next step down in her declining health.

I closed my eyes and we were old and wrinkly, sitting side by side, watching reruns of *Wheel of Fortune* or something.

Shadows passed beneath her bedroom door. Alice's mom, Bernie (short for Bernice), walked down the hallway, talking on the phone in a hushed voice. "It's not a good time." Pause. "She's already asleep, Mom." Pause. "Maybe tomorrow."

Bernie's family lived on the other side of the country, and as far as I knew, Bernie didn't mind. She hung up the phone and a few minutes later she and Alice's dad, Martin, flicked the hallway lights on and off, talking loudly about going to bed. A little show to let me know it was time to head home even though they would never come in and actually tell me to leave.

I swung my feet off the bed and tied the dirty laces on my sneakers. I got up and immediately sat back down and did something I had never done before. I woke up Alice to say good-bye because these bad nights reminded me that we only had so many nights left. When I squeezed her bony shoulder, she moaned in protest. Her lips were dry and cracked, the sound barely escaping her mouth. I dipped my head down next to her ear, my cheek pressed against her bare skull.

"Alice," I breathed. The buzzing TV cast a blue light over her. "Alice, don't leave, okay? I'll come here every day, just don't leave." A single tear cut a path down my cheek, and I wiped it away before it felt real. This seemed like good-bye, not good night.

But then she opened her eyes. "Hi."

I tried to smile.

"That movie sucked."

I laughed. "Yeah. It sort of did."

Her eyes crinkled a little and her lips curved upward, like she'd remembered something funny from a time that wasn't now. "I'll miss you most, Harvey." She sat up on her elbows. "I don't know what it will feel like after, but I know I'll miss you most."

We'd gone through so much shit together, but this was the first time she'd ever told me that I was important. And that I mattered to her. I wanted this. I wanted to keep it forever. But you don't ever get what you want how you want it.

I cleared my throat. "Alice, I—"

"Don't." She leaned forward and kissed my cheek. "Save that for someone who's not about to bite it."

I nodded. I loved Alice. It was so obvious that I didn't even need to say so out loud. I stood and opened her bedroom door.

"Harvey," she said.

I turned.

"Me too."

Alice.

Now

Before I could stop myself, I reached for my hair, my fingers smoothing over my naked scalp. Gone, it was all gone. Even now, over a year later, it still came as a shock. I did this several times a day, like clockwork. It was a phantom limb, my hair.

My oncologist for the last year or so, Dr. Meredith, bustled into his office. Noise from the hallway bled through for a moment before the door shut behind him, sealing us in. My mom drummed her fingers on her leg, a nervous habit. Dad reached over and took her hand in his, absorbing her tension.

Dr. Meredith was a large, robust man, and jolly too, with rosy cheeks and this perpetual baby-powder smell. I always thought he would be better suited as a Santa Claus at the Green Oaks Mall rather than a doctor charged with the duty of delivering earth-shattering news. Maybe his appearance was supposed to soften the blow. *The bad news is you have cancer. The good news is Santa Claus is your doctor. Peppermint stick for your trouble?*

I almost laughed out loud, remembering that stupid Christmas movie I'd watched with Harvey last night. Well, he watched it and I slept through it. But that wasn't all that happened. I always knew how he felt about me, and I finally told him that I felt the same. Telling him that seemed like my final task—well, almost. There was one item left on my list. From where I stood, it was likely to remain my only unfinished business.

My dad spoke up first. "What is it, Dr. Meredith?" Then, a little quieter, almost to himself, he said, "I thought we'd heard the worst of it."

Dr. Meredith squeezed behind his desk, sweat gathering at his brow, huffing between labored breaths. My parents occupied the two chairs directly in front of his desk. I sat in the middle of the small loveseat in the corner of the office; stacks of folders and papers sat on either side of me. Dr. Meredith had been my specialist for over a year and neither of these stacks had moved an inch. The couch was stiff and, I suspected, rarely used. It was one of those deceptive couches that looked like it should be much more comfortable than it really was. Typical doctor's office furniture, something I was all too familiar with.

Dr. Meredith looked at me directly while I stretched my long legs out in front of me, pointing my toes hard, like I would in my pointe shoes. (Now stuffed away in the back of my closet along with some old recital costumes.) Long out of practice, the backs of my calves stung.

All the news Dr. Meredith had given us had been delivered to my parents. I'd always been in the room, but not *really*, not to them. It must have been easier for him to say those things to my mom and dad. It removed me from the situation. But whatever it was he had to say this time, it was me he wanted to say it to. He'd called us early this morning and told us we needed to come in as soon as possible. In my experience, phone calls made outside of office hours never led to anything good.

Flipping through my charts, Dr. Meredith said, "I see your temperature's a little high."

Instinctively, my hand flew to my forehead. Still clammy, but not as bad as last night when Harvey had come over. I'd gotten so used to being ill that now I had trouble telling the difference between being sick and being Sick.

My dad cleared his throat, loudly.

Dr. Meredith took a deep breath. "Alice." His brown eyes found mine, and it was only me and him. He exhaled. "You're in remission."

For a moment, it was quiet and everything felt okay. But then my mother began to sob, her entire body shaking in response. It was a horrible noise that made the room feel too small. Dad coughed, trying to bite back his emotions. He pinched the bridge of his nose, like his fingers might absorb his tears, but instead they rolled down his hand and into the cuff of his jacket.

Oh shit.

This, I did not expect. This was not on my list.

Harvey.

Now

My eyelids hung heavy from staying too late at Alice's last night, again. I jogged down Aisle 9 (soup, canned vegetables, and dressing) toward the employee break room, with the Christmas Muzak crackling over the speakers. Pushing the door open with my back, I called to Dennis as he restocked the prepackaged lunchmeats. "I'm out early, man. Heading to Alice's. We're watching your favorite, *The Life Aquatic with Steve Zissou!*" One of Dennis's life goals was not to be *like* Bill Murray, but to *be* Bill Murray.

A couple nights ago we'd watched *Jaws*, and afterward Alice said movies about the ocean were "lame," but I promised *The Life Aquatic* would be different. Even if she would never say it, she had always been scared of the ocean or any other unchlorinated body of water. It was the one thing I ever knew Alice to be scared of, and not even she realized that I knew.

"Restock Aisle Six for me?" I didn't wait for him to agree. "I owe you!" He waved me on and said something under his breath.

I slid my time card into the clock and punched out. Only an hour and a half today. Shit. These short after-school shifts were killing me. Normally, I worked five to six hours, four days a week after school. Lately I had been leaving early and sometimes not even coming in at all.

Grocery Emporium was the last family-owned grocery store in Hughley. They had a strong local following, but in order to keep the big supergrocery stores at bay there were some modern conveniences we went without—like a new time clock. And vending machines, digital produce scales, working barcode scanners . . . You know, all the things necessary to actually run a modern grocery store. I couldn't complain. They worked with my fucked-up schedule, and given all that was going on with Alice, they'd been cutting me a lot of slack lately.

Alice. She would miss me. She said she would. And now it was all I could think about. And she loved me. At least, I thought she did. She didn't really say so. The whole thing gave me these bursts of stupid happy, which were always followed by guilt because it didn't feel right to be happy.

I was thirteen years old when it changed.

Alice's birthday was in eleven days, making it the middle of January.

I remembered playing some Chopin for the intermediate class at my mom's dance studio. All Mom's studio rooms had these old beat-up stereos, but the main studio where the intermediate class usually met had a piano. We'd bought it off one of my piano teacher's friends a long time ago. Mom had always hated dancing or instructing to anything but a live accompaniment. So, a piano-playing son had been no accident.

I never knew who my dad was, but I always thought he must have been a piano player since pianos were the only thing my mom loved more than ballet.

Warm-ups had wrapped, and each student took turns with a forty-five-second solo in preparation for spring auditions. My mother was handing out a ballet solo, which Celeste and Alice were the top contenders for. The tension between them had always been a continuous competitive cycle that only escalated with age.

Celeste stood with her arms spread and a smug expression on her face, waiting for some kind of praise. Ever since we were kids, she would show up to dance with her portfolio of sheet music and monologues tucked beneath her arm, ready for voice and acting class too. For Celeste, dance was one piece of the puzzle. She wanted to be famous, and I'm not even sure that she cared what for.

My mother, Miss Natalie to her pupils, clapped to the beat and said, "To appear effortless requires much effort! Alice, next!" There was no way to tell if that was meant as a compliment or a criticism of Celeste's form. Knowing my mother, silence would have been more positive feedback.

Like Celeste, Alice wasn't en pointe that night. Being the youngest in the class, the two of them didn't always practice with their stiff-toed ballet shoes for the sake of preserving their still-growing feet. I always preferred to watch Alice when she wasn't en pointe anyway.

On a typical day, she wore her hair slicked back into a bun, an impeccable ballet bun. But Friday had become my favorite day of the week, because it was the only school day Alice didn't have dance classes, which meant she wore her hair down. With our last names so close in the alphabet— hers, Richardson, and mine, Poppovicci—we always sat near each other in class. When Alice's light brown, wavy hair hung loose, it hit the middle of her back, the place where her leotard usually met her ivory skin. She almost never wore it down, but when she did, it was the single thing about her that ever looked out of control. It would swish between her shoulder blades, calling to me. And I would have followed her too, anywhere. On Fridays, dur- ing class, she would constantly massage her scalp, and more than once I had to stop myself from running my fingers through her hair.

She was tall and slender, with just a whisper of curves. We were the same height, and I hoped I'd be able to keep up. Her nose was small and sloped a little too far out, squaring off at the tip. Her pale blue eyes, they always swallowed me whole. They were my road map. Alice's lips were full and pouty and she rarely smiled, but when she did it was worth all the eye rolls, bossy demands, and sharp words combined. It was worth it because her smile was genuine, and if you made Alice smile, then you'd earned it. Everything with

Alice was earned. But her scowls were more easily earned than anything else. I'd learned the language of each of her expressions.

Still, I thought she was perfect in every way, but en pointe her perfection was a blinding sun. If I stared at her long enough, the piano keys would play themselves, fueled by her. En pointe she was a force, a tornado: safe to look at from a distance, but in close proximity, you risked being just another piece of her debris. Some days I thought I could only be so lucky.

Her toes bent at the balls of her feet as she rose nearer to the ceiling. She wore lyrical dance shoes in black. They reminded me of gladiator sandals. Thin leather straps wrapped around her feet. Her unpolished toes were red and bulbous; her feet calloused. Most people would say they were ugly, even disgusting. But she wore them proudly, like a badge, a display of her hard work. Without her stiff satin pointe shoes with their stubby toes, she was closer to earth. Closer to me, a little more in reach.

She was in a class of fourteen other students, all by herself.

I'd known her my whole life. Other girls didn't exist for me in the same way she did. They had been there all along, these feelings; the only thing that had changed was my understanding of them. My whole body finally connected the dots, and I realized that even if we were never together, she'd ruined me and I'd never feel that way about anyone again.

On that cold night in January it all slipped into place for

me and she became my everything and my everyone. My music, my sun, my words, my hope, my logic, my confusion, my flaw.

I was thirteen years old, and she was all these things to me.

And I was her friend.

Alice.

Now

Mom and Dad cried freely now, and rightly so. I wasn't dying.

I wasn't dying. Not actively, anyway.

"You're sure?" I asked in a quiet voice.

Somehow Dr. Meredith heard me over my parents' celebratory tears. His glasses had slid down to the tip of his nose. He flipped through the stacks of papers in my thick file. "I'm positive, Alice. Your white blood cells are regulating, and in your most recent bone marrow sample, there was no trace of cancerous cells. I had the lab techs double-check and triple-check. Remission is constituted by shrinking or lack of growth, so there you are. Of course you'll still be going in for scans and blood work on a weekly basis. We'll be keeping a very close eye on you. It can always come back stronger, so it's always best to be aware and prepared." He closed the file sitting in front of him—my file.

My stomach twisted. This should have felt good, but it didn't.

"You'll need to start intensification therapy followed by maintenance therapy, but not until we know what triggered the remission. We're at the peak of the mountain, folks, but let's not relax yet. Thankful, but mindful. That's going to be our mantra these next few months."

My parents sobered up at that and turned in their chairs to face me. They looked at me, really looked at me like they hadn't seen me for a year, and I guess in a way they hadn't.

After I got sick, I wondered if they tried to stop loving me a little bit. Not on purpose, but maybe in the interest of them surviving this thing. I mean, my parents loved me. But wouldn't anyone try to distance themselves from something they knew they were about to lose entirely? I was their only child, but my life had never consumed theirs. Then I got sick, and for the last fourteen months, my disease had become the axis of their world. They'd gotten to this point where they started looking through me, rather than at me. It wasn't anything I fully realized until this very moment, this moment when they were really looking at me again, their daughter. It made me want to be anywhere but here. With a handful of words my life had fallen off the rails.

I'd wondered what would happen to them after I died. Would my mom have left my dad for that guy? But, now, what would happen now? Would she tell us that she'd been having an affair? Would she leave us after we'd weathered this storm together?

I opened my mouth to speak, but swallowed my words when I realized I had no idea what to say. My body was being stretched in every direction, begging to be felt. The list—my final to-do list—had fixed almost everything. But nothing could fix this.

My vision blurred, and all I saw was everything I'd done over the last year. Everything I'd said. *Harvey.* I didn't know how to live with the weight of what I'd told him last night, what I'd said without words.

"That being said," the doctor continued, "in all my years I have never . . . I've never seen anything like it. My profession frowns upon this word, but, Alice, it appears to be what some call a miracle. You hear about these things from time to time, circumstances that defy science. It seems that after we had decided to suspend your chemo-therapy treatment, your body began to fight back. I could go on for days with theories and possibilities, which I will do next week during our official appointment. And I do apologize for the last-minute call, especially right before the holidays. I wanted you all to know the moment we were sure."

After we had decided to suspend your chemotherapy treatment. The day we stopped, none of us had said we were giving up, not out loud. But we did, I did. I had given up the day I was diagnosed. The chemotherapy was horrible and, in my eyes, made the act of dying that much more degrading. After almost a year of chemo, I had to put my foot down.

All of a sudden, the room and everything it contained rushed to meet me. I emerged from underwater, hitting the surface after having been submerged, and the sound of nurses in the hallway and the smell of disinfectant clogged my senses. Everything had been muffled and blurred, but now it was all too sharp and overenunciated.

I'll miss you most. I didn't know how to be with Harvey

now. Not without ruining us. What if I already had? We had nowhere else to go.

"Motherfucker," I mumbled.

My mom heard me and turned back around. My name formed in her mouth like an old habit as her lips parted. But she stopped herself. I could even hear it. *Alice Elizabeth,* she would say in a vicious whisper that I could hear even in my sleep. But no, instead my mother was utterly confused, like I was an equation with no answer. It wasn't the cursing that bothered her; it was me saying it here in my doctor's office after he'd told me I was some Lifetime miracle. *Yell at me,* I wanted to say. *Make this normal.*

After wiping his tearstained eyes in the crook of his elbow, Dad stood up to shake Dr. Meredith's hand. "Thank you so much, Dr. Meredith, we're so . . ." He reached out for my mother's hand and she was at his side in an instant. "We can't believe it," he finished.

Over the last year, I'd watched my parents transform into magnets defined by the length of space between them, letting this tragedy hold them together. But no matter how dependent upon each other they seemed to be, all I saw was the truth that had become the lie my mother lived. It was the truth I'd never been able to tell my dad, even if he deserved to know.

Dr. Meredith grasped my dad's outstretched hand. "Now we'll see Alice next week. We'll stick to the regular schedule," he said, "because you never know. This could be the eye of the storm. We don't know. That's the hard truth. But be happy for today."

Mom doubled back to me and ushered me forward, nudging me with the tips of her fingers at the small of my back. I knew what she wanted, so I played along. It had been quite a while since I had made nice for Mom and Dad, and now it looked like there would be some making up to do. I reached up to pat Dr. Meredith on the shoulder and thank him, but he pulled me into a bear hug instead. The sweat seeped through his dress shirt, and I wanted to pull away, but I didn't. Because if I did, my parents would have seen the few tears rolling down my cheeks and onto Dr. Meredith's lab coat. I'd grown so used to the terms of my life—the conditions—that now I didn't know how to tell the difference between the good and the bad. But I knew, unless the cancer came back, that I was going to live. Now, I had to decide who and what I could live with.

Harvey.

Now

After grabbing my keys, I headed out to my hand-me-down car. I had parked out by the buzzing Grocery Emporium sign with the rest of the employees. I spent most of my childhood with this car, a midnineties red Geo Metro. It was small, but it'd always been me and my mom so it was never a problem. For my sixteenth birthday my mom bought herself a shiny new Jetta, slapped a Miss P's Ballet Academy car magnet on the driver door of the Geo, and called it my birthday present.

Technically, it was more than a ballet academy. When I was younger, my mom had all these requests for jazz and tap classes, so she expanded her courses after her first couple years in business. Not until I was about nine or ten did she hire a hip-hop–and–jazz teacher and a lyrical/ modern dance teacher. I tried to convince her that changing the name of the studio to Miss P's Dance Academy would bring in more students, but she refused. The name was something she wouldn't budge on. When she'd first decided to open a ballet school, she wanted to call it the Poppovicci School of Ballet, but Bernie told Mom that people don't like to do business with a place whose name they can't pronounce. Eventually Mom caved and settled on Miss P's.

The bumper of the Geo was covered in recital stickers (Martin, Alice's dad, designed new ones every year). One day I tried to scrape them off, but my mom threatened to take the car right back if I touched her stickers. So, essentially, my car was on loan from my mom until further notice.

It wasn't really a *guy* car, but it was my car. The fact that it had an engine and wheels outweighed the fact that the steering wheel bumped against my knees when I turned and that I always hit my head when I got in and out of the car.

Before reversing out of the parking lot, I glanced through the call history on my cell. No missed calls. I'd spent the last couple months teetering on the edge of insanity, so scared of getting *the* call.

I took the back roads to Alice's house, hoping to beat the five o'clock traffic, which sounded more pressing than it was. We lived in a small suburb, where traffic existed solely because modern roadways did not. Every street was a two-lane street, and many streets were one-way.

Racing past the studio, I prayed my mother wasn't outside greeting students at the door. If she was, she might see the Geo speeding down Little Ave and know that I'd skipped out on work early. Again.

I didn't really have big plans for tonight, but Alice had been so tired lately and I was scared. Every night could be the last. By the time my shift ended at seven thirty she was usually about to fall asleep, so I tried to cut out early as much as I could. Her body was starting to wind down on her, drowning bits of herself a little more every day. It wasn't what I'd expected, dying.

As I shifted the Geo into park, Alice's front door closed. Either Bernie or Martin must have just gotten home. Like I'd told Dennis, on the menu tonight was *The Life Aquatic with Steve Zissou*. Dennis said it was hilarious and a little sad too. The sad I could handle; it was the hilarious that worried me. The funny movies had been the hardest to get through, because you're supposed to laugh and Alice was too tired to laugh. When she couldn't laugh, I tried to remember her laugh for her, and for me too, in case I forgot it. But every time I recalled it in my head it sounded distorted and faraway, like the screams you hear when you're waiting in line outside a haunted house.

I grabbed the DVD from the passenger seat, not even bothering to take off my Grocery Emporium apron. Running past Alice's mom's car, I could still feel the warmth transmitting from the engine.

I knocked on the door as a formality. I had my own key anyway. But before I had a chance to shove the key into the lock, Bernie answered the door, her normally smooth face a red mess.

"Harvey, we just got—"

I interrupted her because I was scared of what she would say. "Hey, Bernie, I brought over another movie." I began to step toward the front door, looking down at her as I asked, "Alice in her room?" But Bernie wasn't shifting to let me through. Her body stood wedged in the crack between the door and the frame, like I was a threat.

"Stay put for a minute, Harvey." She shut the door without giving me a second to respond. Then the lock clicked.

The muscles in my back tensed.

Through the door, I heard Bernie say, "It's Harvey. You should tell him."

Silence.

My throat closed and my heart hammered a hole in my chest.

"You should be the one to tell him," she said, more insistent this time.

Dead air.

I tried peeking through the curtains, scared of what I might find, but the blinds were pulled down too tightly. I heard hushed voices. And I knew. They were trying to figure out how to tell me she was gone. I wanted to walk right in and tell them I knew. I knew last night when she told me. *I'll miss you most.*

I was a stranger on their doorstep, certain that I'd lost my connection to Bernie and Martin that mattered most. Sticking my empty hand in the pocket of my jeans, I shook around some loose change and thought about the list. When she first told me about it, I told her she was crazy. But if it hadn't been for the list, I might not have had her all to myself this last year. So, I guess we both got a little bit of what we wanted. She got the last word and I got her.

A minute later, Martin came to the door. Of course Bernie would send Martin out here to tell me, but I didn't want to think of this moment every time I saw him. He wore his usual ripped jeans, an old, threadbare T-shirt, and loafers. He looked even more exhausted than Bernie. As he stepped out onto the front porch, he closed the door behind him. No one had ever called Martin the father figure in my life or my male role model or some crap like that, but he was. And I didn't want him to be tied to this memory, the moment I found out she was gone.

What if she's in there? Her lifeless body might have still been in there—maybe in her bed, tucked in like she was asleep—waiting to be picked up by the funeral home or the ambulance or whoever did that sort of thing. I closed my eyes, but panicked when my memory of her face was fuzzy. I wanted to see her, but it would be all wrong and I was too chickenshit for that. I couldn't see her like that. Seeing a dead body outside of a funeral home would be like seeing your teacher out at a restaurant or at a concert.

"Hey, Harv," said Martin. He rubbed his hand up the back of his short-cropped hair and puffed his cheeks full of air before slowly deflating them.

He smiled. He was smiling.

No. That had to be wrong. *You can't smile—she's dead. Don't tell me her pain is gone. Don't tell me she'll be at peace. Because she's not at peace, she's gone.* I wanted to scream all these things at him. My blood boiled and my knuckles begged to connect with his face. All that anger felt sour in my mouth, but Alice was gone, and now I was waiting for that other half of me to disappear.

"It's gone, man." Martin wasn't the type of guy who spoke like a teenager so he could be hip and "connect with the kids." He talked like a teenager because he still was one, in a way. But I didn't hear Martin call me *man*, which would normally lift at least a corner of my lip. I heard *it*. I didn't know what *it* meant.

"It?" I asked. My voice was too high and strangled, like puberty wasn't done with me quite yet.

A whole river of tears loomed behind my eyes waiting for the word. I tried to picture myself falling apart on their front porch. I didn't even care about what I would look like or who would see me. Would they invite me in to comfort me or were they bandaging their own wounds now? Maybe they'd send me back to my car, then call my mom to warn her of the storm. What really stung was that if she was gone, I should have known. I should've felt it.

"The cancer." Martin choked on his words. "She's in remission."

Three words. Three words I never thought I would ever hear. Three words that could build enough tomorrows to last me forever.

"Can I come in and see her?" I asked, reaching for the door. Really, I needed proof that she was still here and alive.

He opened the door and stuck his head inside. After whispering a few words to whoever stood in the entryway, he turned back to me. His eyes shifted a little. "She's resting. Her body's still got a lot of work to do, but we'll call Natalie and plan a celebratory dinner." He shrugged his shoulders, like he was trying to communicate something else to me, but I didn't get it.

It was the first time they'd ever told me no, the only time they'd ever not let me into their home.

But she was alive. Martin reached for me, and I stood there, shocked, as he hugged me with my arms glued to my sides. He squeezed me so hard that the DVD in my hand slipped from my fingers and clattered to the front porch.

I walked to my car, my feet knowing what to do without my mind ever telling them to do so. We could be together. Alice and I. That could be my life. I unlocked my car and sat behind the wheel for a moment, letting all of last year flood me. She'd have to make up for a lot of lost time at school. But it was okay. It would all be okay. My white-knuckled fingers gripped the peeling steering wheel as a smile tugged at my lips. Pulling the rearview mirror down to face me, I saw that I wore the same stupefied smile Martin had worn moments ago.

I shifted gears into reverse, and squinted at Alice's house before rolling down the driveway. And there she was, watching me through a crack in the blinds of the big bay window in the office. The blinds shifted and she was gone. I told myself every reason why she might not let me in. Especially now, after everything. And then I told myself, it was okay, because now we had time on our side.

What should have been our end had become our beginning.

Alice.

Then

I was dizzy, my sixth dizzy spell in three weeks. The first had been that day in Luke's car after I'd seen my mom with that man. I thought it was just a reaction to being so overwhelmed, but after the fourth dizzy spell during World History last week, I started to think something might be wrong. But it felt like a dumb thing to go to the doctor for. What was I supposed to say? I saw my mom with some guy, and I've been feeling dizzy ever since? I probably needed more iron or something like that. Then last night I woke up shivering and covered in sweat, and now I didn't know what was wrong.

I sat down on the bench in the locker room. Everyone else had already changed into their school-issued gold shorts and gray T-shirts and left for gym. Closing my eyes, I pulled at the neck of my T-shirt. It felt too close to my throat, like I couldn't breathe.

"You look really tired."

I recognized that voice. I took one more deep breath before opening my eyes. Celeste stood a few feet away from me, holding her arms to her chest as she tried to find her T-shirt in her gym bag. She wore a black-and-white-striped bra, the straps cutting deep into her shoulders.

"What are you staring at?" She rolled her eyes as she maneuvered, trying to hide her stomach. "Is that your thing now? Staring at girls in the locker room?"

Celeste had always been the thickest girl in ballet. When we were in sixth grade, I heard Natalie telling my mom that she had to select a different costume for our entire class because Celeste didn't fit into junior sizes anymore and the costumes didn't come in regular adult sizes. It's not like she was fat. She just didn't have a ballet body, and that was something she would never get by practicing. Height and curves, that was Celeste. She would do things like eat lettuce and drink lemon juice for six weeks and call it a "cleanse." I wanted to feel bad for her, but she made it so damn hard. She might not have had the body of a dancer, but Celeste was good. When I was still in ballet classes, the solos always came down to me and her. Ballet was different for her than it was for me. Ballet was my life. For her, it was a vehicle. Celeste wanted nothing more than to be a triple threat—dancer, singer, actress—and it killed her that, when it came to dance, I'd always have her beat. She probably thought our competitive rivalry was over when I quit right before freshman year. But then I started dating Luke and it got even worse because Luke wasn't something Celeste could audition for.

"Yeah, I just want you so bad," I said, my voice monotone. "That's why I have a boyfriend."

She flinched for a second, but made an effort to act cool

as she searched her gym bag for her T-shirt. "You really do look like shit."

I touched my fingers to my cheeks, warm and clammy. "Luke doesn't seem to mind. What are you doing without your one-girl minion anyway?" I asked, referring to her eternal sidekick, Mindi, who was best known for her runner-up beauty pageant titles. The only thing worse than losing was almost winning.

Celeste ignored my question and pulled her T-shirt on over her head. She bit down on her lip for a second before she said, "I heard about your mom."

I stood. I wished I hadn't, but it was like a reflex and it was the exact response she was looking for. "What are you talking about?"

She threw her bag into her locker. "That's got to be hard," she said, "catching your mom with some other guy."

Luke. Oh my God. I didn't think he'd actually seen anything worth remembering. I ground my teeth as panic, betrayal, and rage coursed through me. "I don't know what you're talking about. Those batshit cleanses must be going to your head."

Her lip twitched and she took three steps toward me. We stood nose to nose, a few inches apart. "Really? No idea? I can't even imagine. Skipping school to lose your V-card to your boyfriend only to find that your mom's getting more action than you ever will." Her lips twisted into a pout and she shrugged. "Rough stuff."

I hadn't told a single person—not even my dad—about what I'd learned that day. Luke must have seen her. Why would he have told Celeste? I didn't know, but I wasn't going to give her the satisfaction of me asking. "Fuck you, Celeste."

"No," she said, "your boyfriend's got that pretty much covered." She turned and walked off toward the gym.

I sat. Not on the bench, but right there on the floor. Her words hit me like a gunshot, so quick I hadn't noticed it, until blood had pooled around the wound. It would have been easy to call her a liar, but I didn't see any other way she could have known.

Maybe Celeste was lashing out. Maybe Luke had just told her for the umpteenth time that he was going to break up with me for her. Maybe I'd sent her over the edge or maybe she hated me that much. I wouldn't ever know, but it was in that moment that she and I went from frenemies to mortal enemies. I could believe that Luke was fooling around with other girls. The doubt had already been there. But he was cheating on me with *her*. Her, of all people. And on top of that, he had shared a secret that wasn't even his to share. I wanted to destroy them both, but all I felt was powerless and foolish. A burning sensation spread across my chest as I began to cry.

You start high school and it feels new and shiny, but what no one tells you is that the sophomores, juniors, and seniors all have these tricks and games they've been playing for a while now. That's the thing they don't tell you at freshman orientation. And everyone is totally aware of this stuff except for the doe-eyed freshmen. I should have known better than to date Luke. Laurel had warned me, and I should have believed her.

It hurt to know the truth. Not because I loved Luke, but because I was mad at myself for not knowing any better. I had to break up with him and it had to be public. I was going to send a message.

The next morning, he found me at my locker again.

"I'm bored," I announced, my voice carefully controlled.

"You want to cut out of here early today? Maybe go do something not so boring?" asked Luke, and his eyebrows rose with expectation.

Two days ago I would have thought that he was kind of adorable, but now I thought he looked like a severe case of herpes. I rolled my eyes. "No, Luke, I'm bored. *With us.* We never do anything anymore that doesn't involve the backseat of your car."

"So we'll grab some dinner on Friday and go to a movie."

"I don't think you understand," I said, raising my voice. "I'm more bored with the *you* part of us."

Luke leaned toward me. "What the hell, Alice?" The words spilled out of his mouth in a rushed whisper. "Are you trying to break up with me?"

"I'm not *trying* to. I *am* breaking up with you."

Bodies froze all around us, and life felt slow like when you turn a snow globe right side up and everything falls into place again. Onlookers whispered behind us, and a few girls pointed at us. To the side of me, some guys whistled, saying things like "That's busted." Another group of girls directly behind Luke smiled, ready to pounce. I hoped Harvey was watching too, but I couldn't risk a glance.

"What are you looking at, homo?" yelled Luke.

I looked over my shoulder to see Tyson—one of the few openly gay students at our school—rushing off in the other direction. I rolled my eyes. "You're such an ass."

Luke slammed his hand against the locker, catching my eye for a second before glancing over my shoulder once more. "Is it some other guy?"

I wanted to scream at him and tell him of course there weren't any other guys, but all I could think of was Celeste saying *Rough stuff.* The cheating hurt, but him telling Celeste about my mom was unforgiveable. "Oh, Luke," I said, "there are plenty of other guys."

I turned around and walked down the hallway with the eyes of the entire school on me. Without turning back, I lifted my hand and gave a little wave. *Good-bye, Luke.*

Harvey.

Then

The roads were a little slick, but they were nothing I couldn't handle. I'd always been a good driver. My mom had hated driving for as long as I could remember. I don't think she ever had to do a lot of driving until she had me.

Mom flipped the radio over to some easy-rock station and leaned back into the passenger seat, closing her eyes. Not normal behavior for a mother while her fifteen-year-old son sat behind the wheel of the family car.

Every night after we closed down the studio, I would say, "Hey, Mom, I'll drive home tonight."

"Ha-ha, Harvey. Get in," she would reply.

But one night when I was fourteen years old and about halfway through eighth grade, she tossed me the keys and said, "Back roads only. Don't forget, gas is right; brake is left."

This became our nightly ritual four days a week. Before then, my mom had let me skid around parking lots, but this was the first time I was ever allowed to drive on real streets.

Every night after that, her body seemed to melt into the passenger seat. Once I had a solid handle on the drive to and from the studio, she got in the habit of tilting her head up and closing her eyes the whole way home. Sometimes she was sleeping, other times just relaxing. I think my mom had been waiting a long time for me to be old enough to drive because by driving us home every night, I was fulfilling one of her needs. It wasn't the first time I had felt like that. We'd had this partnership. It was hard not to share responsibilities when it was only the two of us. She didn't talk much about her life before me. It's weird to think that your parents had this whole world and you had nothing to do with it.

When I was four years old, my mom decided it was time for me to learn her craft. This was fine with me; it was. I wasn't like most boys. I had grown up with ballet and even my four-year-old self knew that both boys and girls could be dancers. The problem being: I was horrible at ballet.

Sure, every four-year-old is horrible at ballet, but I was exceptionally tragic. I begged my mom to let me quit. I never took an issue with ballet; it was the me-being-horrible-at-it part that made it unbearable.

A few weeks after my fifth birthday, my mother took me to Mrs. Ferguson's house for my first piano lesson. It wasn't love at first sight, but it wasn't as gruesome as ballet had been. By the time I was eight years old, I was playing piano for a few of the intermediate classes, and most of my after-school time on Tuesdays and Thursdays was spent at Mrs. Ferguson's house. At the age of twelve, my lessons were limited to Sunday mornings, and I spent Monday through Thursday playing the piano for most of my mother's classes. She had always loathed the bulky black stereos usually found in the corners of dance studios, but hiring a pianist would slice right through her budget. My playing the piano for her was sort of like that night when I was fourteen years old and she tossed me the keys. She was waiting for me to be ready.

With just the two of us, we had no other option except to be resourceful, but sometimes I wondered what it would be like to go home after school and watch TV or play video games with Dennis.

"Can I talk to you, Mom?" I asked as we rolled out of the parking lot and toward home. With my driving test coming up in one month at the end of October, I was careful to use my blinkers and look both ways.

"Harvey, you don't have to ask me if we can talk." She paused. "Of course we can."

"I'm thinking that maybe when I turn sixteen, I'm going to get an after-school job. I could pay for my car insurance and gas, you know?" I tried my best to sound casual, like it didn't matter either way. But it did matter. Big-time.

"Harvey, you don't really have time for that. I appreciate you wanting to help out, but it's not necessary. We're doing okay. What about piano?" The minute the question left her mouth, she seemed to have answered it herself. "Oh."

We drove in silence for several minutes before either of us uttered a word.

"I don't really enjoy it, Mom." I idled at a stoplight, waiting for it to turn green.

"And you've always felt this way?"

"I don't know. I guess I want a break." The older I got, the more aware I became of time and how I was wasting mine. I didn't want to fill my time with a new hobby—at least not right away. I wanted to fill my time with something that fifteen-year-old Harvey chose to do, not something five-year-old Harvey did because his mother told him to.

I was a pretty decent pianist. I had these long, slender fingers, perfect for playing, and it came naturally to me, but I wasn't a prodigy or anything. If you're going to dedicate your life to something like music, it had to be an all-consuming thing. It had to be the reason your body got out of bed every morning. Maybe it would have been different if I had stumbled upon piano on my own; I didn't know.

I knew this would be hard for her to accept. Mom had always known she would be a ballerina. I wondered if this whole thing would be easier for her if I said I was quitting piano in favor of theater or art or something like that. Maybe she just wanted a talented son, but my talent for the arts was mediocre. Maybe I wanted the chance to find the thing I loved, like she had with ballet. And, yeah, I didn't want to be that guy in high school who hung out at the ballet studio every day after school.

My mom thought for a moment, then said, "You'll get a job when you turn sixteen and have passed the state driving exam. Until then you'll continue playing the piano for classes. I'll cancel your lessons with Mrs. Ferguson."

I was a little shocked that she had agreed to this so easily. "Thanks, Mom."

"I'm not your captor, Harvey. We're not a traveling circus. If you're not happy with the piano, then there's no point in you doing it." I pulled into the parking lot of our apartment complex and she added quietly, "But it would really mean a lot if you continued to help out at recitals."

I placed my hand on her knee. "Yeah, Mom. I can do that. No problem."

She was sad, I could tell.

Piano had always tied me to her, almost in the same way ballet tied my mom to Alice. When Alice quit ballet the summer before freshman year, my mom was heartbroken. Dancers had this secret language that you couldn't understand unless you were a dancer too. But playing the piano for my mom and Alice let me in on their secret, if only for a moment. The two of them were alike in so many ways. When I played piano for them it felt like I was in on it. Like, for a few minutes, I could be a part of this world that was outside of mine. In that world, though, where I was only a guest, I was their accompaniment. And I was tired of being everyone's damn accessory.

It tied me to my dad too. I couldn't picture what he looked like, but I could picture his fingers—close-trimmed nails, with knobby knuckles, dry with use—and I thought if all I got out of piano was having it in common with my dad, then it was worth it. But he'd left us, so I shouldn't have to stay for him.

Harvey.

Then.

I watched Alice from across the cafeteria as she walked to the trash line to dump her leftovers. It'd been a few days since telling my mom I wanted to quit piano. I wondered what Alice would have to say about that, if anything at all. It didn't matter, though, because we never really talked much anymore, not since starting high school. I saw her every once in a while when my mom dragged me over to Bernie and Martin's. The three of them would sit around the table drinking wine while Alice and I sat on the couch watching TV in silence—and not the comfortable kind. There was none of the easy laughter we'd grown up on. Lately, though, I'd started making excuses. Homework, plans with Dennis, job interviews—all reasons why I couldn't go.

Noise bounced off the linoleum floors, traveling, as the fluorescent lights buzzed overhead. I'd heard about her and Luke breaking up. It took a few days for the news to trickle down the social totem pole to Dennis and me. I wasn't sure exactly what had happened, but I did know that Celeste now occupied Alice's seat next to Luke with Mindi at her other side. Mindi had always taken dance classes at my mom's studio, but she'd never been very serious about it.

She was there for Celeste and because she needed a talent for all the pageants her mom entered her in.

Since she didn't sit with Luke anymore, Alice sat at a table by herself. But, every day, people sat with her. She hadn't really talked to any of them, but they all sort of talked around her, waiting for Luke's ex-girlfriend to make her next big social move.

The last time I really talked to Alice was the week before high school. Bernie had made partner at her law office, so Martin threw a party for her. The attendees were basically old fat men wearing khaki pants and dress shoes without socks and accompanied by their wives. The backyard smelled like barbecue, cigars, and beer.

Alice had reached this point in the night where she'd stopped verbally responding to all the old people trying to ask her questions about school and ballet—especially since she'd just quit.

The old guys who'd managed to leave their wives at home flocked to my mom in her usual all-black attire with her hair done up in a bun.

Alice's eye caught mine from where she stood next to the dessert table. She mouthed to me, *Driveway. Question game.*

I nodded, unable to stop myself from smiling.

I may have been a mediocre piano player, a horrible dancer, and a little too easygoing, but I had always been a supreme lip reader.

I sat in the grass waiting for Alice since the driveway was full of cars.

She plopped down next to me and handed me a beer.

"How'd you swing this?" I asked. Bernie was careful to separate the beer cooler from the soda cooler so she could police us. Alice's parents may have been cool with swearing and stuff, but drinking was not on the okay list.

She shrugged. "Old guys love me."

"Gross!" But it was probably true.

"Not like that," she said. "Okay, well, maybe like that. But who gives a shit?"

She wore cutoff denim shorts and this really tight navy blue tank top with little flowers. I wanted to kiss her so bad. I wanted to know what it would feel like to lie in the grass with her on top of me and nothing but clothes between us.

She held her bottle up to mine. "Cheers!"

It wasn't the first time I'd ever had a beer, but it tasted as sour as I remembered.

"Question game," said Alice.

The question game was a game we played growing up. Really, I guess it wasn't a game, just a conversation. But when you're a kid, everything's more fun if you can call it a game. My mom used to call cleaning the clean-up game. Alice and I would race to see who could clean up their mess of toys or construction paper first. We never won anything. Well, except gloating rights—which, to Alice, was the only thing worth winning.

Alice asked first. "If you had to choose to sleep on your back or your stomach for the rest of your life, which would you choose?"

"What about my side?" I asked.

"Not an option."

I took a sip of beer. "My stomach."

"Me too."

"My turn," I said. I wanted to ask her why she quit ballet, but Alice quitting ballet felt a lot like me not knowing who my dad was. We tiptoed around it. "If you had to choose a brand-new first name right now, what it would be?"

"Joey," she said without pause.

"That's a guy's name."

She stretched her legs out on the grass. "I think it's sexy when girls have boy names."

I didn't know if my hormones could survive her bare legs and the word *sexy* all in one moment.

"What would your name be?" she asked.

"I don't know," I said. "Something like Mike. Something normal and not old."

She laughed and her hand brushed mine. "I love your name." Sounding out both syllables, she said, "Har-vey."

If she kept saying my name like that, I might not mind it so much.

"If you could take a test right now and skip all four years of high school, would you?"

"That's a good one," I said, feeling the bubble of beer in my chest. I thought for a second. "I would . . . not. It's going to suck so hard. That's all anyone tells us, but I think maybe there's some stuff that might be worth it, and I don't want to miss out just in case. What about you?"

"In a freaking heartbeat," she said. "I wish I could wake up tomorrow and be on the other side of graduation."

I didn't know what to say back to that. "It'll be okay."

"Alice," called Bernie from the side of the house. "There's someone who wants to meet you."

"Oh, shit. Dump these." Alice handed me her half-empty beer and ran off to the backyard.

That was the last conversation we had. It all made me wonder if maybe the Great Alice and Harvey in my head was a distorted version of reality—reality being that we were two kids, forced to hang out with each other because our moms had become best friends, but now we weren't even that.

Dennis sat across from me at lunch, rehashing some stand-up act he'd watched online last night. I nodded my head along, but didn't really catch what he was saying. Alice, her lips pressed together in a thin line, rolled her eyes at something one of the girls behind her said, and then I lost sight of her. I tried focusing my attention back on Dennis, doing my best to push her out of my thoughts. It was one of those stupid moments when nothing at all is really happening, but you'll always remember every detail because you're trying to hold on to all that was solid in your life before it exploded. It was being in an awful car accident and remembering every lyric to the song you were singing before the crash. That's what that moment was for me, my last memory of Alice pre-cancer.

Then the scream—an earth-shattering scream, followed by multiple shrill screams. I stood, trying to get a better look at whatever was going on. My chair clattered to the floor behind me.

It was quiet for a second before the tidal wave of gossip began to roll through the cafeteria.

"She, like, passed out!" one girl said.

Some guy yelled, "Someone get the nurse!"

"Call 911!" shouted another panicked voice, prompting an army of technology-armed teenagers to reach for their cell phones.

I searched for Alice's crown of hair, but nothing.

I don't know how I knew it was her, but I did. Like I could recognize her absence as much as her presence. I pushed through hordes of kids to get to her. People yelled at me and pushed back, but I didn't care. I saw familiar faces, like Celeste and Mindi, but I shoved my way relentlessly to the front of the crowd. Everything went dead quiet, and all I could hear was the pumping of my blood in my ears.

I pulled up short, in front of her body splayed out on the ground. It looked unnatural, with her knee bent all weird. Her bottle of water had spilled all over her stomach and now rolled around at her side back and forth, water dribbling from the open top. I wanted to clean it up. Her skirt was flipped up, revealing more than I wanted anyone to see. I threw my jacket over her lower half and sat there on the floor next to her until the paramedics came, like me sitting there would change something.

When the paramedics arrived, they enlisted a couple of guys from the wrestling team to pull me back, which said a lot because I wasn't ripped or anything. The paramedics kept asking if we were related.

"We grew up together," I said over and over again.

"You her brother?" the youngest paramedic asked as he held open the cafeteria door for the gurney carrying Alice.

"She was my friend. She's my . . ." I didn't know *what* Alice was. The guy shook his head and let the door swing shut behind him.

I should have lied. I should have said I was her brother, but I didn't. It was one of those stupid mistakes that plays over and over in your mind for days.

The next week, she came back to school and didn't even look at me. She acted like nothing had happened, and I began to wonder if I had imagined the whole thing. It was an earthquake, one that only I seemed to feel.

Alice.

Now

I still *felt* sick.

I knew I would, but I couldn't separate the act of *being* sick from the act of *feeling* sick. It didn't make any sense to me. When would my body stop dying and start living? Or did it even work like that?

The plan was to start more chemo this summer, as long as my "condition" stayed consistent, which it had so far. Dr. Meredith told my parents that it would be in my best interest to get back into some sort of routine as soon as possible. I'd been dragging my feet for weeks, hoping I could get at least another two weeks out of my parents. And today was my seventeenth birthday, a day I had never imagined living to see.

My body may have been in this great state of in between—neither healthy nor sick—but my mom had definitely moved beyond me being sick. She was ready to push forward. We never really talked about the whole remission thing, which I guess was another issue, but her totally out of character "handle Alice with care" haze had begun to fade. Even so, yesterday when she came home with a manila envelope from the principal's office, I felt betrayed.

She held it out to me and said, "They're expecting you back on January eighteenth."

I stood with my hands in tight fists at my sides.

She sighed. "Let's concentrate on getting you back on track. If you do summer school, you might be able to graduate on time. And then there's college, too. You're not that far behind. Still lots of viable options available."

I crossed my arms over my chest. *College.* I hadn't thought too much about college except for the fact that I wouldn't be going. All of a sudden I had this future and everyone seemed to know what to do with it, except for me. I didn't have to talk to Harvey to know what he expected from us. He would want permanence. I'd even promised him that—when it hadn't been mine to promise. And now my parents with school.

When it became clear I had no intention of taking the envelope from my mom, she dropped it on the counter and turned to walk down the hallway toward her room. From outside her door, she called to me, "There's no hiding from life, Alice Elizabeth. It always finds you."

Then why hasn't it found you? Why do you still get to live a lie?

I took the envelope to my room. According to the papers from the principal's office, I would pick up mid-junior year. I had been homeschooled the last few months of sophomore year, and over the summer I'd rot in summer school while I made up the first half of junior year. It all sounded so easy, like nothing had ever happened. Between chemo and summer school, my vacation was already shaping up to be top-notch bullshit. But then again, the cancer could always come back. In a deep corner of myself that scared even me, I thought that maybe if the cancer did come back it might not be so bad. I knew how to die. It was the living that scared me.

But right now I was faced with two hurdles. Tonight, the Alice's-Seventeenth-Birthday/Not-Dying-Anymore Party, and in the morning I would have to face school. And with school came Luke and Celeste and Mindi. Suddenly, life was at my doorstep, waiting to be answered, but all I had were questions. It's a hard thing to explain unless you'd ever gone through something so life altering as toeing the line between life and death.

I still couldn't wrap my mind around it, being in remission. I'd been going to doctors' appointments biweekly, and everyone there treated me like a bubble that might burst at any moment.

The doorbell rang, and I heard the sounds of Natalie and Harvey letting themselves in, slipping off their boots at the door, and locking the thumb lock behind them. I didn't really know why I was so stressed about this party thing. It wasn't even a party. It was only me, Mom, Dad, Natalie, Harvey, and some ice-cream cake. Minutes passed, and I thought maybe they had forgotten me back here in my room. Relief as true as a lie settled in my chest as someone rapped on my bedroom door.

"Come on, Al," said my mom. She stuck her head into my room, her wavy blond hair bouncing around her chin. It was starting to grow out. She had cut her long, untamed locks into a bob when I lost my hair. I bet people at work assumed she'd cut it for the sake of solidarity with me and my bald head. But I was pretty sure it had to do with her boyfriend or whatever the hell he was. Her eyes crinkled as she bit her lip, studying me.

I sighed and looked down at my jeans. I'd had them since I was thirteen. A little short, but they fit in the waist. I had put on about three pounds since going into remission, but most food still made me queasy. After sliding on my slippers, I followed my mom out the door and down the hallway. I couldn't look at her without seeing him. That man. In our house. Now that I wasn't waiting for the end, I would have to live with this.

Nearly a month after Christmas and our house was still decorated. The dust had settled on the ornaments and garland. The out-of-season decor was a longstanding tradition in my house. My parents always waited to take down everything until after my birthday, saying it added to the festivities. I thought they were just lazy, but still, a birthday without Christmas lights would feel flat-out offensive.

Since being told I was in remission, I'd been poked and prodded more than I had when the cancer in my blood was actually detectable. Between doctors' appointments and feigning tiredness, I'd been able to just miss Harvey. I avoided him for nearly a month, although he called every day. I wanted to see him, but I didn't want to talk to him, like any words might break us. I saw him on Christmas. It was weird this year. There had been so many presents, more than any other year, and I wondered if my parents had gone overboard before or after Dr. Meredith's news.

Harvey's face lifted the second he saw me. "I missed you," he said, and hugged me tight. Over his shoulder, I could see tears streaming down Natalie's ivory face. Harvey held his arms so closely around me that I felt the weight of his forearms overlapping across my back. It made me feel paper thin, breakable.

When he finally let go, it was Natalie's turn. I hadn't seen her for over a month, and I had assumed I might never see her again. She curled her long, lean arms around my shoulders and placed her chin atop my head. She was a gazelle of a woman, standing at least a few inches taller than my five foot nine inches. "Welcome back," she whispered into my hair.

Everyone in my life was ready for this except me.

"Happy birthday to you . . . ," my dad began to sing as he approached us from behind. His voice was a little unsure at first but rose in volume when everyone else joined.

I turned to him. He held out a huge strawberry-ice-cream cake, my childhood birthday party staple. Natalie squeezed my shoulder, telling me to make my wish. Heat warmed my face, and the countless candles made everything and everyone look fuzzy. I closed my eyes and pretended to make a wish, but I didn't, not really. I had nothing left to wish for, and even if I did, I wouldn't wish for it; I would *do* it.

My eyes must have been closed for too long because my mother cleared her throat. My eyes sprang open. They all stared at me, waiting. It took me three puffs to blow out all the candles but one. Without missing a beat, Harvey swiped his tongue over his thumb and pointer finger, using them to snuff out the last stubborn flame.

Next, we opened presents. My parents gave me cash, which was what I asked for every year. From Natalie and Harvey, I received a generic Happy Birthday card and a rectangular box wrapped in champagne-colored wrapping paper. I knew what it was before I opened it, but I still went through the motions. Tucked into a small brown box and shrouded in white tissue paper was a pair of brand-new pointe shoes.

The minute I opened the box, Natalie tried to explain herself. "I know." She stopped, collecting her thoughts. "I know that you don't dance anymore, but I read somewhere that your body would recuperate more quickly if you exercised."

Natalie was never verbally confrontational. In fact, she might even come across as shy at times, but she let her feelings show in her actions. So while this seemed like a nice gesture, it was also Natalie's way of saying, *It's time to get back to the studio.* I picked up the shoes, the silk smooth against my fingers and the leather soles blemish-free. My throat went dry and my fingertips numb. Anxiety sank deep into my abdomen like a set of hooks. One more expectation I didn't know how to live up to. At least this one could exist in a box beneath my bed.

I wanted to be that person for all of them—the person they'd painted into their memory, the memorialized version of Alice—but that girl wasn't me. And that scared me. As it turned out, my greatest fear in life had become expectations.

Natalie looked back and forth between my parents. Dad

patted her back. And Mom looked at me with anticipation. My forehead knotted in confusion, not sure what she wanted me to say. She raised her brows and tilted her head to Natalie.

"Oh," I said. "Thanks."

Like an old friend, I wanted to keep ballet within reach, but this was too close. With this defunct body, I wasn't all that interested in testing my limits. I slid the shoes back in the box, and gave Natalie and Harvey a stiff-lipped smile.

The summer before freshman year, I'd told my mom that I wanted to quit ballet. She agreed as long as I told Natalie myself. On the surface, I think I wanted to start high school fresh. I was done being the girl who had to go to ballet class every day. We lived in a small town and, yeah, I was considered good here. But in comparison to whom? I couldn't be like Natalie, teaching pupil after pupil, hoping something might stick. If ballet was going to be my life, I'd only be happy living it on a stage. I preferred to accept the disappointment now rather than waste more years in a studio and have a casting director or an admissions board tell me I wasn't good enough.

On that day, I ran through the front door of the studio and into the changing room, bobby pins slipping from my bun as I changed out of my denim shorts and tank top and into my black leotard. I slid my black convertible tights on over my leotard and threw my backpack beneath Natalie's desk.

"Alice, get back here with that nest of hair," called Natalie.

Without a word, she rolled her office chair out for me and I sat down. She placed her hands on my shoulders and squeezed some tension from my sore muscles. Gently, she took out all my bobby pins, and my head screamed with relief. Taking down a ballet bun is sort of like a brain freeze, causing a brief but intense headache. I held out my hand for her to place the discarded bobby pins in. When my hair was completely loose around my shoulders, she massaged my scalp for a minute, and I couldn't stop the sigh that slipped from my lips. Instead of putting my hair back into a tight bun, Natalie placed a straight part in the middle of my head and gave me two long braids on either side. When she was through braiding, she took a couple of bobby pins from my open palm and wove the braids together at the base of my scalp, pinning them in place.

That night after class, and after all the other students had gone home, I sat with Natalie on the floor of the largest studio while Harvey waited in the car. I told her I wouldn't be back for classes in the fall. I sat up straight and enunciated my words, but inside they were a whisper.

She didn't say much of anything until we were standing in the dark with our bags in tow, getting ready to set the studio alarm.

"You can have until Monday to change your mind. I'll hold your place until then." The room around us was pitch-black, so like most things people hear in the dark, I pretended not to hear anything at all.

★ ★ ★

Ever since I was a kid we'd always had cake before the meal at any of my birthday gatherings. One year I'd begged my mom to have cake first. She'd caved and it had been a tradition ever since. Besides, I'd always hated the idea of saving the best for last.

After eating cake, Harvey sat right next to me with two plates of pizza—one for each of us. He wolfed down his slices and went for seconds while I still picked at my first helping. Our parents huddled around in a circle, conversing in hushed whispers while every couple minutes my dad glanced over his shoulder at me and Harvey.

After his trip for seconds, Harvey ducked beneath the low-hanging light dangling above the kitchen table and asked, "Do you want me to pick you up for school tomorrow?"

"I think my mom wants to take me because it's my first day back," I lied, rubbing my hands up and down my arms trying to warm myself. I wasn't ready to be alone with him yet.

With a slice of pizza hanging from his mouth, he shrugged out of his zip-up hoodie and draped it around my shoulders. I resisted rolling my shoulders back and letting the jacket slip to the ground. Instead, I pulled the fabric tight around myself. It smelled like Harvey. Like spilled gasoline and produce and boy deodorant.

Tonight, I was cold. Tomorrow, I would deal with Harvey.

"Are you nervous?" he asked.

"Why would I be nervous?"

He scooted his chair a little closer to me and took my hands from where they sat in my lap. Beneath the table, he held my fingers, warming them, and said, "I won't let them near you. Not Celeste. Not Luke."

"Don't. Just don't." I pulled my hands away and pushed my plate to the side and rested my cheek against the table, turning away from him. All that lay ahead of me tomorrow weighed on my shoulders, and I could barely pick my head up. Beneath the table, he squeezed my knee. I jerked away. Harvey did too, doubling the gap between us. It hadn't been so long ago that Harvey's touch had been the only cure I'd wanted.

Still, he sat silently by my side all night, reaching beneath the table for my fingers every so often. I wavered between hot and cold. Between wanting to lean into him and wanting to shoo him away. Our parents stayed huddled in the kitchen, their voices growing louder and more boisterous as the wine disappeared from their glasses.

Finally, at a quarter to eleven, Harvey dug the keys out of his mom's purse and escorted her to the car. On the porch, both my parents and Natalie wore rosy cheeks and drooping smiles as they said good night. Harvey hung back with me in the doorway.

The January cold tinged his cheeks and nose red as he rubbed his hands together. "We can sit together at lunch tomorrow. And I was thinking we could do something this weekend. Dennis is going to ask out Lacy from work— she graduated last year, so I doubt it'll happen. But if she says yes, I thought we could go with them. I guess, like, a double date or whatever. Make it less awkward for them."

I sucked in a breath and turned my gaze to our parents, still laughing, not quite ready to say good-bye. "It's cold out. Take this," I said, pulling off his jacket.

"Keep it till tomorrow."

I shook my head. "I'm fine."

His jacket draped over his arm, he took a step forward and kissed the spot where the corner of my lip met my cheeks. "Happy birthday." He paused. "I love you."

His words sucked the air out of my lungs. My heart pounded, echoing to every crevice of my body.

He ran down the steps to his mom's car, not waiting for me to say it back. "I'm going to warm it up," he called to her, the keys dangling from his fingers.

I slammed the front door behind me, my parents still outside. I ran upstairs and, in my room, I melted into my desk chair. I had Harvey, and I had him for good. Hadn't that been all I wanted? To make those perfect moments last? But now I felt trapped, like a homeless person who'd been given their dream home only to suffer from intense wanderlust because we always want something until we have it.

I thought about something I could control—my hair. Or lack thereof.

Since my treatment was suspended months ago, my brows had grown back and my hair was on the mend too. I'd kept shaving my head, though. I would have rather died bald than with some random wisps of hair. After finding out I was in remission, I'd stopped shaving my head.

Although it was sporadic and splotchy, my hair had now started to grow in.

I dug through my closet until I found a red beret that must have once belonged to my mom. Not that it would do much good. I was the girl who had cancer. That shit's sort of hard to hide.

After Harvey and Natalie left and my parents had turned off all the lights, there was a quiet knock on my bedroom door. I slumped down in my bed and pretended to be asleep. I developed that little gem of a habit while I was sick. People love to talk to sleeping sick people. It's like talking to a dead person, but a breathing dead person, so it's not so bad.

From the sound of the footsteps, I knew it was my dad. My bed creaked beneath him as he perched on the edge. He took my cold fingers, enveloping them in his, and I wished I hadn't pretended I was asleep.

"Alice Elizabeth, you fooled us all." For a second I thought he'd caught me, but I realized he wasn't talking about my sleeping act. "If anyone could beat it, it *would* be you," he said, his voice slow with wine. "You're tough as nails, Al. Tough as fucking nails." The springs in my mattress squeaked as he stood.

Both my mom and dad had never tried to censor themselves around me. That included everything from curse words to financial woes. My mom, especially, believed that hiding things made them that much more illicit. She was right, in a way, but my mom always thought everything to the extreme. And maybe feeling illicit was why Mom hadn't told us about her affair. Maybe she liked having a secret.

All the honesty I'd become so accustomed to made being sick that much harder, because suddenly I was a damn egg with a flimsy shell. I stopped getting in trouble—well, not really—I still got into trouble, but I was never punished for anything. I never heard a peep about hospital bills. And my mom stopped arguing with me when usually every morning was a contest to see who could pick a fight first.

Now everything felt wrong, and nothing was the same. My parents and school. Harvey and us. Natalie and ballet. All these plans and all I had to work with was a big, fat question mark. Even though cancer was the hulking monster in the closet, it wasn't a relapse I was concerned about. Lying there in the dark with the creaking sounds of my house settling, I saw what only ever haunted me in those moments when my body was asleep and my head was still wide-awake. The unknown. It consumed me.

Harvey.

Then

Alice sat on the foot of my bed. It was the first time I'd seen her since she passed out that day in the cafeteria. Seeing her so alive, right there in front of me, eased every muscle in my body. I'd asked my mom every day since then if she'd found out what happened to Alice, but she only told me that they were still running tests. All I could think of was the paramedics asking me over and over again if we were related. Then today, after school, Alice found me at my locker and asked what time I was through with work. She said her dad was going to drop her off for a little while later that night. My mouth had stopped working, so I'd only nodded.

I had spent the hours between then and now wondering what had changed and why she was coming over. Since we'd started high school, I'd get these urges to go up and talk to her, but any time I came close she was with Luke. And even when she wasn't with Luke, I couldn't think of anything worth breaking the silence for. I kept thinking that if I was going to say something to her, it'd have to be a little more groundbreaking than *Hi*.

That night Alice let herself into my room with her hand

covering her eyes and said, "You have five seconds to hide your porn."

"You're going to have to give me more than five seconds," I said, trying to play along.

She didn't laugh, but plopped down on my bed.

"Do you remember when we were kids and your mom was watching me and she had to take you to a doctor's appointment, so she took me too?"

I didn't answer. Things like that had happened all the time when we were little.

"Your mom went to the bathroom for a minute while we waited in the examination room. You sat in the chair, and I walked around looking at everything, sticking my hands in the cotton balls. You kept telling me to sit down." She turned to me. "Do you know what time I'm talking about now?"

I laughed. "Yeah," I said. "You told me the rubber doorstop on the wall behind the door was a nose-cleaner. And then you kept saying, 'What's that on your nose, Harvey?' so I knelt down in front of the doorstop and rubbed my nose around inside."

"And then the nurse came in and hit you with the door. Oh my God, and then your mom came in!" She pressed the tips of her fingers to her smiling lips. "She was so pissed."

I sat down next to her. "Yeah. I didn't figure out that you were making it up till I was, like, ten." I wanted to ask her why she was here, but I didn't want this moment to end.

She had probably said fewer than twenty words to me

since the beginning of freshman year. I was trying hard not to count her words now. *One hundred and thirteen.*

"You don't even like playing the piano, do you?" she asked, changing the subject.

I like creating the rhythm of your body. That's what I wanted to say. If I was suave I would say shit like that, the kind of stuff that made girls' clothes fall off. I wanted her to keep talking so I told the truth. "I don't know. I quit."

"That's dumb."

I needed her to say it. Whatever it was she came to say. Because after a year of silence, why else would she be here? "Alice—"

"I have leukemia, Harvey."

Your life changes sometimes and it only takes a few words to bridge the gap between now and then. My first instinct was shock. It didn't make sense. She didn't *look* sick. "I'm sorry." It was all I could think of to say.

"Yeah," said Alice, "because I must have caught it from you." She slid in closer to me. "Don't be sorry."

I nodded. "So, is this, like, the type of cancer they just cut out of you and then it's all 'Hey, everybody, remember that one time I had cancer?' Or is this, like, the bad kind?" The type of cancer that decimates you and everyone you know.

She didn't answer, and because she didn't say so, I assumed it to be the latter. If it was okay, if she thought she would be all right, she would have said something like *but it's not serious.* I tried to talk, but the words stuck to the back of my throat. This wasn't supposed to happen.

"Acute lymphocytic leukemia. I'm starting the first round of chemotherapy next week."

"How do you feel?" Words, sounds I didn't know I was making.

"The same, I guess. I don't know. I can't tell if I've felt like this for so long that I can't tell or if I genuinely don't feel any different. Does that make sense?"

One hundred and ninety-six words. All those words in a matter of minutes but only four words that mattered. Only four words played on repeat in my head.

I have leukemia, Harvey. I have leukemia, Harvey. I have leukemia, Harvey.

I wonder if she practiced how she was going to say it. *Harvey, I have leukemia. Leukemia have I, Harvey.* Maybe she tried different inflections of each word. I would have. *I have leukemia, Harvey.* I thought about all the other people she might have told before me—the list was short— and I hoped that, besides her parents, I was the first to know. It was selfish, but I wanted to know I came first even if it was only when shit was falling apart.

I ignored her question because I wasn't sure if what she said *did* make sense and, too, I thought maybe it was the type of question you didn't answer. "Is it bad?" There should have been an online course that covered appropriate questions to ask when someone tells you they're terminally ill, but nothing could have ever prepared me for the hole that was growing inside of me. The absence I was already feeling at the thought of losing her.

"It's not good." She licked her chapped lips and even

now, when she was trying to tell me that some disease was eating away at her, my fucking hormones took over.

I thought about my mom because if anything could extinguish my sex drive, it was her.

I wondered if my mom knew. Bernie probably figured out a way to time it so that we both found out at the same time. That would be fair, and Bernie was nothing if not fair.

"They said the younger you are, the higher your chances are for recovery. But, I dunno. The doctor said it can be dicey. Dicey," she repeated to herself. "All the good shit is supposed to happen when you get older. Driver's licenses, concerts, sex. So that's really fucking ironic," she whispered.

"Did they do, like, a bunch of tests?"

She flexed and unflexed her feet. "Yeah. They kept saying things like 'inconclusive' and this 'warrants further testing.' They did a bone marrow biopsy and finally came up with something."

It sounded painful. "Did it hurt?"

"They gave me stuff for while they were doing it, but now it's just sore."

I wanted to have an answer to that, a way to fix everything. "What do we do now?" *We.* It sounded presumptuous, but it'd just come out. And even though I knew it shouldn't have been the case, the last year felt inconsequential—minuscule in comparison to the weight of her confession.

"Let's turn off the lights and look at the glow-in-the-dark stars on your ceiling."

It wasn't the answer I was looking for, but I wanted to do it all the same. "Okay."

I turned off the lights and navigated my way back to my bed by moonlight. Alice lay on my bed and patted the empty space next to her. Didn't have to ask me twice.

"Are you scared?" It was the question game, but this time I was asking all the questions.

"I don't want to be." I heard the words she didn't say.

"I am."

"Good," she said, her voice a whisper.

"Are you staying in school?"

"My parents haven't said otherwise." We were quiet for a moment. "Do I tell people at school? How does that work?" She hadn't told anyone else.

"The booster club is going to have a field day with this."

"*Oh God,*" she groaned, rubbing her eyes, and when she did, her T-shirt shifted, revealing a sliver of cream skin in the moonlight. I slid my hands beneath my back. *Look, but don't touch.*

"I think I'm going to die." There was an eerie calm to her voice that terrified me more intensely than any cancer.

"Don't say that, Alice."

"We all die. We *are* dying. I'm just in the fast lane, I guess, dying faster than the rest of you slugs."

My knowledge of leukemia was limited. I knew that leukemia involved blood and that there were two major types of leukemia—chronic and acute. And I also knew that Katie Cureri's little sister Emma had leukemia when

71

we were in fifth grade and she was in third. The elementary hosted a ton of events and fund-raisers for her and her family. The more money they raised, the better Emma got and now she was fine.

Money was the cure to cancer.

I wished I was rich.

I couldn't think of anything that would piss off Alice more than a charity event in her name. I cracked a smile and laughed.

"What?" she asked.

I shook my head. "Nothing," I said. "Do you think you'll be eligible for handicapped parking?"

"You're kidding, right?" Without giving me a second to respond, she continued. "That would be incredible." She paused. "I don't drive yet, though."

"Yeah, but I bet your parents could get one."

"Yeah," she agreed, and then after a moment, "I could, like, sell it online."

"I don't think it works like that."

She sighed.

I wanted to ask her if whatever was going on right now, between us, would end when we turned the lights on and she walked out of my room.

"I have something I want to talk to you about." Her voice filled my dark bedroom.

My stomach flipped in anticipation. "Okay."

"I've got some research to do first." She shimmied down to the edge of my bed and made large steps over piles of clothes and books, ranging in height and mass. She headed for the door, and I wished there was a dead bolt on the other side so she could never leave. So we could never leave.

"Good night, Harvey. I'll be in touch," she said, like she was the godfather of cancer. She flicked the light back on and slunk out of the room. Did girls with cancer even slink? Alice did.

This felt like a dream. Tonight had been the best and worst night of my life, and the only logical explanation was that it had been a dream. I stretched out my limbs like a starfish with my feet hanging off the edge of my bed, staring at my plastic stars, their colors muted and dull beneath the bright lights. My room was too small for everything inside of me.

After a while, my mom came in my room without knocking. Normally, I would have made some smart-ass remark about things teenage boys did behind closed doors, but not tonight.

She sat on the edge of the bed, right where Alice had been only a little while ago.

With her eyes glued to the empty space ahead of her, my mother wiped a tear from each cheek. She squeezed my hand once, stood up, and left without a word. On her way out the door, she flicked off my bedroom light, leaving me to my stars.

Alice.

Then

"Harvey, I appreciate you being here," I said, taking a seat at my kitchen table.

I had seen Harvey at school, but I hadn't talked to him since last week when I told him I'd been diagnosed. In the last year, his obnoxiously curly hair had relaxed into waves, but his face would always have that permanently sleepy look to it. His thin, muscular build had finally stretched past my five foot nine by at least two or three inches. When we were kids, Harvey used to say we were going to get married, as if it was predetermined, like the color of your eyes. "Not going to happen," I would say. "You're shorter than me, and girls can't marry boys shorter than them."

When I told him, last week, that I had leukemia, it was the first time that the cancer had belonged to me, the first time the news was mine to share. His optimism broke me, but I didn't have time to be broken.

"Yeah, why aren't you in school right now?" he asked, sitting down at the kitchen table.

I guess he wasn't impressed when I phoned the school claiming to be Natalie and said that there was a family emergency. The good boy that he was, Harvey had turned his phone off during school hours, so I went about getting him out of class the old-fashioned way. After turning his phone on, he would have found this text from me: Call me. And call me he did, but amused he was not.

"Faked sick. Told my parents I didn't feel well. They propped me up on pillows with stacks of magazines, Sprite, and a bag of mini marshmallows."

"Seems a little callous, Al, don't you think?"

"What do you mean, *callous*?"

"You just found out you have leukemia, and you lied to your parents about being sick. I think they're on edge enough as it is without you lying to them so you can skip school."

In light of recent developments, I could see his point. "I hadn't thought of that." And really I hadn't. Technically, I hadn't lied. I had leukemia, therefore I was eternally unwell. I only took advantage of my circumstances, but still, a small bit of guilt twisted in my stomach.

I'd stayed home for two reasons. One, to snoop around my mom's office, which yielded no evidence of her cheating. And two, I needed time to gather my thoughts. Since being diagnosed, no one had left me alone, and I just wanted one day. Dad had been home twice to grab "some stuff" he'd forgotten. I knew he was here to check on me, and him not saying so irked me.

"I needed the house to myself."

I scooted my chair closer to Harvey. Animosity seeped through his roll-with-the-punches exterior. Turning into him, I pressed my full body against his side and placed a hand on his thigh. His resolve crumbled beneath my touch and his whole body tensed. I loved the way this control over him made me feel. The feeling scared me, but not enough to do anything about it, because now all I felt was assurance and purpose.

"I need your help," I told him with my hand still on his thigh.

He watched my hand. "With what?"

"I'm sick. You know that. And because of that, there are some things I need to do, and I need to know that you'll be there to help me when the time comes."

"What do you mean, *things?*"

I shrugged.

"What do you mean, like, a bucket list?"

"Well, I guess you could call it that, but I think Just Dying To-Do List has a better ring to it."

"No," said Harvey, his voice solid. "Those are for old, retired people." He leaned back in his chair and crossed his arms, shaking his head; my hand fell away. After a moment, he threw his arms up and said, "God, what the hell, Al? This is so screwed up. You don't talk to me for a year and now—no, this is ridiculous."

He didn't get it yet. He didn't get that the blood inside of my body was revolting against me. He hadn't been there for the cold sweats in the middle of the night. He wouldn't have to go through chemo so that he could be made even sicker for the sake of some sad sense of hope. I had to make him understand this, for me. "Harvey, what about 'I have leukemia' don't you get? I mean, maybe we should all have a list. You could get hit by a car tomorrow and die a virgin."

"How would you know if I'm a—?"

"Harvey."

He looked the other way, out the window above the sink.

"Harvey, if I . . . if I die and you don't help me with this, you will always regret it. Doing these things with you, that's part of my list in a way." I bit down on my lip. "Maybe there are some things that you want to do with me that are on your list, ya know?"

He sat in silence, watching his fingers, woven together in his lap. "What's on the list?" he asked, his voice low and scratchy.

"I can't tell you."

He laughed to himself in a sad way and rubbed his eyes. "You want me to help you with a list of things you won't disclose to me." He leaned forward and bit the skin around his thumb. "Classic."

"I would tell you on a need-to-know basis."

Writing down a list and showing it to Harvey made this thing more tangible and more of a commitment.

"This isn't going to be, like, riding-a-horse-bareback-down-the-beach type of shit, is it?"

I smiled and leaned in to him, only a few breaths between us. "No," I said. "No, it's not." Cancer would take away plenty. My hair, my body, my life. What I'd never realized, though, was that there was one privilege to dying: the right to live without consequence.

"I'm in." He said it like it was inevitable, like he could

say no, but it wouldn't matter.

"You won't regret it."

"You have a plan, though, right?"

"I'm still working on the logistics."

"But—"

"Harvey," I said, my voice low. "Trust me."

I knew what this looked like. It looked like I was using Harvey. But here was the reality of the situation: the minute my life went from semipermanent to most likely temporary, I decided to latch on to everything in my world that had always been permanent, and for me, Harvey was so permanent he was concrete.

Harvey.

Now

Today was Alice's first day back in school. I didn't see her until third period. I wanted to pick her up that morning. I could feel us slipping again, like freshman year. But this time was different. It was worse. This time there was so much more to lose. Last night, I told her I loved her. I'd said it in a no-big-deal kind of way. She'd always known, and I'd practically said it before she went into remission. But last night I needed her to know in case there was ever any doubt.

When she entered the classroom, her eyes traveled the rows of desks and barely flickered with recognition when she saw me sitting in the third row. She wore a red beret, baggy jeans, and a striped purple sweater that I recognized from seventh grade. Alice was always thin, but now she was transparent. Still, even in her mismatched ensemble, she looked cool.

She walked down the aisle without acknowledging me. Just when I thought she was going to pass me by altogether, she slid into the desk I'd saved for her. She sat with her legs crossed at the knee and with her head on her desk, one hand resting beneath her cheek and the other arm stretched out so far it hung off the desk. And closed her eyes.

Last night, she'd acted so bizarre, and before that she'd avoided me for weeks. I could understand, in a way. I saw how all this might be difficult for her, like the shock of a bright light in the middle of the night. But now, here at school, her avoidance felt so deliberate. And she seemed . . . mousy, which was the most un-Alice word I could think of.

Before the final bell rang, Celeste appeared in the doorway with Mindi at her side, who happened to be in this class.

With a vicious smile, Celeste whispered in Mindi's ear. She nodded and walked past us to the back of the classroom, kicking the leg of Alice's desk on her way.

Alice startled a little, but turned to see the back of Mindi's head and then spotted Celeste outside the entrance to the classroom.

They had this weird girl moment. No one said a word, and the only thing that broke their stare was Margaret Schmidt—class treasurer and member of the world's saddest color guard—as she shouldered her way past Celeste.

Margaret gasped when she saw Alice. "We all thought, like, you know, that you were still sick." Margaret's springy curls bounced, not because she was moving, but because they seemed to move with energy. Dennis said she probably snorted her prescription Adderall every morning. "So, are you better?"

The whole class turned.

Alice watched each of their faces and seemed to shrink back a little. "That's what they tell me."

"Oh my gosh," said Margaret, clutching her notebook to her chest. "That's so incredible. It's, like, a miracle."

Alice bit her lip and nodded.

More students—who I was sure Al had never spoken to in her life—began to crowd her desk, like they hadn't even seen her until Margaret Schmidt had to make a goddamn scene out of it.

"Yeah," said Doug Halbert. "My dad talked about you in church on Sunday."

"Could you feel it? Like, the cancer?" asked Tasha Wenters.

Yeah, she can feel the earth orbiting too.

It was rapid-fire. Two girls leaned on my desk trying to get a better look.

"How soon will your hair grow back? My aunt's didn't grow back the same," said some guy I couldn't see but wanted to kick the shit out of.

I was overwhelmed, so I knew it could only be that much worse for Alice. She didn't answer any of them, not based on what I could hear. And I don't think the fuckers cared because none of them even gave her a chance to respond.

Some were genuinely nice. Things like "I'm glad you're okay," or "I prayed for you," or "If you need help catching up on schoolwork, let me know."

I wondered if every single class Alice went to today had been like this one.

"Class, seats."

A teacher. Thank God.

While Mr. Slaton settled into his chair, the thrum of voices leveled out and everyone trickled back to their seats. Alice trained her eyes on the top of her desk. One lone pencil sat tucked behind her ear. She squeezed the back of her neck, her fingertips going white. I wanted to protect her.

Mr. Slaton clapped his hand loudly against his desk, giving one last warning for everyone to shut up before roll call. He called name after name and then Alice.

"Miss Richardson?" called Mr. Slaton.

She barely moved at the sound of her last name.

"Welcome back," he said, smiling. "I'm sure you've heard this a thousand times today, but we're glad to have you back. Quite a bit to catch up on. See me after class. We'll get you squared away." He waited for her to nod before smiling and calling the next name.

If it hadn't been for the Algebra 2 book on my desk, I wouldn't have been able to say exactly which class I'd been sitting in for those forty-five minutes. I spent the entire period staring at Alice, and Alice spent the entire period pretending to sleep—I could tell by her breathing. (Weird, I know, but I'd seen her do a lot of sleeping in the last year.) When class was dismissed, she stood and waited for Mindi to pass her. With her shoulder, Alice rammed her from behind. Mindi tripped and dropped her books. I picked one up and then practically ran over her to try to catch up to Alice, but she didn't stay after class like Mr. Slaton had asked her to. She disappeared, making whatever loomed between us grow a bit bigger.

I searched for her all day, but she didn't show up for any of the other classes we had together. After last period, I turned my phone on and found I had a voice mail from Martin explaining Bernie had gotten tied up in court and they wondered if I could give Alice a ride home. I would have been cool with giving Alice a ride, if I could find her in the first place.

I covered every square inch of school, including janitorial closets and girls' bathrooms, in forty-five minutes. Alice was nowhere in sight. I even checked the groundskeeper's shed out past the track. I'd done as much looking as I could on foot and decided to head out to the parking lot.

Her phone sent me to voice mail over and over again. She was probably screening my calls. Either that or her phone was dead. Both were entirely plausible options. I left four voice mails. My artfully composed messages sounded something like this:

Voice Mail One: "Alice."

Voice Mail Two: "It's me, Al. Where. Are. You?"

Voice Mail Three: "I'm sorry, where did you say you were again?"

Voice Mail Four: "Alice, in case you were wondering, you're not in the guys' bathroom, but whoever was here last pissed all over the floor. I'm really hoping that wasn't you. I give up. I'll be in the parking lot."

The cold air slapped me in the face, and I slid my gloves on, pulling the collar of my jacket up around my face to shield my cheeks from the burning wind. As I ran down the aisles of cars belonging to kids staying late for rehearsals and practices, I saw two figures sitting on the ground huddled together between a truck and an old Cadillac. I thought I recognized a spot of red on one of their heads, so I doubled back. I found Alice sitting on the freezing pavement, but without her beret on. Her cheeks and nose were bright red. And looking at her made my bones chatter even more.

"Hey," she mumbled, and wiped her running nose in the crook of her elbow. "This is Eric," she said, nodding to the guy sitting next to her.

From where he sat on the ground I could tell he was scruffy and broad with thick muscles. Thicker than my body could carry. Basically, he was all the shit you didn't want to see in the guy sitting next to the girl you love. He was more man than boy, and he wore Al's beret, while her nearly bald head was exposed to the freezing cold. Either he was even more selfish than Al or he was that stupid.

"Hey, guy," he said.

Guy? Who called people that? There was something slightly familiar about him. "Are you in any of my classes?" I was really hoping this guy wasn't some creepo Alice had picked up in the parking lot.

"It's possible," he said, shrugging his shoulders with a calculated effortlessness. "I guess I'm new."

"Eric, this is my . . . this is Harvey."

I flinched. "But you can call me *guy*."

Alice crossed her arms tightly over her chest. She was not amused.

Then it dawned on me. "Study hall! You were in my study hall last Monday. Did you get moved to Johnson's study hall or something?" I'd only seen him the once.

"Something like that," he said, not even looking at me but at Alice, like it was some kind of private joke only they shared.

I wanted to drive an entire continent between them, but instead I extended my gloved hand. Scruffy man-boy stared lamely like it was some kind of inanimate object.

"Right . . . okay," I said, stuffing my hand in my pocket and directing my attention to Alice and away from His Royal Scruffiness. "Al, I've called you a billion times. I'm supposed to give you a ride home."

"I'll meet you at the car." She didn't even look at me; her eyes were locked on Eric Guy.

"I parked far away."

"Sure, yeah." She gave me a small smile.

I shook my head at her, but she'd already turned back to Eric. "I'll be right back."

I pulled the car to the front of the lot, giving the heater a chance to warm up. With her back turned to me, I could see Alice had no intention of getting into the vehicle any-time soon. She was talking to Eric Guy. She couldn't talk to me, but she could talk to this asshole. So I honked. For thirty seconds straight. And then one more honk for good measure. Alice turned and narrowed her eyes at me.

Normally, I would have given her an apologetic smile, but not today. I rolled down my window and breathed in the cold, fresh air. I gave her a grin so big I was sure she could see all thirty-two of my teeth. She rolled her eyes and continued on with Eric Guy.

"Alice, come *on!*"

She held a finger up to me while Eric Guy grabbed her hand and pulled a permanent marker out of his back pocket. As he was about to press the marker to her palm, she pulled her hand back like she'd changed her mind.

I exhaled.

But then she took the marker from his hand and pushed up the sleeve of his jacket, scribbling her name and number down the length of his forearm. She tossed the marker to him and sauntered over to my car with a prowling grin on her face.

She slammed the passenger door shut. "Hey, guy!" I yelled through my still-open window. "The hat!" I said, motioning to my head. "Hand it over." Alice punched me in the thigh. "Now." He took his time walking to the car, trying to make a sad display of James Dean cool, and tossed the hat into my lap.

"I'll be calling you, Allie."

"Her name's Alice, you turd," I said, and sped off.

"Jesus, Harvey. What's your problem?"

"You're my problem!" The words were out of my mouth before I could calculate them. "You are so obviously my problem." I paused. "Why are you acting like nothing happened between us when something did?"

She didn't answer. So we acted like adults and gave each other the silent treatment. Her eyes followed the blur of trees and buildings outside her window as her fingers traced patterns on her seat. It felt good—standing up to her, like I'd won something. But that didn't last for long.

When I dropped her off, she gave me a quick kiss on the cheek, a small gesture that she knew would appease me. I hated myself for letting it be this way, and I hated her for making it this way. But, really, I loved her, and that hurt the worst of all because I was tired of being her debris.

Alice.

Then

Most everyone who's undergone chemotherapy has a hair story.

Plenty of people had told me that when my hair grew back, after all the chemo was said and done, it would look and feel a little different, a new texture or maybe even a whole other color altogether. The first person to tell me this was a stranger, a random woman at the Grocery Emporium. I was in the juice-and-soda aisle when she came up behind me, touching my elbow lightly, like I might break. She had had breast cancer and rebelliously curly hair, but after remission it all grew back straight as a board. Then she gave me a reassuring smile and hugged me, which honestly creeped the shit out of me.

Harvey stood a few feet away, stocking apple juice in his Grocery Emporium apron with his name tag hanging upside down, witnessing this exchange. With my chin resting in the dip of this stranger's shoulder, I watched him concentrating on his task, avoiding my gaze.

I had lost my hair a few weeks before. Most people let their hair fall out slowly—clogged in a bathtub drain or clumped in a hairbrush—until it was time to let go and shave it all off. But I guess I've never been very patient.

It was Christmas Eve, and I had finished up my first round of induction chemo the week before. I'd seen enough Lifetime movies to know it was coming—plus it was a major bullet point in the "So, you're going through chemo" pamphlet. The pamphlet also said that the process of losing hair can feel more manageable if the patient cuts their hair first. I'd stood in the bathroom the night before starting chemo with the scissors in my hand. Before I'd made the first cut, I noticed my pile of hair ties next to the sink. I couldn't do it. The pamphlet also said I should be attending a support group, but I didn't take that advice either. Nothing would have made me feel dead faster than sitting in a room full of dying people talking about their feelings.

At treatments, I'd see girls with scarves wrapped around their heads, and they looked at me like they knew all my secrets. And they probably did.

We usually spent Christmas Eve at home. Natalie and Harvey would come over and we'd have a big dinner and take family pictures, blending the six of us together for various combinations. Natalie would make lots of traditional Romanian desserts, like amandine—which translated to *insanely delicious chocolate cake*. When we were kids, Natalie and Harvey used to stay the night and we'd all open presents together in the morning.

I stood in front of the bathroom sink, splashing water on my face. I'd spent the entire previous day puking up every piece of food I'd ever so much as looked at. The prospect of Christmas Eve felt better, as long as the nausea didn't kill me.

Pushing my hair back to put it half up, I ran my fingers through to the ends to find a clump of hair in my fist. I'd noticed it before, in the shower and in my brush, but this was the most at one time. I dropped the hair into the sink, wishing I could count the strands. I closed the lid to the toilet and plopped down.

I'd never been all that vain.

Okay, that was a lie. But I'd never had to try with my looks. They just were.

Tucking my knees into my chest, I pulled on another small patch of hair, just to see if maybe it was a fluke. A drill. I loosened my fingers and let the strands fall to the ground, hitting the white tiles of the bathroom floor.

I was fine.

I was absolutely fine until I realized the last person who had played with my hair had been Luke. And I would never put my hair into a sleek dancer's bun again. I had this certainty about death, and, for me, there was never a possibility of it growing back. I knew it the way most people expect they'll wake up in the morning.

"You all right?" called my mom through the door. "Everyone's ready for pictures."

"Just a minute," I said, my voice a little shaky.

I pulled my fingers through my hair once more and a fistful of hair fell into the sink.

My mom knocked on the door. "Alice?"

I turned the thumb lock, unlocking the door, and the minute it clicked she twisted the knob. She looked me over once before noticing the hair in the sink and the loose strands on my shirt. Reaching for me, she tucked me beneath her arm. I was too tired to pull away. She spoke to me in a soothing language only she and I knew. For that moment, her lies dissolved and I melted into her side. She held me, as though the sheer force of her could keep me on this earth.

The next day, we shaved my hair in the kitchen with the brand–new electric razor my mom had bought my dad for Christmas.

There were no family pictures that year.

Alice.

Now

Harvey was pissed at me. I really didn't care, though. My first day of school was horrible, even worse than I'd expected. And Harvey's feelings weren't at the top of my list right now. He was livid the entire way home, making sharp, jerking turns and shifting his foot between the brake and the gas.

When he pulled into my driveway, he didn't even cut the engine to come inside like usual. He sat there with his hands on the wheel, drumming his long fingers. I leaned across the center console and gave him a kiss on the cheek. That was exactly what I needed to keep Harvey in reach. Not too close, but still in my line of sight.

My mom watched from the porch.

"You're home late," she observed as she followed me into the house.

"Yeah, lost track of time."

"I see. Got home a minute ago—court was shit today. I knew I wasn't going to make it in time to pick you up."

I doubted court was the only reason she was held up. *How's your boyfriend, Mom?* I'd carried this knowledge of her with me for so long that it had become as much a part of me as the cancer had. And now when I saw her, I saw nothing else.

"It was very nice of Harvey to drive you home." My mother was impatient by nature, and her job always showcased the worst sides of people, so she wasn't very forthcoming when it came to caring for others. But she loved Harvey. In the eyes of my dear mother, Harvey hung the moon. Hell, he *was* the moon. "Why didn't you invite him in?"

"I don't know, Mom. Why didn't *you* invite him in?"

"Drop the attitude, Alice." She thumbed through her box of teas and pulled out two different individually wrapped tea bags. "After school teatime. Lavender or hazel?" she asked, holding them up.

"Neither," I said. "Hot chocolate."

She closed the tea box.

"With extra marshmallows," I added.

When our bags of grainy powder had turned into steaming mugs of cocoa, she sat down next to me at the kitchen table.

"Talk to me."

Talking. It's something we used to do all the time, just talk. I'd tell her all about school and dance and even Celeste. Two summers ago, when I was headed to tenth grade, we even talked about going for birth control soon. I told my mom over and over again that Luke and I weren't having sex, but she insisted that we take the precaution and that I could always be honest with her.

"How was it?"

Horrendous. "Nothing to report."

"Anyone give you a hard time?"

"Not really." Lie.

"And Celeste?" she asked.

"Didn't see her." Another lie.

"Girls can be barbarians. But you know that—you are one."

"A girl or a barbarian?"

"Both." She paused. "I talked to Natalie on my way to work this morning. She's not doing any spring-break camps at the studio this year. She was thinking maybe the five of us could go on a little mini vacation. What do you think? I mean, if you're still feeling okay."

What did I think? I thought that sounded great and horrible all in the same breath. "I don't care."

My mother pursed her lips. She probably wanted to tell me to stop acting like a brat, but she didn't. "We'll play it by ear." With her still sitting there and neither of our cocoas barely touched, I got up to go to my room. But my mother wasn't done. "Do you have any homework?"

"I guess," I called over my shoulder. Instead of replying with an equally biting remark, she let me walk right out of the kitchen without a word left between us.

I wanted her to yell at me. I wanted to hear the truth. The lack of truth—that's how I knew she was still having an affair. And today, with her getting stuck in court, I couldn't believe it. No matter how true it might have been, I would always be suspicious. Because if she'd ended it, she would have told my dad, and then they would have told me. Working in criminal law, my mom saw the fruit of lies every day, and she wouldn't tolerate it at home. Growing up, she would say, "Inside our home, we always tell the truth. Even when it does more harm than good."

In my room, I checked my cell phone and found three missed calls from the same unknown number, presumably my newest acquaintance, Eric. Funny, I hadn't taken him for eager.

After having been out of school for months, I started my first day back with Luke in first period. Since he was a senior, we shouldn't have shared any classes, but he'd always been horrible with dates and names, so I wasn't surprised to find him in my eleventh-grade history class. I sat in the only seat available, which was about midway to the back of the room. When our teacher, Mrs. Morrison, told us to break into groups for a project, I excused myself to avoid the risk of ending up in a group with Luke. I needed some serious air anyway. In the hallway, I dug around in my pocket for the tiny slip of paper with my locker number and combo.

After some trial and error, my locker sprang open, and I realized I didn't have anything to put inside of it. All I had brought with me to school was a single pencil. I laid my pencil down in the locker and spun it between my two fingers. *College.* It'd been gnawing at me since last night. College could take me away. Far, far away. But college meant making plans. And plans meant hoping for something. Unless medical science had been magically revolutionized and remission was now synonymous with cured, I was wary of plans and all the goddamn hopes that came with them. I sighed, tucking my pencil back behind my ear, and slammed the locker door shut.

"Never thought I'd see you again," said a voice.

I turned around to see Luke.

"Get the hell away from me," I said coolly, even though I was fully aware of how alone I was, here in this hallway with Luke. I'd never been conscious of things like that, but I'd never had good reason to be.

He laid his hand on my shoulder. "Hey, now, Alice, I'm just the beginning of the welcome wagon." I slapped his hand away.

He stepped back. "You'll be seeing me around. I haven't forgotten," he said, "and I don't think Celeste has either."

This was Luke's senior year, so if I could survive until May, I'd be fine. If the cancer didn't come back, I'd be here next year with Celeste and I could handle her. I wondered if Celeste got her wish and finally got to do Luke. Luke didn't really have standards anyway.

Of Celeste and Mindi, only Mindi was in any of the classes I'd attended. I saw Celeste for a brief moment, though, sneering at me from the doorway of my classroom. The scene with Margaret Schmidt had been the same version of scenes in my first- and second-period classes. The questions, the few well-wishes—authentic and not. It all made me feel like someone else, someone I'd never wanted to be, someone fragile and lonely, who went home to scrawl all her feelings in her fucking journal.

After second-period algebra with Mindi and Harvey,

my school day was o-v-e-r. Well, not technically. I skipped out on the rest of the day, including my little meeting with Mr. Slaton.

On my way to anywhere that wasn't class, I stopped by the bathroom. As I washed my hands, the door swung open.

"I thought that was you."

From the mirror, I watched Celeste. She stood with her arms crossed and her little designer wristlet dangling from her wrist.

"You know, I'd already bought a dress in case you didn't make it. I mean, it was such a steal, and who doesn't need one more little black dress?"

"You're sick."

"I wore it for New Year's instead. Luke took me to Three Forks off I-9."

I laughed. "Oh, so that little charade is still going? Do you guys like to do it with the lights on? We never got that far, but I always wondered."

She didn't answer my question, but her lip twitched for a second, making me think that Celeste's dreamboat might not be such a dream after all. I blinked and her vicious smile was back. "How's your mom doing?"

I turned around and crossed my arms, mirroring her, as I leaned up against the sink. I wanted to say something equally low, like how it must be really nice for Luke to be dating someone his own size. But I didn't and it was Harvey's fault. He was the closest thing I had to a damn conscience. "What do you want, Celeste?"

"All I want is for you to feel welcome. It's cute how

people are so excited to have you back." She took two steps closer to me. "They don't know what I know. The cancer might be gone, but the bitch isn't."

I'd met Eric under the bleachers in the gym after my run-in with Celeste. I'd never seen him before. He looked as though he hadn't been to class in weeks, if not months. A few copies of *SPIN* magazine sat piled up beside him, like he'd set up a little home there. He was playing a game of solitaire and chewing on sunflower seeds, spitting the shells on the floor for the janitors to clean up.

When I saw him there, I almost told him to leave because I intended to stay there until May. But before I did, he sprang up from his spot on the floor. He wore jeans tucked into combat boots and a black T-shirt. He looked older than most students, and I wondered if he was even a student at all. On the floor next to his pile of magazines were an olive green army jacket and a bright red scarf.

"Hey," he said after looking me over, like he was trying to figure out if I posed a threat. He must have decided he was more interested than threatened because then he spread his arms out, displaying his little area. "Looking for a place to hide?"

"Yeah, I really am." I pulled my red knit beret off my sparsely haired scalp as a warning: damaged goods approaching.

He didn't flinch. I liked that.

After I sat down, I expected him to ask me about my

wisps of hair, but he just offered a handful of sunflower seeds.

"I like to suck the salt off of them and that's it. They'd be a waste on me," I said.

He was unperturbed. "So suck the salt off and give them to me. I just care about the seeds."

Normally, this would gross me out, but I had a feeling we'd be sharing germs before long anyway. Eric rolled over on his stomach, holding his face up by his knuckles, like a little boy watching Saturday-morning cartoons.

"First day of school?" he asked.

I thought for a moment. "Yeah. Yeah, it is. You?"

"Nah. Started two weeks ago."

And for the first time ever, I was the new kid. I didn't ask any more questions and neither did he because I don't think either of us was all that interested in answers.

We hung out for the rest of the day, under the bleachers. At lunchtime he treated me to a vending-machine buffet. My beret stayed on the floor all day, and when I shivered, he tossed me his jacket, which was big enough to use as a blanket. Without asking to, he put on my bright red beret, like we were even, and we continued our game of Go Fish. By the end of the day, Eric must have thought we were at the point in our relationship where we would trade "Daddy doesn't love me" stories, because he asked me out of the blue, "Who are you hiding from, little girl?"

"The boogeyman. Go fish."

Alice.

Then

After Christmas, I started school a week later than everyone else because of my second round of chemo. It felt pointless to keep going, but my parents didn't seem to think so. Besides teachers and administration, no one had known I was sick. But when I came back to school without a head of hair, my health was no longer a private matter. There were whispers and questions, which at first I'd ignored, but then I figured the fastest way to stop the whispers was to answer the questions.

Within a week, I was Hughley High's poster child for cancer. People offering to stand in line for me at lunch or carry my bag to and from classes became a regular occurrence. I usually declined, unless it was Harvey doing the offering.

I didn't know how to explain it, and only the doctors seemed to understand, but my body always ached, and for the pain I was prescribed Tramadol. I wasn't allowed to carry it on school grounds, so Miss Shelly, the school nurse, always held my stash for me and let me hang out in her office for as long as it took to shake off the dizziness brought on by the meds.

Today, I skipped out on English lit in favor of the nurse's

office because I couldn't take the echoing sting my body felt every time I moved. Miss Shelly doled out my meds and set me up on the cot farthest from the door with the curtain pulled shut in front of me.

"Do you need anything else for now?" asked Miss Shelly.

I shook my head, my eyes closed.

"There's a cup of water and some crackers on the counter if you need them." The curtain rings scraped against the metal rod. "I'm going to run down to the teachers' lounge for lunch and a slice of Mr. Welston's birthday cake. I won't be long."

My brain told my head to nod, but I didn't feel the motion of it. Drifting, my mind went places I wished my body could follow.

"Hurry, come on," said a voice, interrupting my pharmaceutically induced sleep. "She just went to the teachers' lounge."

"I don't want to do it," said another voice. "I don't want to know."

"Oh," said the first voice, "and you'd rather wait and find out when your clothes don't fit in six months and you can't see your freaking toes?"

From the other side of the curtain I heard a whimper.

"Come on," said the first voice again. "You're probably not even pregnant."

My eyes flew open, my mind suddenly registering that this wasn't a dream.

"Okay." It was the second voice. "But you'll keep an eye out, right?" The voice was panicked, but familiar.

"Mindi, yes. Of course I will." Mindi. It was Celeste and Mindi. I held my breath, trying my best not to make a sound. Holy shit. Mindi might be pregnant. Quietly, I let my chest fall.

"You're the one who didn't want to take the test in one of the main bathrooms."

"I can't pee in public bathrooms like that," said Mindi. "I have a shy bladder. You know that."

I heard a zipper and papers rustling. "Here."

"Do I just pee on it?" asked Mindi.

"I think you can use a cup if you want." A cabinet door creaked open. I closed my eyes and could practically see them standing right there outside Miss Shelly's bathroom, next to the cabinets full of supplies. "Pee in this if you want."

"How much was the test?"

"I didn't pay for it," said Celeste.

"You *stole* it?"

"Uh, yeah, I did. I wasn't about to be seen buying that thing. Hurry up."

The door to the bathroom closed and opened again a few minutes later.

"I used the cup," said Mindi.

"Now we let it sit for ten minutes."

"Ten minutes? Are you serious? I can video chat someone in Russia in real time, and it takes ten minutes for a stick to tell me if I'm pregnant?"

"Like five minutes ago you didn't even want to know," said Celeste. "Come on. Sit down."

Mindi sighed as one of Miss Shelly's stools creaked, and they sat in silence for a few minutes.

I hadn't pegged Celeste as the type to risk stealing a pregnancy test for a friend in need. I never really had a girl friend like that, though. Growing up, I was always sort of friendly with Celeste because we went to school together and spent so much time together in dance class, but as we got older, the competitive tension between us swelled. A month before freshman year and a few weeks before quitting ballet, Mindi invited all the girls from dance class to a slumber party for her birthday. After her parents had gone to bed, we piled up on the couch with liters of soda and bags of jawbreakers. We flipped through channels until we found *Carrie*. For the most part, we laughed and made fun of the clothes, until the prom scene at the end where those skanks drop the pig's blood on Carrie. We watched, our jaws slack, as the high school gym went up in flames and Carrie turned everyone else's joke into their nightmare.

After the movie, I found Celeste in the kitchen, tears spilling down her cheeks as she held her phone to her ear. When I asked her who she was calling, she told me she was asking her mom to pick her up. The movie had freaked her out and she wanted to go home. I told her that if she left, none of the girls would ever let her live it down. After a few seconds, she nodded and hung up the phone. And that was it.

I was the first to fall asleep. And when I woke up the

next morning, I was covered in shaving cream and permanent marker. Celeste had been the ringleader. I guess she was ashamed of how I'd found her in the kitchen. It took me hours to rinse off the permanent marker so that my parents wouldn't see what had happened. That day changed everything for me. I would never make the mistake of trusting Celeste again.

It had been at least three minutes before Mindi began to cry. "How am I supposed to tell Drew? And what about my mom?"

"Hey," said Celeste, her voice dropping an octave, and I had to strain to hear. "It's going to be fine. You're on the pill. You're probably just late, and it's not like your parents will make you keep it anyway. Drew's nowhere near ready to have a baby. He goes to a freaking community college."

"It's just . . ." Mindi paused, and when she spoke again her voice shook. "I really liked him, and now . . ." She paused. "I'm going to get huge. And I'll have stretch marks and my boobs will get gross. And he won't stay with me. I wouldn't want to stay with me. And I'll have to do, like, night college—"

"Okay, stop. No more crying. In four minutes you're going to feel so ridiculous when you find out you're not pregnant."

Mindi laughed a little.

"You're totally wrecking your pretty makeup," said Celeste.

It was so weird to hear Celeste like that, being a friend.

Mindi took a few deep breaths. "Okay, I'm good. I'm good. I didn't even ask you—how did you feel about the *Oklahoma!* auditions?"

The school musical. Of course Celeste had auditioned.

"I've totally got it. I mean, the only person who can even compete with me is Tyson, and as much as he'd love to play Laurey, it's not going to happen. And then there's the ballet number. I'm without a doubt the most qualified. There's no way Mr. Achron doesn't see that."

"What if you don't get it?" asked Mindi.

"Not going to happen. I won't let it. And neither will my parents. They're sponsoring the play, and I don't think they'd be too willing to keep their commitment if I'm just some chorus member. Worst case scenario: I make up a story about Achron inappropriately touching my leg or some bull and threaten to take it to the school board."

"No," gasped Mindi. "You would not."

"Someday this is going to be my career, and I'm not about to let some washed-up theater teacher jeopardize it." If I didn't hate her so much, I would admire Celeste's ruthless drive. "I don't think it'll come to that, but I'm prepared to do whatever it takes. Musical theater programs need to see me as a leading lady. I'm not doing all this shit to play someone's dopey best friend."

"Yeah," said Mindi. "How much longer?"

"Two minutes," replied Celeste. "So, Luke's been a little weird lately. I feel like—" She stopped herself. "It's nothing."

"Come on," said Mindi. "I spilled my freaking guts to you."

"It's, like, when we were hooking up before we were together, it was so hot. He would call me while I was at dance and be like, 'Meet me in the parking lot. I need you.' He'd do stuff like that and it was such a turn-on. But now we sit around his house and watch movies and it's— Wait. Oh my God, wait. Get the box! What does one line mean?"

Shoes squeaked against the linoleum floor. "Pregnant," said Mindi, her voice hollow. "No, hang on. No! Not pregnant! I'm not pregnant!"

Their words turned into incoherent squeals.

Mindi let out a heavy sigh. "I am so relieved. Shit. I didn't even realize how tense my whole body was until it relaxed."

"God, do you realize how *over* your life would have been?" asked Celeste.

Mindi laughed. "Bitch."

"Whatever, we've got to get out of here."

"Wait," said Mindi. "What were you going to say? Before the test results showed up."

Celeste sighed. "We haven't really hooked up since he broke up with *her*."

I smiled. They deserved each other.

"Oh my God," said Mindi, "can you believe it? She has *cancer*."

"That's what my mom said. So freaking crazy. It's sad, in a way." She paused. I waited for her to say something about my mom. "And I'm not a bad person for saying this, because you know what I mean, but karma's a bitch."

Mindi laughed. "That is so messed up."

"Oh, come on, you were thinking the same thing."

She was right. Karma was a bitch, but so was I.

Alice.

Then

Over the last few weeks, and between sporadic vomiting and spells of nosebleeds, I'd become very well acquainted with the various girls' bathrooms and their locations.

I'd never been the type to stop and ask someone what was wrong when they were visibly upset. I am, however, the type to wear emotional blinders and mind my own damn business, which is exactly what I planned on doing the day I found Tyson Chapman bawling his eyes out in the girls' bathroom. Tyson and I had taken ballet together in first grade, but eventually he'd found his niche with theater.

Most girls might be alarmed to find a boy crying in the girls' bathroom, but finding Tyson there on the floor was no surprise. You didn't want to be the guy crying in the bathroom, but you especially didn't want to be the gay guy crying in the guys' bathroom. Tyson had come out of the closet the summer before freshman year, and he'd been getting shit for it ever since.

After spending ten minutes kneeling in front of the toilet bowl, I realized there was nothing inside my stomach to throw up and that I would just have to live with the nausea.

And, thanks to the chemo, I had puffy chipmunk cheeks, another chemo pamphlet bullet point. Seriously, my cheeks looked like they were storing three gum balls apiece.

I walked out of the stall nonchalantly, like I didn't just have my fingers down my throat. Tyson still sat there in the same spot on the floor. I did a good job of ignoring him as I studied my scalp in the mirror. After two rounds of treatment, I'd made no progress, living up to my grim prognosis. We'd recently found out that I wasn't a bone marrow transplant candidate, but Dr. Meredith had suspected that from the beginning. Since the start, chemo had felt more like a participation grade, except without the gold stars. Now, faced with the decision of our next step, my parents asked me to continue treatment. I didn't know how to say no to them. My time was running out, though, and I had things to do.

I shook my hands dry, then pushed the swinging door open with my back when Tyson said, "I thought the day you broke up with him was the best day of my life."

I took a step back inside. "What?"

"When you broke up with Luke. I saw it all happen in the hallway. He called me a homo, remember?"

I nodded. "You've got my attention," I said, and dropped to the damp floor next to him. It smelled like mildew covered in bleach, and I tried not to think about it. I already felt queasy enough.

"Okay. So, this last weekend I was at this house party out in Alton. I guess he had been at some other party, because he was plastered. Anyways, he kind of wandered

in all by himself. I swear to God, I thought it was a sign."
He scooted closer to me. "Alice, I've been in love with him
since the *third* grade." He said it like it hurt, and I bet it
did. Tears pooled at the corners of his eyes, making me feel
uncomfortable, like I shouldn't be seeing this.

I knew what house party Tyson was talking about. It was
a weekly thing at this old drag queen's house. You didn't go
there without knowing what you were getting into.

"My friend Courtney has always known how much
I loved him, so she went over to him and dragged him
onto the dance floor. Well, the center of the living room,
but you know what I mean. She danced with him for
a little while, but made sure I was right by her side the
whole time. There were people, like, everywhere, so he
didn't notice when Courtney left him in my very capable hands." Tyson leaned even closer to me. "I was kind
of freaked out, but he was dancing with me so I kept
going along. It was like he was still dancing the way he
would've with Courtney, but he was dancing with *me*.
There was no way he didn't know I was a guy. We were,
like, grinding and—"

I shook my head. "No further explanation necessary,
thanks."

"Anyways," he said, rolling his bloodshot eyes, "I went
to go get a drink from the keg outside and he followed me.
We didn't really talk. It was just us back there. I was crazy
nervous. I was about to ask him why he was there when he
sort of leaned in and kissed me."

I waited for some kind of an explanation. This was

the guy who had practically begged to get into my pants. He even slept around with other girls. "Hang on," I said, holding my palm up. "*Luke* sort of kissed you?"

"Yes, and it was earth-shattering. Everything I had dreamed of since third grade. Okay, well, I didn't realize people used their tongues to kiss when I was in third grade, but you get the idea. After that he kind of freaked out and took off."

I recalled all those times Luke and I had kissed, and it was okay enough, but nothing I could ever imagine someone dreaming of or hoping for. The thought actually made me want to gag, and I wondered if Tyson and I were even talking about the same guy.

Luke had kissed a boy. I couldn't believe it, couldn't understand how I didn't see it. A girlfriend would have known something like that.

"Courtney couldn't believe it either, so she snapped a picture with her cell from inside the house."

The wheels in my brain began to spin. "Does it look like him?" I asked.

Tyson's head cocked to the side, and his brows furrowed in confusion.

"The picture," I said, "can you tell it's him?"

"I can," he said cautiously, as he pulled out his smartphone. My breath caught in my throat as he showed me the picture. It was a little blurry, having been taken with drunk goggles, but, oh God—it was definitely him. He even wore his letter jacket with the unmistakable MVP varsity soccer patch emblazoned on his bicep.

"So what happened next?" I asked, handing the phone back reluctantly.

"Well, today I went up to him in the locker room before gym. Everyone had cleared out but us. When I asked him if he was okay, he said, 'Okay with you being a faggot?'" Tyson choked out a sob.

I hated that word.

Tyson sniffed and continued. "Then I reminded him that he kissed me in the first place. He told me to keep my mouth shut, and then this happened," he said, lifting his shirt to reveal a long, colorful bruise that stretched the entire length of his left side and seemed to continue well past the waistband of his jeans. The bruise yellowed at the edges, getting darker and angrier toward the middle.

"Wow. Are you okay?" I asked.

"Yeah. A little sore, but okay."

"So, you still think you're in love with him?"

"Probably." His face was severe and now free of tears.

Sometimes love is so intense that it turns into this gray area that borders on hate. That's what happens when the people you love have that type of power over you.

"I'm sorry, you know," he said, motioning to my scalp.

I nodded. "Can you send me the picture?"

He narrowed his eyes at me. "Why? What do you want with it?"

"Oh, I want to ruin that asshole." I felt bad for Tyson and even for Luke, but that didn't change what he had done to me.

He chewed on his lip for a second, thinking. "Yeah, you can have it. Let me know before it goes public, okay?"

I stood. "I will."

He nodded. "Hey, isn't your birthday this week?"

"Next Monday, sweet sixteen." I'd be spending my sixteenth birthday at the treatment center. "Sorry about the bruises, Tyson."

"It's okay. Suddenly, the pain is starting to fade."

"Yeah, revenge does that."

Harvey.

Then

I opened the picture on Alice's phone again. "And you're sure this is real?"

"One hundred percent," she replied.

Alice sat in the passenger seat of my car with a quilt wrapped around her legs, the hot air from the vents blowing stale as we idled in the school parking lot. She'd finished her most recent round of chemo a week ago, and this time she wasn't so quick to recover. Before, she had looked okay—not good, but okay. Now, the disease was tattooed all over her. She was always shivering and nauseous. There was nothing I could do about the nausea, but I had started to keep blankets in my backseat for her.

I couldn't make sense of it all. The chemo was supposed to help. The chemo was supposed to kill the disease, but it felt like Alice had become her disease. Her doctors told her to consider homeschooling as an option, and everyone tried to act like that wasn't bad news.

"Alice," I said, turning to face her, "are you sure you want to do this? I don't know that this is entirely ethical." I wasn't sure of Alice's entire plan, but I knew it involved a picture of Luke kissing a boy. The boy was sort of hard to identify, unless you knew it was Tyson, but anyone would recognize Luke.

"Luke's never been nice to you, or anyone else for that matter. He doesn't deserve to have secrets, Harvey."

Alice had given me the play-by-play of everything that had happened with Tyson, including his unfortunate bruises. I'll admit it, I had always hated Luke. He had never abided by any type of moral code, and even Alice had a line. "You're sure Tyson's okay with this?"

"He's completely on board with this. You know that."

The only concrete detail I knew of Alice's plan was that we'd gone to Alice's dad's print shop last night to upload the photo and make it as clear as possible with his high-end photo-editing software and that we'd transferred the photo to a disc. Three copies existed: one in my backpack, one beneath Alice's bed, and one in my closet.

I felt kind of bad about sneaking into Martin's shop. I hated going behind his back. He'd always been so good to me. When Alice and I were in second grade and in different classes, we had career day. As soon as I told my mom, she asked Bernie if Martin would talk to my class for her. I was never ashamed of my mom, but she knew that her coming to career day as a ballet teacher would only get me bullied on the playground. Bernie spoke with Alice's class about being a lawyer, and Martin spoke with my class about running a print shop. He brought free slap bracelets for the whole class. The week that followed was the closest I'd ever been to popular, until Mindi and Celeste told everyone that Martin wasn't even my real dad, and I got bumped back down the social ladder.

Not having my dad around was the type of thing that didn't matter to me until I figured out that it should. The more anyone tried to compensate for it, the more I realized that I might have something to miss. I'm sure there would have been ways to find him, but since he never tried to find us, I thought maybe he didn't want to be found. When I was younger, we got a few sporadic child support checks, but those stopped coming in the mail around the time I stopped believing in Santa Claus—which was pretty early on, thanks to Alice. It hadn't bothered me so much when I was a kid, but in the last few years I had started to wonder again. It's not that I had this hole in my life that needed to be filled. I had a family. For me—Alice, my mom, Bernie, and Martin—we were our own family. But I wondered sometimes, the way your mind asks those big questions, like whether or not there's a god or how a girl can think she's ugly one day and pretty the next.

I sat in the car with Alice as other cars began to trickle through the school parking lot. Today was the yearly drunk-driving seminar where the student government and the booster club teamed up with local police officers to do a cautionary skit and presentation in the gymnasium. All that really meant was that everyone got out of at least one class today.

I turned off the car. "We better get inside."

Alice threw the blanket into the backseat while I grabbed her notebook and my backpack from the trunk.

"Al, what if someone gets hurt?"

"No one is going to get hurt."

My feet stopped, anxiety bearing down in my chest.

Alice turned around and sighed, doubling back to me. "What is it?"

"What about Tyson? He has to live with this too."

She took the last step between us and held my face in her chilly hands. "I swear to you, Harvey, no one will get hurt. The only person who will have to live with what happens today will be Luke."

I didn't know how she could promise me that. Of course someone would get hurt. I shouldn't have given in so easily, but it was her touch that convinced me. All I could think about was her breath on my lips and her skin against mine. "Okay," I said.

We went our separate ways for first and second periods but met back up for third period, like she'd told me to. Because of the all-day seminar, the student body was on a rotating schedule so that not everyone missed class all at once. My and Alice's classes were scheduled for some time in the afternoon, but that didn't matter. What mattered was that Luke had third-period weight training.

Alice and I met outside the gymnasium door. When she walked up, her skin was a little yellow and her breathing ragged.

"You ready?" I asked.

She nodded and tried breathing through her nose.

Alice slid a key from her back pocket and unlocked the windowless door in front of us. I followed her up the back stairs to the gymnasium sound booth, which was set up so that we entered through the hallway outside the gym and took a steep set of stairs to the box above the bleachers. We couldn't see the presentations since the booth sat behind the makeshift stage, but it was the same thing every year. Four students—usually seniors—would stand in blue jeans and white T-shirts with fake blood and bruises all over their faces, pretending to be dead drunk drivers. It was dark, except for a few emergency lights. Each student held their own flashlight and flicked it on, holding it beneath their chin, when it was their turn to speak. Above the students onstage hung a large projector screen, flashing images of totaled cars. On the desk in front of Alice and me sat the laptop controlling the pictures on the screen. If it wasn't for the nerves, I would have felt like God.

Each of the four students said the same things but with different words. *I should have known better. One drink wasn't worth it. I killed myself and my girlfriend. There was a whole family in the other car, and it wasn't their fault I was drunk, but it's my fault that they're dead. I should have listened. I should have stayed.*

I guess if I hadn't heard the exact same thing at the seminar last year, the whole thing would have been a little more impactful. But the scare tactics didn't really work on the student body, and the faculty usually spent the entire time milling through the bleachers, threatening students with detention if they didn't shut up.

"You have the disc?" asked Alice, with her hand out.

I unzipped the front pocket of my backpack and handed it over. Alice hit the button on the side of the computer and the CD-ROM tray slid open. Looping her finger through the center of the disc, she used her other hand to pull out her phone and dialed a number she knew by heart. Hitting the speaker button, she said, "Here we go."

I began to sweat. From everywhere. My hands, my back, my head.

The phone rang so many times I thought he might not—

Luke picked up. "I think you have the wrong number."

"Oh, no," said Alice. "I most definitely do not."

I looked out over the gymnasium; it sounded like this part of the presentation was almost done.

"Whatever, psycho," he said. "I'm hanging up now."

Alice smirked.

My stomach turned.

"I don't think that would be a good idea, Luke. Now listen to me very carefully." She stood.

He said nothing, but I could hear him breathing into the receiver.

"I've come across quite the interesting picture of you swapping spit with someone of the same sex."

Silence.

"Now, Luke, I have no problem with this. But I happen to know that your small mind does and that you've fucked over one too many people for this to end neatly for you." Alice paced back and forth. "Still listening?"

He grunted. "You're lying. There is no picture. I'd never kiss a dude. That's disgusting."

"You have—" She glanced at the clock on the computer. "Three minutes to get to the gymnasium and stop this picture from going public."

"What the fuck is your problem, you crazy bitch?" His voice was low with urgency and terror. He sounded like I felt.

This was wrong. I shouldn't have agreed to this.

"Well, I'm dying, so that seems to be a problem. But the pressing issue here would be the bruises you gave Tyson Chapman. These pictures of cars are getting awfully tedious. I think it's time we spice things—"

The phone went dead. Luke knew the picture was real.

I bit down hard on my lip, the taste of copper in my mouth, and shook my head. "How do you know he won't come up here?"

Alice slid her phone into her pocket and sat down next to me. "He's not that smart." Touching her hand to my leg, she said, "Harvey, trust me. For two minutes, trust me."

We watched from the booth. The timing couldn't have been more perfect. The lights were dimmed so no one saw him, and we could only make out the outline of him, but Luke hauled ass out of the locker room and ran for the ladder to the projector, which ran up the back of the bleachers opposite us. To Alice's absolute delight, he wore nothing but a towel. She bounced up and down and clapped her hands, giggling.

When the lights came on he would be positioned above the bleachers where everyone could see him. Luke continued to climb, checking the towel at his waist every few seconds. I craned my neck to watch him.

Alice spun the disc around her finger.

I couldn't take it. "Al, you don't have to do this. He's already about to humiliate himself. And isn't that what you want anyway?"

Doubt flickered across her pale face, but was erased by a thunder of obligatory applause from the students and faculty.

The large overhead fluorescent lights began to buzz to life, taking a few minutes to turn on.

Luke's entire body tensed as he took the next rung.

For a second, no one noticed anything as all their eyes adjusted to the light and the officer who would speak for a few minutes took the stage.

The ladder creaked as Luke froze.

In unison, everyone turned, looking up to see him. The laughter was instantaneous.

I stood and took Alice's hand, hoping my touch impacted her in a fraction of the way hers did me. "Come on."

Luke yelled unintelligible curses as he took a few more steps in earnest. When he was within reach, he stretched for the power cord, his other arm curled around the ladder. It was hard to tell exactly what it was through the glass, but his towel caught on something. Maybe a loose nail or a sliver of wood. Just out of grasp, Luke leaned forward a little farther and his towel began to slip. He wasn't fast enough to catch it. We all watched as the white piece of fabric drifted slowly down to the bleachers below, leaving him in nothing but his skin.

I could imagine the rush of hands to pockets as students searched for cell phones to memorialize this moment. My cheeks burned. I'd always hated watching others be humiliated, even if they deserved it.

One of the police officers helping with the presentation started yelling up the ladder for Luke to come down.

Alice watched the computer, the disc hovering in her hands.

"Al, come on." My voice was desperate.

Shutting the tray with a push of her finger, she said, "Let's go." She led me to an empty classroom where she took out her cell phone and called Luke again.

I leaned against the teacher's desk, waiting for our next move.

When it went to voice mail, she waited for the beep. "Whoops. False alarm. Sorry about the embarrassing towel incident. That was so not part of my plan, but kudos! Now, just so we're on the same page, if you ever even think about seeking out retaliation against Tyson or anyone you think might be related to this little episode, this picture will go public. Whether I'm dead or alive." She took a second to let that sink in for him. "And, Luke," she said, "if girls aren't your thing and you realize you're lying to everyone including yourself and you decide to be honest, just remember I saved that moment for you. I kept your secret, which isn't something I can say you did for me." She hung up the phone.

I tried to process her words. *Secret.* "Alice," I said, "what secret are you talking about?"

She looked down at her feet. "Nothing. It's not important."

I watched her, waiting for her to talk.

"I don't want to talk about it," she said.

I nodded. I could wait. "The picture," I said. "I'm proud of you."

"Everyone was distracted. It would have been a waste. And at least now I've got some leverage on him."

I covered her hand with mine and she didn't pull away. "Let's skip and hang out at my place." Alice yawned. "I'm tired and my head hurts."

"Yeah, that sounds good."

We walked to my car, and I didn't let go of her hand once.

The next day, I headed to gym with Dennis as he told me what had happened after Alice and I left.

"He got suspended for a week, ya know?" said Dennis. "Apparently, the police sent him to the lockers to get changed and he punched one of the mirrors above the sinks, so Principal Kirby said he'd have to sit out the first three baseball games this spring too."

"Wow," I breathed. "How did you find all this out?"

"Debora was in the office when the whole thing went down. She said Luke's hand was wrapped in gauze." Dennis stopped in the middle of the hallway, letting everyone else on their way to class pass us. "I don't know what he did to Alice, but remind me never to get on her bad side."

Before gym class, I stopped in front of the only sink missing a mirror. Small shards of glass that the janitor had neglected still glistened against the white porcelain. I turned on the water and guided the last bits of glass down the drain with my thumb, wondering what hell I'd gotten myself into.

Alice.

Now

"So, Allie Cat, what does your weekend look like?" This was Eric's attempt at making plans, and I was over making plans. Plans were promises in disguise. "Maybe I could take you out Saturday?"

I had to hand it to Eric. Without an "umm" or a pause, he had asked me out.

"I'll let you know Saturday," I said as I climbed out of his old Range Rover.

Eric didn't seem bothered. "Saturday," he said.

Eric had started driving me home on my third day of school. I'd been back for about three weeks now. Every day I seemed to pull farther away from Harvey. I'd never had a problem with confrontation before, but I didn't know how to tell Harvey that the idea of "us" terrified me. I couldn't promise him the things he wanted because Harvey wanted forever. And that had been so much easier to give him when forever had an expiration date. Still, I missed him, and I didn't expect for it to hurt so bad.

Yesterday, I watched him in the hallway from an alcove of water fountains. He walked out of the bathroom and to his locker. I started to follow him. I didn't know what

I would say, but I thought that maybe I was ready to say something. I was a few steps away from him when Dennis's sister, Debora, walked out of a classroom and into step with him. She touched his elbow and stood on her tiptoes to tell him something. He leaned his head over a little so he could hear her. My stomach twisted, and I felt my ears turning red. I spun around and went back to the gym to find Eric.

The novelty of me coming back from the dead had worn off, and now everyone at school was more concerned with whether or not the vegetarian sloppy joe in the cafeteria was actually vegetarian. I hadn't seen much of Luke or Celeste, but I hadn't written them off either. That would have been stupid of me.

Eric reversed down the driveway. I wondered what his story was, but I didn't plan on asking. If we got personal, our friendship would no longer be one of convenience but instead something to maintain. Before unlocking the front door, I checked the mailbox above the doorbell. All junk mail and advertisements. At the bottom of the stack was a giant postcard folded in half. The postcard showed families on mini trains and in spinning teacups. It read:

Chill of winter got you down?
It's never too early to book your summer vacation
to Lake Quasipi Family Amusement Park!

Below that was all the booking information, including local lodging rates and a list of some other nearby attractions.

Once inside, I dumped all the mail in the trash and walked to the living room. Up until fifth grade, we'd gone to Lake Quasipi every summer. It was this old, rundown amusement park that never had any lines. My memories from Lake Quasipi were perfect little slices of nostalgia where everyone got a happy ending. I remembered riding the mini mine train with Harvey when we were kids, which was basically a mini wooden roller coaster with tunnels like a mine would have. It was Harvey's favorite, and he would beg to ride it again and again. One time the bar that sat in our laps got stuck, so we couldn't get off the ride. The manager had to come over and help the teenager manning the ride jimmy the bar up. We both howled, thinking we would be stuck forever. My mom stood next to us, calming us down as my dad told us jokes and Natalie held our hands.

Sighing, I doubled back and fished the postcard from the trash can. I smoothed it out and laid it on the kitchen counter. Then I called Harvey. I missed him and that was worse than not knowing what to say to him. After four rings, it went to voice mail, and I fumbled with the phone, unable to hang up before leaving a four-second message of silence.

I waited, but Harvey didn't call me back.

When my parents got home from work, they said they were going out for dinner and asked if I wanted to join. I passed, unwilling to play a role in their sham of a marriage.

The two of them rushed out the front door after making a last-minute reservation. As I locked up behind them, the doorbell rang.

Harvey stood on the front porch, waving to my mom.

"Hi," I said.

He turned to me. "Mind if I come in?"

I opened the door and he followed me through to the kitchen.

The house felt even quieter than it had when I was alone.

Harvey leaned up against the kitchen counter. "You called me, but I figured I'd stop by on my way home from work."

"What made you think I'd answer the door?"

His jaw twitched with the promise of a smile. "I don't know." He drummed his fingers on the countertop. "I haven't seen you much these last few weeks."

"Yeah. Lots of catching up to do with school." That was a lie. There was plenty of catching up to be done, but I wasn't really doing it.

He nodded and pushed off from the counter, walking to the other side of the kitchen where the postcard from Lake Quasipi sat. "Alice—" The way he said my name. It was the way you say someone's name when you have something to say that you've been sitting on for a while. But then he saw the postcard and held it up. "Feeling sentimental?" he asked.

I shrugged.

"You hungry?"

"I guess," I said. "Let me get a jacket."

I went upstairs for my maroon peacoat and a scarf. The coat was big and the scarf didn't match, but right now, I didn't care. I touched my fingers to my hair, which had begun to grow out into a poorly maintained pageboy cut. I took kitchen scissors to it the other night to even it out.

My mom asked if I wanted her to take me for a haircut, but I declined. I had so little hair that getting a haircut would have felt like buying a picture book for a blind guy. Unnecessary.

Outside, the wind was biting and relentless. Harvey ran ahead of me and opened the passenger door.

His heater made more noise than it did heat. I didn't ask him where we were going, but was unsurprised when we pulled up to Prespa's. We came here every year for Harvey's birthday. It was a little kitschy Italian place with over-buttered garlic rolls and grapes painted on the wall, not to be overshadowed by the giant mural behind the bar that showcased everything that might in some way be Italian, from people to landmarks.

Inside, we waited for a table even though every single one was available.

When we sat down, Harvey asked, "What are your specials?"

The waitress, with her short, curly, black hair peppered gray, had worked here for as long as I could remember. And because the specials never changed, she pointed to the dusty chalkboard on the wall.

"I'll have the chicken marsala and a Coke," he said.

"And I'll take the spaghetti and meatballs and a water. No ice. Extra lemon."

The waitress nodded and walked off to the bar to retrieve our drinks. After she'd brought those back with a basket of microwaved bread, Harvey said, "Question game. What do you want to be when you grow up?"

You'd think that after all these years of playing the

question game there would be no questions left to ask, but that wasn't the case. We'd asked each other this same question—*What do you want to be when you grow up?*—a million times, but the answer seemed to change every time.

"This time last year I might have said 'alive.' But I don't know," I said, sitting in silence for a moment, trying to mentally sort this. I'd never thought about professions or anything. I guess when I was little I wanted to be a ballerina, but no one ever does anything they plan on, so I never thought much of it. Thinking about it seemed like a waste of my *now* time, but I guessed there was one thing I always wanted to be. "In control," I said.

The corner of his lip lifted and he shook his head, like he'd won a bet.

A gust of wind blew in as our waitress went outside for a smoke break; I shivered.

"What about you?" I asked.

He shook out of his jacket and tossed it to me. I used it as a blanket on my legs. The lining of the jacket was warm with Harvey.

"I think," he said, "I think I want to do lots of things, but I want to own something. Like a business or, I don't know. I'd like to learn to play another type of instrument. Like the guitar or whatever."

His fingers traced paths on the sticky plastic tablecloth. I wondered if they missed that act of creating, like my toes did. The healthier I got, the more my feet ached to move.

It was my turn now, and I wanted to ask him about

everything that had happened between us those last couple weeks before I found out I was in remission, but I didn't know how to. So I asked, "Freeze to death or burn to death?"

"Too easy, Al. Burn. What about you?"

"I've already done the dying-slowly thing, so burn."

"We can burn together," he said.

"Thick as thieves," I mumbled. Skimming the edges of my memory were recollections of us whispering in the backseat while my dad watched us in his rearview, a smile on his lips as he muttered, "Thick as thieves."

"My turn. Was there ever a time when you actually enjoyed playing the piano?"

He leaned back in the booth. "A few times."

"Oh, come on, Harvey. That was awfully vague."

"Well, so was the question, and I answered it," he replied smartly.

"No you didn't. Now answer my question."

"When it was for you," he said, his voice soft. "I enjoyed playing the piano when it was for you. Are you happy now?"

His words made my rib cage hurt, like it was too big for my body, but I didn't answer. "Why did you quit?"

"It's not your turn anymore."

The waitress brought our food out along with a round of refills.

I took a sip of my water.

Harvey practically face-planted into his dish, shoveling food into his mouth. "Why did you quit ballet?"

I took a deep breath and decided to be honest. "I would never have been good enough."

"What do you mean?" His face scrunched up.

"I wasn't ever going to be good enough to make a career of it." I paused. "I love your mom, Harvey, but I could never teach like she does. It wouldn't satisfy me. Performance or nothing." And I was never going to be good enough for the stage.

He leaned forward. "But you were incredible, Alice."

I smiled. "In comparison to who, Harvey? All fifteen girls in my class?" I would never go back to ballet. Especially not now, when my body was still weak and out of practice. No matter how much I convinced my brain not to, my muscles still missed ballet. Then there were the pointe shoes Natalie had given me. I tried to hide them from myself. But it never worked, because all they did was haunt me every time I opened my closet or looked under my bed.

I was done thinking about this. I was done talking about this. "Now, you have to answer. Why'd you quit?"

He took another bite and swallowed. "Because I got tired of doing it for other people."

We were quiet as we ate the rest of our dinner. Harvey finished before I did. He pushed his plate aside and said, "I think my father played the piano too."

I didn't know what to say. Harvey never really talked about his dad. I figured he'd always thought about it, but I felt wrong asking.

"Do you wonder where he is?" I asked.

"I try not to."

I wasn't a very good person unless I really made the effort to be. But I'd always wanted to solve this problem for Harvey. Because I had a pretty okay dad and Harvey deserved that—probably more than I did. But I had no idea where to start.

It was such a frank moment between us that I almost told him about my mom. But if I told Harvey that, there would be no more secrets and he would move in even closer. And that couldn't happen. The closer he got, the more answers I owed him.

When our check came, Harvey insisted on paying. I argued, but finally said thank you.

We stood and I gave him his jacket back. Outside he hesitantly took my hand. The touch of his skin against mine sent a shot of electricity up my spine followed by the sheer relief that his feelings for me hadn't changed.

We walked to the car, but he didn't open the door for me. Closing the space between us with one step, he pressed me up against the car with the length of his body. I knew it was freezing out, but only because I knew it should be and not because I could feel it. He brought his hands up to my face, holding my cheeks in his hands; I tucked my arms inside his jacket and around his waist. It was a reaction, nothing my body gave my mind a chance to decide.

"I've missed kissing you," he said. One hand slid around to the back of my neck.

My stomach tightened and my fingers tingled against his

back. I should have stopped him right there and told him the truth—that I couldn't promise him what he wanted. Because I wouldn't let myself make promises any longer. Not when they could be broken.

Instead I replayed his words in my head because they were so delicious.

The heat from my chest filled my cheeks, and Harvey leaned into me. Even if I wasn't pressed up against his car, I wouldn't have moved. I stayed perfectly still except for the beat of my heart pounding in my ears, like someone was inside of me banging on the cavity of my chest, begging to be let out. He was so warm and near that when I inhaled, it was his breath in my lungs.

The car next to us beeped, the headlights blinking, and we jumped apart.

We drove in silence the whole way home, not because it was awkward. We didn't have to talk and the not talking felt good.

When we got home, Harvey followed me inside, and I tried to count the hours until my parents might be home. I felt like I was at war with myself. I wanted nothing more than to feel something, but I didn't know how to deal with what came after the feeling.

"You want some hot chocolate?" I asked.

"I'm okay," he said, looking out the kitchen window, like he could see whatever was out there in the darkness of our backyard.

All I saw was the reflection of him in the window.

I poured a cup of milk and put it in the microwave.

"Alice," he said slowly, "why have you been avoiding me?"

The question made me testy, like a cornered animal. "I'm not," I said. "I called you tonight, didn't I?"

He took in a sharp breath and exhaled. "You called me because you decided you wanted me here *tonight*, not because you wanted me." His voice got louder with every word. "You don't get to be the only person to decide when *this* works for you," he said.

The microwave dinged as I closed my eyes for a moment and said, "Good night, Harvey." I couldn't look at him and say it at the same time. I wanted so badly to tell him to stay and that I was sorry, but calling him had been a mistake, and I didn't know how to make him understand that. He had to leave because if he didn't, I wouldn't be able to stop myself from falling down this slope and into him.

"You never surprise me, Alice, which is such a disappointment."

His words pinballed in my chest, every syllable hitting harder than the last, but I kept my back straight and my expression unmoving as I opened the microwave.

He turned, walked a few steps, and then spun back around long enough to say, "I can't pretend to forget anymore."

Alice.

Now

I went to bed before my parents got home from dinner. I wasn't sure when I fell asleep, but it was somewhere in between thoughts of Harvey and my mom.

The next morning I slept in and found a note from my mom on the kitchen table.

A—

Doctor's office called, had to reschedule your blood work for Tuesday.

Big case on Monday. Went to office to prep. Dad came to help sort papers (and order Chinese food, yum!). Be home late. Call Dad's cell if you need us!

Love you.
P.S. Left cash in case you go out.

There was a crisp twenty lying on the counter.

"Nice," I murmured to myself. "Unsupervised Saturday."

I used to love being home alone. Our house always felt full, especially over the last year. Everyone seemed scared to leave me alone, but today being alone in my house was as good as a clean bill of health.

I spent my morning trying out each of my mom's nail polishes and watching reality shows about hoarding and people staging interventions for others with drug addictions. Those shows were a giant time suck. Anything I did was a sad attempt at avoiding thoughts of last night.

These last couple weeks, I'd pushed Harvey farther and farther away while keeping him barely in reach. Then last night, I really fucked up when I almost let him kiss me. I felt weak and wanted to let him in. In the parking lot, it was like we would be okay, like we *could* be okay. Under the night sky, everything looked so much better. So much more manageable.

The show went to a commercial break when the doorbell rang. My first instinct was to pretend like I wasn't home.

It rang again, then three times in quick succession. "Okay," I called. "Cool it." I looked through the peephole and saw Eric on my front porch. His messy hair flipped up around the edge of his beanie. He rubbed his hands together.

I cracked the door open. "Hey."

"I didn't feel like waiting until tonight. You free now?"

Rather than respond, I waved him in with one hand and shut the door behind him. I'd forgotten about tonight and our supposed plans.

"God, it feels so good in here," he said, and then suddenly took notice of my bare legs. "Cute."

I always felt like that word was an insult cloaked as a

compliment, but I swallowed my annoyance and led the path to the living room.

"Cool," he said, "I love this show. Have you seen the one where this guy saves all his toenail clippings in mason jars? Crazy."

"Gross." At least we didn't talk about cancer. Actually, we never talked about cancer, and that was one of the things I liked best about Eric. "Sit down."

He sat right next to me, half on my cushion and half on his. "I think I like you," he said. It was more statement than confession.

I flipped through channels, trying to pretend like I hadn't heard him because I didn't know how to respond.

"So what's up with you and that Harvey guy?" he asked.

"Nothing at all." I'd never been charitable with words.

"So, um . . . ," said Eric from the corner of my vision, and he actually looked a little nervous, which was alarming and endearing all at the same time. He slid closer to me until the bare skin of my thigh touched his jeans. He felt warm, and his closeness made my heart skip. I didn't feel butterflies or anything like that; he made my skin feel antsy, like I might jump out of myself.

"I'm going to do this, okay?"

He curled his arm around me so that his hand was on the small of my back, pulling me to him. He kissed my neck and unzipped my hoodie a little so his lips could travel farther down. A sigh escaped my lips. His kisses became more feverish as he unzipped even more of my hoodie. As he kissed my body, it occurred to me he had never kissed my lips. But the thought vanished as his mouth traveled up my neck to my lips and he kissed me deeply. The feel of him was a magnetic charge, humming my entire body to life.

For a moment, my thoughts shifted to Harvey and the way he was so carefully deliberate with me last night. How he'd taken it so slow—so slow we never reached our destination—and how he seemed so present for the moment, so ready to experience every single touch.

Pushing away my memories of Harvey, I shoved Eric's shoulder back and straddled his lap. This wasn't scary or complicated like being with Harvey. This didn't have to mean so much. He took my face in his hands while I tugged the hat from his head. His fingers moved through my short hair and down my back, bringing me closer to him. I needed his body to be seamlessly connected to mine, to feel something physical, without the anchor of emotion. I tugged his jacket off his shoulders and broke the connection between our lips while my lips concentrated on his jaw and neck, nibbling and kissing. He moaned into my ear, and the sound alone just about broke me in half.

"The doorbell's ringing," he breathed.

"Ah, hang on," I said. "Stay back here." I zipped my hoodie all the way up to my neck.

Without thinking to check the peephole, I swung the door open to find a deliveryman jogging back to his truck and an overnight package addressed to my mom with the word CONFIDENTIAL stamped across the overstuffed manila envelope. Probably something for work.

I tossed the package on my mom's desk in her office.

"Swank office."

I turned to where Eric stood in the doorway. "I told you to stay in the living room."

He shrugged.

"Come on," I said, and tried to squeeze past him, but he didn't let me. Eric picked up exactly where he'd left off, pressing my body against the door.

He lifted me off the ground, and I draped my legs around his waist. Carrying me back to the couch, he stumbled backward a little and we crashed down on the cushions. Our limbs were a tangled mess, and our kisses didn't feel quite as potent as they had before our interruption. But I was willing to work up to that. Coming up for air, I unzipped my hoodie completely and threw it somewhere behind me. Eric took in a sharp breath as he devoured the sight of me. I wasn't wearing a T-shirt, just a plain yellow cotton bra. I felt uncomfortable, though, but made a conscious effort not to cover myself with my arms. Just because I felt uncomfortable didn't mean I wanted to look like it.

The hunger in his eyes ignited my entire body.

Then the doorbell rang again. Eric sighed in frustration. A small piece of me—the piece that was smarter than the rest of me and knew that Eric was nothing more than a distraction—was a little relieved.

I jumped to get the door. With my hand on the knob, I realized I didn't have a shirt on. I darted back toward the living room and collided with Eric's chest. He threw his jacket around my shoulders and said, "I couldn't find your hoodie."

Behind me, there was a very distinct sound, the sound of a key turning a lock. My stomach clenched and I felt queasy. Only two people rang the doorbell before entering with a key. The first person was Natalie, and the second person was Harvey. And I knew without a doubt that Natalie was not on the other side of that door.

"Fuck!" I whispered. "Shit, damn." I turned to Eric. "Hide. *Now*."

He looked confused, but obeyed, jogging toward the kitchen.

"Alice?" called Harvey. "Oh, there you are," he said as his gaze swept to the side of the entryway where I was standing. "Listen, can we talk about last night? I feel kind of bad. We don't have to talk about . . . well, you know, but I figured I could at least make sure we were okay. Like, friends. I wish—"

He stopped, like his eyes had caught up with his mouth, and he finally noticed me standing there, my hands limp at my sides, in my bra, and with a jacket (that so obviously didn't belong to me) draped over my shoulders. Something clicked for him and he looked at me with flared nostrils before walking into the alcove off the entryway. He pulled down one of the blinds and saw the old Range Rover in the driveway. He had only seen Eric's car a couple of times at school, but I knew he recognized it.

It took another second before it all added up for him and he became the most furious version of himself I'd ever seen. "Seriously, Alice? You're kidding me, right?" His voice made the entire house quake as he stormed back to me.

I owe him nothing, I told myself. I slid my arms through Eric's jacket, wrapping it tightly around my rib cage.

"What are you thinking in that head of yours?" he asked, moving toward me.

I wanted to push him away, because the closer he got the more sharply his disappointment came into focus. But soon he would stop trying, and he would realize that I wasn't worth the heartache, and he'd move on to some other girl. I was both ready for and terrified by the inevitability of that moment.

"I can't do this anymore, Alice; this isn't fair. You know that. Don't pretend you're blind to it. I need you to choose."

It was that feeling again, of being backed into a corner. I stayed silent for far too long, but Harvey waited. And he waited for nothing.

After minutes of thick quiet, he said, "No more, Alice. Good-bye." Then he walked out the door.

"You said you two weren't anything," said Eric from behind me. "That's not how people act when they're not anything." He sounded a little let down, which surprised me. It hadn't occurred to me that Eric might feel something more than hormones for me.

"He's been in love with me forever." I forced myself to keep my voice steady as I swallowed back tears. "But I don't feel the same way," I lied, still facing the door. It was probably the most I had said to him since he'd gotten here earlier this afternoon.

I heard Eric moving behind me, and a minute later he appeared in front of me with his hat on and my hoodie in his hand. Without having to be asked, I shrugged out of his jacket and slipped on my hoodie.

He opened the door and said, "I'll see you Monday."

As soon as the door closed, I locked the dead bolt behind him and crumpled to the floor.

Harvey.

Then

A week after the Luke incident, Alice told me I needed to get off work one Saturday night and tell my mom I was staying at Dennis's. At first I told her I couldn't do it. I didn't like lying to my mom, and I still felt pretty uneasy about this whole list thing; but when Alice told me where we were going, I couldn't say no to her—even if it was 100 percent trespassing. Which, I guess, was no surprise.

Alice sat in the passenger seat. "Lake Quasipi should be two exits down."

"This is going to be awesome!" screamed Dennis from where he sat behind me.

I glanced to the rearview mirror to see Debora sitting next to her brother, biting her lip. She looked concerned. Our eyes met and she smiled for a second, raising her eyebrows. Debora was never very comfortable with breaking rules, so I couldn't really figure out why she'd made us bring her along.

We drove with the windows down, the heat blasting, and music crackling through my crappy speakers. I hadn't planned on inviting Dennis or Debora. But when I told Dennis about our plan to go to Lake Quasipi in the middle of December during the off season when the whole park would be closed to the public, he begged me to let him come. Which was okay, except that Debora caught us leaving and said she'd tell if we didn't bring her with us.

We all had our perfect excuses. I told my mom I was spending the night at Dennis's, and Dennis told his mom he was spending the night with me. Debora told her mom she was staying with her friend Lucy to get ready for the Spring Academic Bowl. And Alice told her parents she was going to a basketball game and a slumber party with some girls from Miss P's—which was less believable, but cancer had bought her a few Get Out of Jail Free cards. Plus she'd been pretty okay the last two weeks. If it wasn't for the lack of hair, I might have forgotten she was sick. Still, I was scared, and I think everyone else was too. But no one talked about it.

Dennis leaned forward with his upper body wedged between my and Alice's seats. "Where should we park?"

I turned my blinker on for the exit. "Uh, in the parking lot?" I looked to Alice.

She nodded.

We followed the signs for Lake Quasipi Family Amusement Park. Alice turned the music down, like we were going through some residential neighborhood and not a weaving two-lane road in the middle of the woods. The road led to the parking lot outside of the park gates. I expected us to have to climb over some sort of gate or maybe even sneak past a rent-a-cop, but there were no obvious security measures. Lake Quasipi was the oldest theme park in the state. None of the rides had ever been replaced, only maintained. There were roller coasters, but nothing huge. Some of the rides were even manual.

It actually made me feel better that Dennis and Debora had tagged along, because they never got in trouble, and if they were here, it felt physically impossible for us to get caught.

The four of us got out of the car, all bundled up in winter coats, hats, and scarves.

"What if there are cameras?" asked Debora, tugging down on her purple knit hat, which matched her gloves and scarf.

"We just have to be stealthy," I said, "right, Alice?"

"Sure," she said.

We walked up to the front gate, which was chained shut.

"I think we can all squeeze through that," said Dennis.

"A camera!" screamed Debora, jumping back enough so she was out of its line of sight.

Okay, so there was a camera, but it was covered in cobwebs and probably hadn't worked since 1983.

Alice picked up a stone too small to be a rock but too big to be a pebble and threw it directly at the camera, knocking it down so that it only clung to the wall by its wires. "Not anymore."

"Are you crazy?" hissed Debora. "That's vandalism!"

Dennis laughed, and I tried not to.

Alice turned back to Debora. "What? You thought you were going to come here and relive my childhood memories with me in the parking lot?" She squeezed through the fence and from the other side called, "Let's go!"

Debora huffed but followed as we all filed in.

It was eerie. The games were locked up, and there were no lights except for the moon and the stars and a little flashlight Dennis had been smart enough to bring. At times, Alice walked ahead of the three of us, scoping the place out, and it made me wish that it'd only been us.

The whole park had this colonial theme, with pastel houses that served as storefronts and little eateries and an old blue Ferris wheel. When we were kids, I thought this place was huge, like its own little country. But now all the doorways were too low and too narrow, the buildings didn't seem quite so big, and the Ferris wheel looked like it probably didn't meet any of the necessary safety regulations.

I ran ahead and caught up to Alice. "Is it anything like you remember?"

"Sort of," she said. "More rundown." She took a deep breath and held her side for a moment.

I hated seeing those little signs of her health slipping, and I knew she hated letting it show. But I've often wondered what was worse: being sick or watching it happen.

"We should climb the Ferris wheel!" said Dennis, running to catch up.

"No. No way," said Debora, tripping behind him. "You would break your neck and die, and then everyone would know we were here and it would be your fault for breaking your neck and dying."

Alice laughed. "I might like her."

Debora rolled her eyes.

"I'm only here for the fucking teacups anyway," said Alice. "This way."

We followed her, and like everything else, the teacups were much smaller than I remembered. But, still, all four of us barely fit into one cup.

"This is an electric ride, guys," said Dennis.

"The platform is, but it looks like you can spin the teacups yourself," said Debora, motioning to the metal circle at the center of the cup. It looked like a little table.

Alice smiled at Debora, but stopped when she realized I'd caught her.

We used to get on this ride and spin as fast as we could. The person to scream *stop* first lost and had to do all the pedaling on the boats.

Dennis began to spin the disk. "You guys ready?"

We nodded.

All eight of our hands tripped over one another, trying to keep the teacup spinning as fast as it would take us. Alice, and even Debora, shrieked. My eyes couldn't keep up with anything except for Alice blurring at the edge of my vision. I wanted to lean over and kiss her. We were moving so fast that no one would have noticed, and Alice might not have even realized that it was on purpose. I slid over a little closer.

On my other side, Dennis screamed, "This is awesome!"

"Watch the sky!" said Alice.

I looked up.

I knew I would never travel through space or fly a plane, but sitting there with the girl I loved—there was no question about me loving her—and two of my oldest friends, the whole universe spinning around me, reminded me how big this world was and how small we were. In a hundred years, no one would know us, but this moment for us would last as long as we did. This. Right now, with traces of Alice coloring my view of the sky, would never be in a history book or a movie, but for as long as I could push air in and out of my chest, I would remember this moment that could never be measured.

I yelled. I howled at the moon, and, for a few minutes, I forgot about how I thought my life hinged on kissing Alice. I forgot about who my dad might be. I forgot about disappointing my mom. I forgot about everything that didn't fit inside of this moment.

"Stop! Stop!" yelled Alice.

I grasped the disk on either side, stilling us.

Alice sat up on her knees and leaned over the edge of the teacup. Her whole body shook as she coughed like a little kid who'd been crying for too long. She wiped her mouth. I put my arm around her shoulder.

Debora moved in closer to us.

"I feel sick," moaned Alice.

"It's okay," said Debora. Our eyes met from either side of Alice. "It'll get washed away by the rain. Just let it out."

Dennis opened the little door to the teacup and ran down the exit ramp. "I'm sorry," he said over his shoulder. "Other people vomiting makes me vomit too."

She kept coughing, but nothing came out. Finally, she said, "Okay, okay. Yeah, I'm okay." She turned around and sat back down, slumping in her seat. "Give me a minute."

None of us said it out loud, but we knew it was the chemo. Alice's body had started to tell her what she could and couldn't do, and she had never responded well to limitations.

I unwound my scarf from my neck and handed it to her to wipe her face.

"Thanks," she said, and rested her head on my shoulder.

Debora scooted back a little and watched the patch of trees beside us that led out to Lake Quasipi.

"We should go home," I said.

Alice sat up. "No," she said. "No, I want to stay."

So we did. We found Dennis not far from the teacups at a row of water fountains. Thankfully, the water was on, so Alice splashed her face a few times and took a few sips of water.

We ran out to the docks and played on the pedal boats until the chill of the water became too much. Then we went to the mini mine train and used the hand pumps to go through the tunnels.

When we were done, it was too late to drive back, so we spent the night in The Tunnel of Love, which was nothing but a really small indoor roller coaster with plywood cutouts of kissing couples. It was really dark, but it was warmer than it would have been outside. The coaster cars were these oversized love seats with red, sparkly plastic upholstery and purple piping.

Dennis and Debora fell asleep first, but I couldn't sleep

and neither could Alice. She crept over to my car, with her finger to her lips. Her breath smelled like spearmint chewing gum.

I opened my mouth to talk—to ask her if she was okay—but she covered my lips with her fingers and shook her head no.

Dennis's snores echoed down the tunnel from the back cart, and I could hear Debora a couple cars back, her breaths heavy and measured.

Alice left her fingers on my lips and leaned forward into my shoulder. She pulled the collar of my T-shirt aside, kissing my neck. I breathed into her fingers and kissed her fingerprints, hoping the proof of her would always stay there on my lips.

I let my hands work up her arms until my fingers found her neck, her face, pulling her to me.

And then we kissed. It was deep and slow, like a first kiss should be. Her mouth melting against mine. I had to stop my head from working because all it was doing was thinking about this moment—*Alice is kissing me. Alice is kissing me. I'm kissing Alice. I'm kissing Alice.*—and not living in this moment. And I couldn't let myself ever forget this.

Alice slid down low in the cart, so I followed. She yanked her jacket off and mine too without ever pulling away from me.

I held her hips and waited for her to push my hands away as they ran up the back of her shirt and over the straps of her bra.

Her hands swept over my chest and down my stomach,

while kissing my neck all the way up to my ear. The feel of her hands against my skin. And the thought of where those hands might go. I gasped.

"Shh," she whispered. "Just kissing tonight."

I fell asleep, with her curled into my chest and my chin resting on top of her head, scared for tomorrow because this was too perfect to last.

When I woke up in the morning, Alice sat in her own cart, wrapping her scarf around her neck.

"I'm starved," yelled Dennis, his voice muffled, from the back of the tunnel.

Debora yawned. "Me too."

The park looked different under the sunlight, a little bit sadder than it had the night before. Chipped paint, splintered wood, cracked sidewalks.

We piled up in the car and Alice insisted that Dennis take the front seat.

Every time I looked for Alice in the rearview mirror, she flicked her eyes off to the road and instead it was Debora whose gaze caught mine. We stopped for breakfast outside of town. There were few words, lots of yawns, and no regrets.

Alice.

Then

I didn't expect for it to feel so good, to see Luke humiliate himself like that in front of all those people. But it did, and I wasn't done yet. I hadn't given Harvey any details—mainly because I wasn't so sure of them myself, but he agreed when I asked him to take me to the Nifty-Thrifty one Sunday afternoon.

Harvey gripped the handle of the shopping cart and pushed me down the aisles of abandoned goods, sneezing into his sleeve. I'd been kidding when I told him to push me around, but when he offered, I was relieved. I didn't know how long I could last walking up and down the aisles of this place. The spring musical was at the beginning of April, and I had a plan, giving me a few weeks to nail everything down and gather some supplies.

Between now and then, I had another chemo session to go, even though it still wasn't doing any good. I'd taken some painkillers this morning, but it felt like my body was getting used to them and now all I felt were the side effects and none of the benefits.

"Jesus, Al, this place is killing my sinuses. Can you at least tell me what we're looking for?"

"I'll know it when I see it," I mumbled.

"I still don't get why we're here."

"The list."

"Oh yeah, Al, that explains everything."

I smiled. We zigzagged up and down aisles of used goods, Harvey pushing the cart with me in it, my knees tucked into my chest. Row after row of crying children, appeasing parents, and none-too-happy employees in red vests.

Again, we paused for a moment as Harvey sneezed into the crook of his elbow. Okay, so maybe the local Nifty-Thrifty was a little bit dusty.

A woman twice as wide as our shopping cart stood in front of us, blocking our path. She wore a faded Nifty-Thrifty vest with *Gwenda* stitched onto the left breast pocket. Her pudgy hands made fists and pressed into the bulge that was supposed to be her waist. She eyed me in the cart, with Harvey at the helm. Two teenagers screwing around. She was not amused.

But neither was I. "Beep-beep," I said, my voice monotone.

Gwenda didn't budge.

Harvey started to back up, pulling me with him.

I looked over my shoulder. "Wait. What are you doing?" I pursed my lips and sighed through my nose. "We weren't doing anything wrong!"

He rolled his neck from side to side. "Alice, there wasn't anything good down that aisle anyway."

I settled back against the metal grates. "You didn't even know what I was looking for." We continued to roll down the aisle of children's clothing. In the bins above the racks were random pots and pans and toys. It was depressing. We turned another corner. "It's like you've got to win everything," he said, not letting it go. He was a little bit right; I did have to *win* everything because this was my last shot, and I wasn't going down without the last word.

"Even when there's nothing to win," he continued. "I mean, she works at the Nifty-Thrifty. I'm pretty sure she's not winning. Not everything is about—"

"Stop," I said a little too quietly. Something had caught my attention.

"You know, it's okay to be nice sometimes. It won't—"

"Harvey, stop!"

The cart stopped with a jolt, sliding me forward against the metal grates. I squatted on my haunches. "Push me closer," I said.

So he did.

The aisle we were in now was lined with tall racks full of dresses. When I was within reach, I stood up right in the cart, my head bobbing above the racks—giving me a view of the entire store, including Gwenda.

I sifted through the dresses methodically. Nothing was sized and most everything was of the plaid jumper variety.

"So we're looking for a dress," Harvey concluded. "What do you need a dress for? You have plenty of dresses."

I continued to search, not bothering to reply.

"You don't even like to shop, Al."

"The list, I told you. It's for the list."

The hangers scraped against the metal bars as I pushed

aside dress after dress, waiting for the perfect one to reveal itself. Each dress was a story, a life. Funerals, birthdays, dates.

Harvey kept his foot on the bar beneath the cart, to steady me. He reached his hand into the pool of fabric and pulled, coming up with something chiffon and delicate looking. He rubbed the material between his fingers. It was the perfect shade of pink. Ballet slipper pink, so light it was almost white. I raked aside dozens of dresses to reach it.

"That one."

He dropped the fabric, like he was scared he might stain it.

I pulled the dress to me. "Take me to the fitting rooms."

"Do people even try on clothes here?"

I rolled my eyes and pointed to the ALL SALES FINAL sign hanging from the ceiling.

The fitting room smelled like feet. I wouldn't have even bothered trying it on, but the dress in question was twenty-three bucks, and the list was being funded by old birthday money, so I would need to spend wisely.

I stripped out of my T-shirt but left my jeans on. The dress was comprised of layer upon layer of chiffon with thin straps and a neckline that dipped down in the front, making my bra visible. I would have to go bra-less, not that it mattered much anyway. My boobs weren't very big to begin with. The fabric gathered beneath the bustline, flowing out around me. I felt ethereal in it, like this dress could change me.

I reached around, trying to search for the zipper, but couldn't quite grasp it. "Harvey, come in here." Beneath the fitting-room door, I could see the wheels of the cart rolling back and then come to an abrupt halt.

"You want me to go in there? With you?"

"Yes, and hurry."

From beneath the door, his dirty sneakers shifted around outside. I slid back the bar lock to let him in.

"Uh, okay. I'm coming in." A smile tugged at my lips and I gave in to it, laughing to no one but myself.

The door creaked open, and Harvey squeezed in, trying to be discreet. The room was barely big enough for one person to stand upright, never mind two.

I turned so that Harvey stood at my back. "Zip me."

He pulled the zipper to the top without any hiccups, and then studied our reflection in the dirty mirror. "You look so pretty." He said it simply. Not hot, not gorgeous. Pretty, I looked pretty.

My chest swelled.

"When are you going to wear it?" he asked.

"Soon."

Harvey didn't know the whole plan, not yet, and if my answer confused him, he didn't say so. I think he was as lost in this moment as I was. I could have said, *To the moon, Harvey. I'm wearing this dress to the moon.* And his eyes would have stayed steady on me, unchanging.

He could probably hear my heart beating against my ribs. All I could think was *This hurts. This hurts so much worse than I thought it would.* I knew Harvey would never hurt me, but he was crushing my heart because I was feeling these things for him that I didn't want to name. This *feeling* that the world was so pleased to call love destroyed people every day, and it would do that to me too. It would disappoint and deceive and manipulate. But then, the part of me that was dying thought, *What would it matter?* If I wasn't going to live long enough to have to worry about the aftermath of it all, what did it matter?

I leaned back against him, still undecided but pushing my limits. He sighed, his breath brushing the bare skin of my back, and then dipped his head, practically pressing his lips against my shoulder. The sensation traveled down my spine, causing me to shiver.

I watched our reflection, and wondered if this was really happening or if it was the mirror playing a trick on me. We hadn't kissed since that night at Lake Quasipi, and I could almost talk myself into believing nothing had really happened. I closed my eyes, and I was falling, tripping into an abyss of unknown.

A violent banging shocked my eyes open. I caught a glance of Harvey in the mirror, wide-eyed, like he had been woken from a hypnotic trance.

The door shook.

"Only one person per fitting room!" Gwenda called out.

Harvey backed up what little the fitting room allowed. "I'll be right out here if you need me."

"The zipper," I breathed.

"Oh, right. Yeah. Sorry."

He unzipped the dress and left in a hurry.

I wondered if this moment felt the same for him.

I stood, studying myself in the mirror, waiting for

something to happen, but nothing did. The straps of the dress began to slip down my shoulders and across the smattering of small red spots accumulating there, little broken blood vessels—a reminder of my leukemia. I blinked, trying to wash away my feelings, but it didn't work—it would never work. Then, through the fitting-room door, I called, "Harvey, we've got some serious planning to do."

Harvey.

Then

"Are you sure I can be here?" I asked, my eyes scanning the treatment clinic. It wasn't very full, and no one had said anything to me when I sat down next to Alice with an IV in her arm, but it still felt like some hushed private place where visitors shouldn't be allowed.

She leaned her head back against the recliner. "Yeah. Nobody cares."

I watched an old bald guy covered in age spots come in by himself with nothing but the daily sports section in his hand. A lady, about the same age as our moms, sat down across from Alice as a nurse rolled over a tray full of utensils.

"Does this place weird you out?" she asked.

"Yeah." Death was everywhere. So much so that I wondered if just her being here made her more dead than alive. More one of them than one of us.

"Me too. It smells weird. Like, too clean."

I laughed. "Would you rather it didn't?"

She tilted her head back again and shrugged.

A few minutes passed, and I thought maybe she'd fallen asleep until she said, "There's a notebook and a pen in my bag. We need to make a to-do list, but first grab me one of those blankets at the front."

Alice had brought her own blanket from home, but I'd heard chemo made you really cold. I went for a second one up at the front where they had water coolers and blanket warmers full of blue hospital blankets. In Alice's bag, I found the notebook and pen.

"Okay," she said, with her eyes still shut and the second blanket spread out across her lap. Maybe it was the fluorescent lights, but her skin was too yellow, her eyes more sunken in than I remembered. "We got Luke, but we're not done. Celeste is going down."

"Seriously, Al? Don't you want to do something good, like, I don't know, hold a canned food drive?"

She smiled and the irony of it against her sallow skin made my chest hurt.

"Fine," I said. Of course Alice would want to have the final word with Celeste.

"Write this down," she said. "We need a DVD of *Oklahoma!* the musical, and we have to find a recipe for fake blood."

"What?"

A nurse hushed me from across the room.

"What?" I whispered.

"Hear me out, okay?"

I huffed.

"Okay, so Celeste is the lead in *Oklahoma!* and their last showing is a few days after this round is over. But I need someone to videotape a dress rehearsal for the ballet scene at the end of the second act. Write that down too."

None of this could mean anything good.

"We also need a third person who isn't afraid of heights."

"For what exactly?"

"To sit in the rafters."

"You're not kidding?" I laughed because all this was so damn absurd. Only Alice would plot someone's social demise while undergoing chemotherapy.

"Of course not. Do you know anyone on the inside? I don't want to get Tyson involved. I need, like, a tech person. Someone who can get us in and out of the back-stage area."

Rubbing my eyes, I took an inventory of everyone I knew well enough to ask for help who also had a hand in the school musical. "I don't know anyone," I said. "But I know someone who might."

Her eyes opened again. "Well?"

"Well what?"

"Call them."

I stepped into the hallway with my phone to my ear. "Hey," I said. "You got a minute?"

"I'm eating leftover onion rings and trying to hack the new parental controls on our TV. I think my mom figured out about the after-hours soft-core porn on the movie channels," said Dennis.

"Sounds really intense over there."

The TV cut off in the background. "Yeah, well, you dumped me today for everyone's favorite cancer patient."

"This is true," I said. "Hey, you know any guys in the theater department?"

So here's the thing: popular people may have status, but the rest of us have power in numbers and, because of that, we have resources. Dennis especially. I guess you could call it, like, the nerd mafia, but Dennis knows someone everywhere—water boys, teacher's aides, theater tech gurus.

"A few," he said. "Why?"

"It's for Alice."

"Of course it is." I could picture his smug smile. "You're my best friend, which means I'm obligated to tell you that she's using you."

"No shit." I didn't know what was worse: the fact that everyone could see that she was using me or that I could so readily admit it. "They need to be trustworthy."

"I know a guy," he said. "But I'm going to need details."

"Yeah, well, I don't have those yet."

He laughed.

"Whatever. I'll call you later." I went to hang up but pulled the phone back to my ear. "Hey, wait. You still there?"

"Here," said Dennis.

"How do you feel about heights?"

"I'm in."

When I walked back into the treatment room, Alice really was asleep. I watched her for a few minutes, thinking about what Dennis had said. She was using me, and I should have been pissed about it, but didn't I know that from the very beginning? Honestly, though, she could use me for the rest of her life if these were the last days I'd spend with her. I wish I had the resolve to say no, but I couldn't. Not if saying no meant saying good-bye.

At the end of Alice's session, a girl about our age came in with her mom. The girl's hair was shoulder length and thick. Most everyone in the room watched her in flickering glances as she tucked a strand of hair behind her ear and her mother squeezed her shoulder. I turned to see Alice with the nurse at her side applying a bandage over the spot where her IV had been. She sat with her mouth open, watching the girl, living in a world I didn't know how to be a part of.

We walked out to my car with Alice bundled in a layer of sweaters and jackets despite it being an unseasonably warm March. Once we were in the car and away from the shadow of the clinic, I turned to Alice and said, "You know you're going to have to give me more details."

Harvey.

Then

"Who are we supposed to be meeting again?" asked Alice.

"Some kid named Glen," I said. "He's the one who got the dress rehearsal video."

We stood in the alley behind the school auditorium, waiting to be let in. It was the first week of April and the last performance of *Oklahoma!*, starring none other than Celeste. Glen was Dennis's inside guy, who did all the lighting design for the school plays. I'd never heard of him, but from what Dennis said he never ventured far from the theater tech warehouse behind the auditorium. When I asked Dennis how we should compensate Glen, he said that these guys operated strictly on favors and that he'd take care of it. I didn't want to know, so I didn't ask.

Alice and I rented *Oklahoma!*, but we only made it through the first half, which was all that mattered anyway. From what I gathered, this girl named Laurey liked these two guys named Curly and Jud, but she *really* loved Curly. Anyway, right before intermission there's this big ballet number, which is some dream sequence where

Laurey realizes she loves Curly. All I can say about *Oklahoma!* is that I officially have no desire to visit the state of Oklahoma.

"Hey, you guys!" I turned to see Dennis jogging up behind us. "I texted Glen. He said we've got about twenty minutes and that he's on his way down to let us in."

And then, as if on cue, the stage door opened. "Come on," said a voice from the shadows of backstage.

I looked to Alice, and she motioned for me to go ahead.

It took a minute for my eyes to adjust, but when they did I found a guy two heads shorter than me with greasy black hair, round glasses, and translucently white skin. He wore cargo shorts and a T-shirt with a fire-breathing dragon flying through a rainbow. He had to be Glen.

"Bro," said Dennis, giving him some kind of handshake-high-five combo. "Harvey, Alice, this is Glen."

"Hey," I said. "Thanks for helping us out."

Alice nodded. "Yeah, thanks."

Glen crossed his arms over his chest and widened his stance, claiming his territory. "No problem," he said. "All the leads are always assholes to us anyway. This should be good." He rubbed his hands together and smiled. "I have to head back up to the booth. Good luck."

We did our best to blend in with the theater kids. Glen had advised us to wear all black so that we might be mistaken for techies. The three of us hid behind a rolling staircase made of plywood that had been painted to look like marble flooring (an old set piece, I assumed).

Alice shed her coat to reveal her pink gown, the one

from Nifty-Thrifty. The dress dipped down in the front, lower than I'd realized at the store. So low that . . . *Alice wasn't wearing a bra.* I felt her eyes on me, catching me staring at her chest. My cheeks flushed, and I pretended to study an old paint splatter on the concrete floor. We were about to sabotage the school play, and all I could think about was her lack of bra.

"Okay," said Dennis, not noticing the tension I so obviously felt. "I'm headed up to the rafters."

I nodded.

Dennis pulled a delicate tiara and a honey-blond wig out of his backpack, handing both to Alice, then left.

A moment later, the stage went black in preparation for the next scene.

"You look fine, Celeste," a girl assured from a few feet ahead of us.

"The skirt feels tighter than it did last week," answered Celeste.

"Totally not your fault," said the girl. It sounded like Mindi. "I think Kinsey screwed up everyone's alterations. And you're going to kill this number anyway."

"I think I might use a recording of one of the performances for my musical theater program audition tape as part of a montage. Like a best-of-moments thing." She paused. "I've heard some people apply as early as two years out."

I looked to Alice, my eyes wide.

The stage lights came up.

She shook her head and mouthed to me, "Don't worry—she has this coming."

I shook my head again and Alice took my hand, pulling me to her.

"Please," she whispered, so close to me that when she spoke, our lips touched.

"Fine, but after this I'm done."

She smiled with her mouth closed.

We stood, watching the scene, waiting for the dream sequence to begin. Finally, Celeste sat down in the rocking chair and pretended to fall asleep—our cue.

"Okay," I said. "I'll be waiting for you on the other side of the stage."

She nodded and tugged the wig onto her head. With the wig, she almost looked normal. Alice was at that good point, a couple days before she would be going back for another round of chemo. Her body had recovered long enough for her to get in a few days of freedom only to return for her next round. Sometimes I wondered if the chemo was too much for one body to handle. And maybe it did more harm than good. Yeah, the chemo might kill the cancer, but it might kill Alice too.

I didn't know either of the guys who played Curly or Jud, but the one playing Curly went out onstage and began to dance with Celeste. Actually, he just sort of stood there while Celeste danced around him. She spun and leaped across the stage, putting her ballet experience to use while making everyone else look like amateurs.

The one who played Jud stood in the wings, waiting for his entrance. I bounced on my toes a little, trying to psych myself up before tapping him on his shoulder. He was huge, the kind of guy who basketball coaches saw on the first day of high school and fawned over.

I just hoped I didn't get my ass kicked.

He turned around and whispered, "What?"

"We're having some issues with your mic. I'm supposed to re-mic you."

He shook his head. "Wait till intermission. There's no singing in this number."

"I've got shit to do at intermission. I'm fast, I swear."

He looked over his shoulder to see Celeste still dancing around the other guy and nodded reluctantly.

I led him to the small dressing room off stage right. Once inside, he unbuttoned his shirt.

"We've got to make this fast," he said.

"Yeah, I'm on it." I dug through my bag, my heart pounding and sweat pooling at the back of my neck. "Oh, hey, man. I must have dropped the cord right outside. Give me a second."

He sighed. "You're killing me, dude."

"Be right back. Don't go anywhere."

He paced up and down the length of the dressing room, doing some voice exercise.

I almost told him to forget it and that I'd get his mic later. But instead, I flipped the thumb lock on the door and left him there in the dressing room, locked inside, as I ignored the twinges of regret prickling up my spine.

Running around to the other side of the stage, I had a second to process what was happening in the play. Celeste danced with a group of girls, holding bouquets while they placed a veil on her head. I remembered this part from the movie. Laurey and Curly had danced around and I guess that somehow meant they should get married, and because girls can smell marriage, all Laurey's friends had rushed to help her prepare for her dream-sequence-certainly-doomed-wedding.

I spotted Alice in the wing opposite me, and for a second that moved so fast it might as well not have existed, she looked nervous. But the moment passed, and soon her icy exterior was back and multiplied. She slid the tiara into her wig and stepped forward.

If this was any other performance of *Oklahoma!*, Laurey/Celeste would be running around like an idiot and then stand with her eyes closed waiting for her groom (Curly), only to find Jud, who would then pick her up and make her his most miserable wench wife.

But that didn't happen because Jud was locked in a fitting room and Laurey/Celeste had bigger things to worry about than that sack of muscles.

From where I stood, Alice looked small and harmless with her light pink dress, blond wig, and tiara.

Then she walked out onstage.

From the back, she wove through the chorus—whose feet kept moving but whose faces said *What the hell?* She mimicked what would have been Jud's choreography as all the techies and cast backstage buzzed with confusion. The stage looked like one of those "Which of these things does not belong?" puzzles, and it was so obvious that Al was the odd piece out. She faked the choreography long enough to weasel in right alongside an unsuspecting Celeste, with her eyes closed, waiting for her groom. The techies argued back and forth, saying "Go get her!" and "*You* go get her!" Ultimately, none of them were brave enough to interrupt the show completely.

The stage manager finally reasoned, "Maybe no one will notice her."

Yeah, no one would notice the girl dressed as a prom queen in the middle of turn-of-the-century Oklahoma.

Everyone backstage went quiet as Alice paused in front of Celeste and lifted her veil. Celeste jumped back, the exact same reaction she should have had to Jud—but more authentic.

Alice's lips twitched as gallons of homemade fake blood rained down directly over Alice and Celeste. I looked up and could faintly make out the figure in the rafters, and only because I knew he was there. Most of the cast members avoided the worst of it, but none of them got it quite as bad Celeste, whose shrill scream rang through the auditorium.

Alice stood facing Celeste and drenched in red. It was so obvious. She was Carrie, Stephen King's *Carrie*.

For a second, the whole world froze with shock. Everyone stared, and no one did anything. Except the orchestra. They kept playing until, one by one, each chair began to falter as they noticed the spectacle onstage. Alice opened her eyes and wiped them with the only part of her arm left untouched by the fake blood. Then she turned and ran directly to me.

I'd stuffed her black coat in my backpack, and was ready

for her with a huge brown fleece blanket. I wrapped it around her body and we were off. She kept tripping over her long dress, slowing us down.

We were nearly to the emergency exit when I saw how exhausted she was. Without thinking, I ducked down and wrapped my arms around her thighs, throwing her over my shoulder with the fleece still pulled tightly around her. Alice shook against my body, laughing so hard I almost thought she was crying.

I stiff-armed the bar on the emergency exit door. The Geo waited for us outside like a chariot. Unceremoniously, I threw Alice into the front seat and raced around to the driver's side. I sped off and headed for my apartment. Alice sat forward a little, doing her best not to stain the passenger seat, but really I didn't care.

We'd made a clean getaway. I glanced at my cell to find a text from Dennis saying he was in the clear too, but the place was A fucking zoo, man.

In the car, Alice and I retold the story of what had happened with huge animated gestures. I felt like we were kids again and the only thing between us was nothing at all. Once we'd exhausted the memory from every angle, a quiet settled between us. All I could think about was the feeling of her hot breath on my back as I carried her to the car, and the way she leaned against me in the fitting room of the Nifty-Thrifty, and how we hadn't kissed since Lake Quasipi. We hadn't even talked about the kiss; I was starting to think I'd made the whole thing up.

Alice bobbed in her seat, unable to keep still. I could feel it too—the adrenaline rush from doing something so completely crazy. It made my head feel busy, like I was feeling too many things at once.

At home, I gave her an old beach towel that my mom wouldn't miss and a clean bar of soap. I closed my door to change my clothes, then opened it and sat on my bed, giving myself a clear view of the bathroom door on the other side of the hall. Steam curled out from beneath the door like an invitation. But it wasn't.

I went to the kitchen to make a peanut-butter-and-jelly sandwich. When I returned, Alice sat on my bed in one of my T-shirts and a pair of drawstring shorts. She was the most perfect thing I'd ever seen.

"I forgot my change of clothes in my locker. I didn't think you would mind," she said, her skin pink and raw. "I left the wig in the tub. We'll have to throw it out later. I need to sit here for a minute."

I sat down next to her on my bed and handed her half of my sandwich. We took turns taking sips from the glass of milk I had poured. When we finished the sandwich, Alice leaned her head on my shoulder and sighed, saying thank you without saying anything at all.

"I'm going to lay down for a few minutes," she said.

"Sure. Okay." I took the empty glass to the kitchen and threw out the wig while she slept. I wanted to ignore these moments and pretend like this wasn't happening, but the truth was that her dying had become too real.

★ ★ ★

On Monday morning, Alice was called into the principal's office. No one besides Celeste knew for sure that it was her, so they couldn't really prove anything. In the end, it didn't matter. The next day her white blood cell count plummeted, and she had to spend a month in the hospital.

When I'd visit her, the nurses would give me this look that was all pity and knowing as they handed me a blue surgical mask to wear inside her room. If she was awake, she'd ask me about school and if people were talking about her and what they were saying. Any time I brought up Celeste or Mindi she'd look at me, her eyes lighting up for a moment, and say, "Bitches." And that gave me a strange sense of comfort. In mid–May, Alice's fever broke long enough for them to send her home. We threw a little welcome home party, like this was a good thing, and she hadn't been sent home to die.

Harvey.

Now

This time last week I'd stood in Alice's entryway asking her to choose me. She stood there in that idiot's jacket while I waited for her answer, but it never came. How could it be that she and I were at our best only when her health was at its worst? How did that make any goddamn sense?

The nice thing about the Grocery Emporium was that it was never quiet. There was always a constant cycle of cash registers, bar-code scanners, Muzak, and the nonstop thrum of voices. This morning, Dennis and I had been assigned to stock the canned food from the pallets in the back.

"Sardines." Just the taste of the word in my mouth made me want to gag.

"I know, man," said Dennis as we filled in back stock, pulling the oldest cans to the front of the shelf in a neat row.

On Monday, I'd asked my manager, Collin, for extra hours, and because Dennis was a good friend he'd done the same. I didn't need free time. I needed mind-numbing work that got me through the hours when I wasn't at school or asleep.

"Why do we even sell these? Hasn't society mutually decided sardines are gross?" I asked.

"Who even buys these things?" he asked, not answering my question. "I mean, obviously someone does, or we wouldn't be filling stock. The better question is *why*."

"The only people who buy sardines are people like Luke and his dumbass friends so they can dump 'em in kids' lockers and gym bags." It was true, happened all the time.

"It's like the solution is so obvious. Stop selling sardines and no more sardine-ing," said Dennis, like he had solved world hunger.

"Sardine-ing?" I laughed.

"Just invented a word," said Dennis. "That just happened."

This was why Dennis was my best friend, because everything else in my life could be shit, but he would still be Dennis.

We'd finished the crate of sardines and moved on to tuna.

"I saw Alice looking at you yesterday," said Dennis.

"That's like saying I saw lockers in the hallway. It was probably coincidental. Plus, she made herself perfectly clear about where we stand." It sucked, but at least she finally did it.

"I don't know," he said. "Maybe it's for the best. You've done some pretty extreme shit for her and—"

An old woman made a "hmph" noise from behind us at Dennis's swearing.

"Crap," he said. "I meant to say crap," he called over his shoulder. "Man, I hope she doesn't say anything to customer service. I'm on my second write-up."

I shrugged, watching the old lady go.

"Dennis! I've been waiting outside for ten minutes," called a voice from the front of the store.

Debora speed-walked down the aisle of canned food, headed straight for us with an armful of dry cleaning. Her corn-husk bob swished with each step. She wore a teal, fitted oxford shirt tucked into a straight black skirt that tapered in at the knees and hugged her hips, with a pair of pointy shoes that made my feet hurt just from looking at them.

Dennis turned to me and tilted his head to the ceiling, letting out a loud groan.

Without any sort of greeting, Debora shoved the dry cleaning into Dennis's chest and said, "Here. You're going to make us late. We're supposed to be at the portrait studio in ten minutes, and unless I hit all green lights, it takes me fifteen."

Dennis looked at me. "Family pictures. Totally forgot."

Debora squinted her eyes and leaned in closer. "You didn't even shave, did you?" She shook her head and sighed. "Go change."

Dennis turned for the break room and Debora followed him, so I did too. Their family did pictures every year at the same portrait place in old downtown. They always wore black bottoms and a different-colored shirt every year. I knew this because the portraits lined their staircase, starting with the most recent picture at the bottom.

Mom and I had never taken real family portraits, only pictures at Christmastime and sometimes for one of our birthdays.

In the break room, Dennis slipped into the small employee bathroom while Debora and I sat down at one of the lunch tables.

Debora took a napkin from the center of the table and pushed a few stray crumbs into a neat pile. "So," she said, "have you thought about where you want to apply?"

I tilted my head to the side. "Excuse me?"

"Colleges, Harvey."

"Oh." I hadn't thought much about the future in the last few years. "I guess I'll go to a community college until I figure it out."

She nodded.

"What about you?"

"Well, Mom graduated from Cornell and Dad's a Dartmouth grad. Personally, I've got my eye on Cornell." She continued to sweep the crumbs into little piles, micromanaging them.

I watched her hands, smiling. "You'll get in. Besides, if you can't get into those places, nobody can."

She smiled with her lips pressed tight together. "What about you?"

I shrugged. "I just hope *a* school accepts me."

"Oh, you'll be fine," she said.

"How do you know?" I asked.

"You're smart and talented and . . . I know these things. If you don't get into a decent school, it will only be because you didn't apply."

I leaned back in my chair. "Okay, what else do you know, Oracle Debora?"

She closed her eyes, still smiling. "I see you volunteering to wear the big foam diploma costume at the college fair I'm planning next Saturday."

I laughed. "So not going to happen."

Her smile widened and, for the first time, I realized she wasn't wearing her glasses. "Hey," I said. "No glasses. You look nice."

"Yeah, contacts irritate my eyes. I only wear them for pictures."

I nodded.

"Come on!" she called to Dennis.

"Chill, sis!"

She rolled her eyes and returned to the pile of crumbs. "I know I'm, like, a year late or something, but Dennis said you quit the piano."

"I did. Yeah, I don't know. I felt like I had no life."

She raised her eyebrows. "I know what you mean." She paused. "I don't really know much about music. I sort of listen to whatever's on, but I always thought you were good."

My lips twitched. "Thanks."

"Okay," said Dennis, bursting through the door. "Who picked the color this year? Because I look *fine*. This is way better than the burnt orange we did last year."

"Let's go," said Debora.

"Later, man!" called Dennis. "I've got to tell the front I'm leaving."

I stood and gave him a wave, but he was already gone. "See ya, Debora."

She turned, before following Dennis out the swinging door. "Bye, Harvey."

I sank down into my chair. The doors to the break room swung back and forth. I'd just had an entire conversation without once thinking of Alice. The knot that had been in my chest since last Saturday didn't feel so big. And, for that, I had Debora to thank. I couldn't help but wonder what else she could make me forget.

Alice.

Then

Prom wasn't always on my list, but after having been released from the hospital two weeks ago, my days felt even more finite. It was the type of thing that I never wanted to go to until I'd realized I never would. Prom was for juniors and seniors and their dates, and I was a sophomore. But that was okay. It's not like I planned to walk through the front door or anything.

I was done with chemo too. Or maybe it was done with me. Either way, chemotherapy hadn't helped. In fact, most recently it had done more harm than good and had begun to attack the healthy parts of me. Dr. Meredith said lots of different things about my blood counts and my immune system, but what I took away from the conversation was: chemo equals bad, for now.

It was almost a relief to find out that the chemo was no longer an option. I knew the treatment had taken a toll on me, but living without the weight of it "added to my quality of life," which was the exact wording Dr. Meredith used when he discussed other treatment options. My parents, though, had left the decision up to me and I decided no more.

With our shoes dangling from our fingers, Harvey and I walked across the golf course behind the Shady Grove Country Club.

"Maybe we should have dressed up," said Harvey.

"We're not going inside," I said. "I just want to see it, that's all." We couldn't have bought tickets even if we wanted to. Only upperclassmen were allowed to buy tickets, and they'd sold out weeks before it even occurred to me that I might want to crash the thing.

"How close do you want to get?"

"I don't know; close enough to see everything." We walked across the green so that the lake was at our backs. In front of us was the event space. The grass was so perfect it made me want to throw my shoes in the lake.

Hughley High's prom was always held inside the ballroom overlooking the golf course. Glass doors stretched from the floor to the ceiling, and girls in tacky dresses and boys in matching ties spilled out onto the ornate terrace.

I took a few steps closer and sat on the ground. "Here. This is perfect."

Harvey sat next to me, with his leg pressed against mine. "I'm kind of surprised that your mom let you go out tonight."

"Why? What am I going to do? Die?"

He turned his head away from me.

"I'm sorry," I said. "You know what I mean."

Touching my leg, he said, "Don't be sorry."

I wish I could say that I said something profound, but that didn't happen. We sat there and watched the juniors and seniors of Hughley High fall in and out of love, say no and say yes, let go and hang on. A few couples tripped off into the darkness together while others stood on the terrace, yelling back and forth as the tension brought on by prom and graduation slipped between the crevices of their cracking relationships. There were groups of friends too, posing for pictures and dancing in circles. Peppered throughout each scene were a few loners, looking for a place to settle for the night. All these people in one room, sharing this same event, while each of them would carry a completely different memory of this one night.

Harvey and I sat there as spectators, watching a show that felt like it had been put on for us alone.

"Thanks for being my prom date," he said after a while.

I smiled. "No way. This isn't a date. This is just a warm-up for when you really go to prom."

Music pounded from the dance, and the sound of girls shrieking echoed all the way down to us.

"Yeah," he said. "I think this is probably as close as I'll ever get to prom."

I lay back in the grass. "You have to go to prom, Harvey."

"When did *you* join the prom committee?"

"If you don't go, you're going to be moping around on your porch with your wife when you're old and gross, talking about how you should have gone to your prom."

Still sitting up, he continued to watch the dance. "If you hadn't gotten sick, you wouldn't say that."

"Yeah," I said, "but I am sick, and aren't you supposed to get some life lesson out of the whole thing?"

He didn't answer.

I propped myself up on my elbows. "What's that big banner say?"

Harvey squinted. "'Heaven on Earth.' It's the prom theme."

I laughed. "That's depressing."

"Seriously," said Harvey.

I don't know how long we sat there before he asked, "What did Celeste do to you?"

I draped my arm over my eyes. I could still see Harvey. I didn't have anything to hide from him, but I'd gotten so used to keeping secrets. "She was hooking up with Luke."

"Oh. I think I heard about that."

"And she rubbed it in my face."

He turned, facing me. "But that's not what you were getting back at Luke for?"

"No," I said. "He saw something I didn't want him to see and told Celeste about it." He was probably in there. Both of them probably were. I hoped they were miserable. From inside the dance, the music transitioned into a softer song that I couldn't quite make out the words to.

Harvey leaned in closer. "What did he see?"

I didn't want Harvey to know about my mom. He loved her so much, and I didn't want to ruin that for him. And part of me also felt foolish. Harvey only had one parent, and here I was, bitching because one of mine had slipped up.

I sat forward and turned to Harvey. "Dance with me. Please."

He stood and held his hand out for me. I took it and let

the warmth of his skin travel through my veins.

"You want to get closer?" he asked.

"No, this is good."

He placed his hands on my hips and I looped my arms around his neck, sinking into him as I did.

This part of dying felt good, the letting go. It made everything easier. Watching his throat, I said, "You can kiss me."

I looked up and his lips met mine. It was soft and quiet.

We danced, and when my body got tired, he held me up. I wanted to dance every dance with Harvey. And no one else. For the first time, that didn't scare me.

Harvey.

Now

It had been twelve days since I told her she had to choose. Talking with Debora had been a nice reprieve from this gnawing at my gut, but I couldn't make that feeling last on my own.

There was one blind spot in Dennis's backyard—a small space behind his parents' shed—and it had taken us years to find.

Dennis popped the top on a beer and handed it to me.

I took a sip. And immediately spit it back out. "Oh, gross! This is warm!"

"Well, it's sort of hard to steal a six-pack right off the refrigerated shelves, you freakin' ingrate. Billy will only slip me beer from the stockroom, so suck it up." For the last year, Dennis had been saying he could get us beer from the Grocery Emporium, but this was the first time he'd actually come through. Everyone had always said that Billy, the stockroom manager, sold damaged six-packs to under-twenty-one employees, but I'd never had the guts to ask.

I rolled my eyes and took a swig, making no effort to hide how shitty the beer tasted.

"You talked to Alice?"

"What do you think?"

"Okay," he said. "Let me play devil's advocate for a sec. Were you guys even dating? It's not like she cheated on you."

"Well, no. Not technically, but she knew how I felt and I'm pretty sure she felt the same."

"Did she say so?"

She said she'd miss me most, but now she wasn't going anywhere. I wished I could take back my "I love you" from the night of her birthday, but even that wouldn't make me mean it any less. "I don't know. I guess not."

Dennis took a sip of his beer and shrugged his shoulders like I should say, *Oh yeah, thanks, man, for solving that dilemma for me.*

"I kind of feel like you need to move on, ya know? Maybe date around or something."

I shrugged. He was right, though. I had to force myself to get over her, because it wasn't the type of thing that would happen on its own.

"I took the SAT," he said, changing the subject. "Did I tell you that?"

I shook my head.

"Freaking bombed it. Well, according to my parents' standards. They're making me take three-hour-long SAT classes every Saturday morning starting the week after spring break."

"Blows." I hadn't even thought about the SAT, but I guess I'd have to take it. I didn't know what exactly I wanted to do in college, but isn't that half of it, figuring shit out?

I don't know. I'd told Alice I was done, but I still couldn't figure out how to remove her from the equation of my life. I wanted to be over her. And I wanted to make decisions that didn't involve her.

"Dennis?" called Debora from in front of the shed.

"Hide the beer," he whispered.

"Uh. Okay." I chugged my can and shoved the unopened ones up my T-shirt.

"What are you guys doing back here?" asked Debora, peeking around the corner.

"Talking," I said just as Dennis said, "None of your business."

She took a few steps closer and crossed her arms over her chest. "Mom wants to know if you did your homework."

"Geez. Of course I did."

Debora tapped her foot against the dirt.

"Fine," he said. "I didn't. Tell her I'll be inside in a sec."

Debora turned to walk back to the house. "You guys smell like cheap beer."

I laughed and let the cans roll out of my shirt and into my lap.

"Don't tell Mom!" called Dennis in a loud whisper.

We chugged the last few cans, and Dennis threw the empties over the fence into the neighbor's yard. We chewed half a pack of gum and called it a successful night.

Inside, Mrs. Yates cornered Dennis in the kitchen, so I snuck out through the front door.

I walked through the living room where Debora sat on

the couch with one foot tucked beneath her, reading a thick biography of Hillary Clinton. "Light reading?" I asked.

"Yeah," she said, holding up the book.

I never saw Debora in anything that didn't look like she'd walked out of a J.Crew ad, but tonight she wore a regular sweatshirt and jeans. Everything about her always looked severely precise, but under the warm light of the reading lamp, the angle of her jaw wasn't so sharp and I could see the little baby hairs at her temples curling in a little.

"You want to go out? Maybe, like, next week?" The words left my mouth before I could do anything about them.

She popped up from the couch. "Okay," she said, and bit her lips, like she was trying to hide a smile. "Yeah, next week sounds good. Call me."

"I can talk to you at school," I offered.

"Oh, yeah. Okay, talk to you at school."

"At school," I repeated.

Letting myself out the front door, I walked out to my car parked on the street. Debora was cute and smart, and I was willing to give this a try. I had to try something. If I couldn't stop loving Alice, I could at least learn how to live without her.

Harvey.

Now

"So, Debora, you're doing Model Arab League this year?" I asked.

"Yes. I'll be acting as head delegate." Debora folded her napkin in her lap for what felt like the millionth time.

"Oh. So, like, you guys pick a country? Is it like Model United Nations?"

"Sort of," she said. "But it's more than *picking* a country. This year we've made quite the strategic move and have decided to represent the country of Djibouti. It's a little risky, but I believe it will pay off."

"I see." I nodded. I'd taken Debora to Prespa's. It wasn't very busy, but you wouldn't know that from the sound of Debora's voice. It was loud—I sank down in the booth a little—the kind of loud you are when you're trying to have a conversation in a crowded room. But I'd worn a shirt with buttons and cleaned the pile of soda cans out of my backseat, so this was definitely a date. My first *real* date.

"Last year we were the delegation representing the United Arab Emirates, which was such an amateur move. I mean, everyone goes for U.A.E.," she said as she pushed her glasses up the bridge of her nose. "It's almost as predict-able as being the United States at Model United Nations." She laughed. "But, you know what I mean."

"Yeah, totally." Nope, no idea at all.

Thankfully, Debora and Dennis were not identical twins—is that even possible for brother/sister twins to be identical? The problem was they still *looked* related and that made things a little weird—especially when I tried to strat-egize how I might kiss her at the end of the night. But then Debora would start talking, and I'd remember how big of a slacker Dennis was or at least pretended to be—he was no-studying-required smart—and how different the two of them really were.

We pretty much talked about debate strategies and the value of SAT prep courses until dessert. Our conversa-tion ratio was a solid 10:1. Debora ten, me one. Back at Grocery Emporium, our conversation had sort of flowed, but tonight felt like she'd come up with an agenda for the whole date and hadn't sent me a copy.

When the waitress, the same one I'd had when I was here with Alice, set down Debora's cheesecake and my tiramisu, Debora took a large gulp of water and cleared her throat. "Why did you ask me out, Harvey?"

The good news was my mouth was full of tiramisu, giving me time to process her frank question. The bad news was she had caught me so off guard I was unable to enjoy the best part of our date so far, the tiramisu. "Well, Debora, in many western societies when a male adoles-cent is attracted to a female adolescent the male will ask the female to accompany him on several introductory dates before finalizing the details of their courtship."

"So, you like me and you want to take me on a date before we call each other boyfriend and girlfriend?"

From Rhodes Scholar to sixteen-year-old girl in seconds. "Yeah, something like that," I said.

She thought about that for a moment. "Why me?"

"Are you fishing for compliments here, Debora? You're pretty and, you know, good at stuff. I'm not going to spend our whole date convincing you that you're dateable."

She wasn't buying it. "I'm only trying to understand your motives."

My single motivation was to get over Alice and maybe meet someone in the process. I liked Debora, and I liked that being with her didn't always feel like I was stumbling down a mountain. She was all the things—direct, uncomplicated, reliable—that Alice was not and maybe that would help me forget her. And I didn't want to go searching for some imitation Alice.

I guess she'd taken my silence as a nonanswer, because she said, "You must be really happy about Alice. It's pretty incredible."

I stared out the window and into the parking lot, where Alice and I had kissed only weeks ago. "Yeah, she is." Quickly, I corrected myself. "*It*. It is pretty incredible."

Debora leaned forward, her cheesecake untouched. "Harvey, I'm smart. I don't need you to agree with me or tell me that I am. I know that I am above average. Maybe that's cocky or arrogant, but it's a fact. But there's a difference between myself and others with my same attributes: I pay attention to the human condition. I see actions and reactions; when Alice acts, you always react." The more she talked, the more I realized how much I liked the way her lips curved when she did. "Even if I weren't so astute, I would know that you were in love or infatuated or whatever it is you want to call it with Alice. I like you. I wouldn't be here if I didn't, but I wonder. I wonder so much I have to know: Why, Harvey, did you ask me out tonight?" She took a sip of her water and a bite of her cheesecake.

I sat there chewing on my bottom lip, a little mesmerized. She had this way, when she wasn't talking about foreign politics or global warming, of making sense of all the complex things I never knew how to describe. And, yeah, maybe Debora was giving me shit about Alice, but I liked the way she spoke *to* me and not *at* me. I liked the way she just asked me, and I liked the way she expected only the same honesty she would give.

I'd always known Debora in a third-party kind of way. Passing her bedroom door to get Dennis. Talking to her at school when Dennis didn't feel like she was ruining his life. I wondered how long Debora had liked me and if it was a recent thing or a long time coming. I blinked and saw Alice standing by the front door of her house in that guy's jacket, without a shirt on underneath. I tried to shake the memory.

Debora had been honest with me, and whether or not I knew if it was true yet, I felt like it might be, so I said, "I like you too, Debora."

She watched her cheesecake like it might move. "What about Alice?"

I wanted to lie to her and tell her that I didn't like Alice in that way, but I couldn't. "I don't know. But I'm not on a date with Alice. I'm here because I like you. That's not a good answer, but I won't lie to you."

She looked up. "No lying. You swear?"

I nodded.

"So does this qualify as dating?"

I almost laughed, but I stopped myself. I didn't want to embarrass her or make her feel like this wasn't okay. Smiling, I said, "Like, are you my girlfriend? I don't know." I paused. "Do you want to be?" A weight in my chest lifted, like a person terrified of driving who'd just realized the one thing standing between them and the open road was their own damn self. I'd never asked a girl that question before. With Alice, it was everything or nothing. There was no between. It felt good to take these steps. The crazy thing was that with Debora it was easy.

Her feet bounced beneath the table and her lips did this thing where she was trying not to smile, so much so that the corners of her lips quivered. "Yeah," she said. "Let's try that."

We finished our desserts, and when my foot touched hers, she didn't move.

While we were waiting for our check, Debora scrolled through her phone.

"What are you doing?" I asked.

Not lifting her eyes from the screen, she replied,

"Forwarding you my weekly schedule. I'll need you to send me your work schedule too." She looked up. "Are those pretty consistent on a week-to-week basis? Dennis's are."

Dennis. I'd told him about our date a few days ago during lunch. When he finally realized I wasn't kidding, he told me I was demented for ever wanting to date Debora. Last night, though, at work, we walked out to my car and he said, "Hey, you know I think Debora's totally crazy, but try not to drag her into all your Alice drama, okay?" I nodded, and we drove home like everything was normal.

The waitress brought my change.

"Uh, yeah," I said. "I guess so."

"Perfect."

When I dropped Debora off, I tugged on her hand before she walked up the steps to her front door. I wanted to kiss her, but I couldn't risk Dennis seeing me kiss his twin sister. He knew I was taking her out, and he wasn't protective or anything, but if he saw this, I think he might be eternally grossed out. I didn't touch her face or her waist like I might have done with Alice. I wasn't ready for the two of them to share the same territory. Holding Debora's hands in mine, I leaned down to her and pressed my lips to hers. I opened my mouth a little, and she did too, but only to whisper, "Good night, Harvey."

Alice.

Then

I'd heard people say that being pregnant during the summer was miserable, but that shit had nothing on cancer. The humidity had exaggerated every little side effect of my illness. Nosebleeds, bloody gums, and aching bones combined with the fact that I was always either freezing or boiling meant that I was never quite comfortable. The life I remembered seemed like years away. That's how it felt, getting closer to the end. Maybe it was a self-defense mechanism, but everything and everyone felt distant. Even Harvey. Prom had been a month and a half ago, but it felt like a whole other life—one that was worth living.

Every day was the same thing: sleep, eat, watch TV, barf. And pain. Always pain. Dr. Meredith had tried a cocktail of different painkillers to ease it all. The meds that worked the best always knocked me out and made me someone I wasn't. Even then, though, there were aches that couldn't be medicated. I guessed there were just some things that had to be felt. Sometimes the discomfort was good because it reminded me that if I was going to live with such pain, then my life had to have been worth it. I had to have been worth it. And nothing I'd done lately had made me feel worthy of anything much.

I sat on the front porch, hoping the muggy heat might thaw my bones. At least I didn't have to worry about getting my hair all sweaty, there was always that. Since I'd stopped chemo, small patches of hair had begun to grow back, but it looked so lame that I kept shaving it. Closing my eyes, I let my body feel the noises of my neighborhood—a barking dog a few houses down, a lawn mower one street over, a sprinkler spitting water onto the sidewalk across the street.

"But, Mom-my!"

"Courtney, I'm sorry, but there's nothing I can do."

I opened my eyes, my attention following the voices. My next-door neighbor stuck out her lip and crossed her arms in pure, unadulterated eight-year-old contempt. "They're going to kill him, and it will be all your fault."

"Courtney, our air conditioner went out last week and that was very expensive to replace." Miss Porter had enough patience to sustain a continent. "I just cannot afford the adoption fee until after my next paycheck on the fifteenth." Miss Porter lived in the lone rental house on our street. It had belonged to Mr. and Mrs. Eugene. A few years ago, they both went to live in a nursing home, and their kids started renting out the place. Most of the street was still pretty pissed about the rotating tenants.

"But . . . but the lady at the shelter said they'd have to put him down tomorrow at two if no one adopts him!"

"I shouldn't have taken you to the shelter until after I

got paid, and I really am sorry about that, but my hands are tied until after the fifteenth."

"I hate you," sobbed Courtney. Her voice sounded almost apologetic, like Miss Porter had forced her hand and for Courtney hating her mom was inevitable. She shrieked, stomping her feet, and crumpled up the flyer she clutched in her little fist before pitching it into the street. Miss Porter threw up her hands and followed her very tiny, very angry daughter inside.

I walked down the driveway to the street, past my mailbox, and picked up the crumpled flyer from the ground. I set my fists on my hips, closed my eyes, and tilted my head to the sky to just breathe.

After I made it back into the house, I took a few minutes to catch my breath again. Finally, I was able to sit up on the living room couch and study the flyer. The paper was wrinkled and dirty, but legible. I flattened it out on the coffee table and read over the advertised information. Below the adoption fee was a grainy photo of a black Pomeranian with patches of hair missing. He was adorable—sad, but still adorable. His name was Goliath and he was four and a half pounds. I appreciated the irony.

I called number two on my speed dial, and he answered on the fifth ring. Six rings would have sent me to voice mail.

"Harvey, I need you to come pick me up."

"I'm at work," he whispered. I could hear that he was muffling his voice with his hand.

"This is a time-sensitive issue."

"Are you okay?" he asked, his voice rising a little.

"I won't be if you don't pick me up in fifteen minutes. I'll be sitting on the front porch. Pull up as close as you can to the walkway. I'm having a shit day."

"Al, wake up."

My eyes opened reluctantly. Harvey's hand rubbed the top of my back. I sat on the front stoop with my legs drawn into my chest and my cheek planted on my knees. Wiping the drool from my legs, I handed Harvey the flyer.

"What is this?"

"This is me doing something nice for someone without taking any credit for it." There was always a first time for everything.

"Okay," he said, a faint smile on his lips.

"I forgot my money in the house. Could you grab it for me?" I wheezed. I hated for anyone to see me like this, and he did a poor job of hiding how much my discomfort pained him. Without a word, he opened the front door.

"It's in the Folger's coffee can in my bra drawer."

"I know," he called.

"Two hundred should be good."

"Two hundies comin' right up."

Harvey returned and held out a hand to help me up. I relied on him pulling me more than I relied on my own muscles. Every joint in my body begged me not to stand. His hand fell to my lower back as he guided me into the passenger seat of his Geo.

"It's the shelter on Swanson Avenue," I said once he was behind the wheel.

I didn't sleep, but I did rest my eyes the whole way there.

"We're here," said Harvey after about ten minutes.

The cold air from the AC in Harvey's car sent chills up my spine. I watched my reflection in the side-view mirror. My cheekbones stuck out—an improvement from the chemo chipmunk cheeks—and my eyes looked like blue pebbles sunken deep into my skull. My chapped lips stung. I opened Harvey's glove compartment and dug around until I found his Carmex. The inside of my mouth felt dry, but it wasn't anything that could be fixed with water. A few weeks ago, my gums had started to bleed and it was uncomfortable. Actually, no, it wasn't uncomfortable. It was fucking miserable. And gross too. Really gross.

"What's the game plan, Al?"

"I've got cancer. I don't need a game plan."

"Okay, so if you try to adopt this dog, like I assume you are, then you *do* understand you must be at least eighteen years old to actually do that, right?"

"I know."

"And you have a plan?"

"Yup."

"Am I, in any way, a part of this plan?"

"You're the wheels of the plan. You're my dashing driver, Harvey." I leaned over and kissed him on the cheek. He fished around in his pocket for my roll of cash and slapped it down into my open palm. I smiled a thank-you and got out of the car.

As I opened the depressingly heavy metal door to the shelter, Harvey called out to me. "Please make sure they give you some kind of carrier. I really don't want that thing marking its territory in my backseat."

I gave him a thumbs-up.

After the door fell shut behind me, I pinched both of my clammy cheeks as a last-ditch effort to give myself some color. The smell hit me, that pungent animal-shelter-bleached-feces smell. Nausea rolled my stomach.

"Hey, Allyster," I said as I approached the sign-in desk, thankful that it was him working this afternoon. Allyster was a retired veterinarian in his early seventies. Instead of living the good life in Florida, he spent his days here, caring for the animals no one wanted.

"Well, look who it is! The kennels started going crazy a second ago, and now I know why. They"—he hiked his thumb over his shoulder at the kennels—"must have known you were coming."

We'd never had any pets except for the occasional hamster when I was a kid, but Mom had known Allyster for as long as she'd been a lawyer. He'd been her first client back when she practiced estate law. Now she did general practice, but he'd followed her to her new firm because he liked her so much. He always sent my parents a bottle of wine and a tin of popcorn and me a twenty-dollar check for Christmas.

"My mom sent me in for . . ." I paused, pretending to search for his name. "Goliath? She wanted him for her secretary's son. He's been begging her forever for a dog, and she told Mom that she finally cracked, so Mom wanted to do something special for them."

"Just in time too! He expires tomorrow afternoon. You know," he said, "I'm going to get your mom to take home one of these guys for herself someday." He squinted his eyes. "Is she in the car?"

"No, she couldn't make it," I said, pushing out my bottom lip.

"Could you give her a call? You gotta be eighteen for the paperwork. I could authorize the adoption over the phone for her, not a problem. A one-time exception, though."

"Oh, shit," I said.

Allyster chuckled at that. Old guys love when girls curse. It's the darnedest thing.

"She's in court all day, Allyster."

He sighed, and I knew this was my moment to strike.

"Can't you let me take him? Just this once? He's a purebred and young too. Come on." I rubbed my bald head, like I'd expected to find hair there.

He glanced back at me. "Ah, hell," he said as he shook his finger in my face. "I'd hate to see this little guy get put down. This will be our secret?"

I lifted a finger to my lips.

He slid the clipboard across the countertop, and I filled out the necessary paperwork. When I was through, I smoothed out my bills and paid the hundred-and-fifty-dollar adoption fee. Allyster completed the transaction and left for a minute, then returned with a white carrier that looked like a mini cardboard house. On each side of the box, in big red letters, were the words: *I LOVE MY PET*.

The box panted and shook as Allyster handed him over.

He squeezed my shoulder and looked at me in a way only people over the age of seventy ever did. He understood. Allyster, like me, was only a couple steps ahead of death. He narrowed his eyes and motioned to my scalp. "Beat this thing, would ya? You're too young for all this baloney." I assumed he was talking about the cancer and not the dog.

The exchange left me feeling uncomfortable, and all I could offer him was a single nod and a quick wave as I backed out of the door with Goliath in tow.

Harvey had practically pulled the Geo up onto the sidewalk. He jumped out of the still-running car and rushed around to the passenger side. I handed him the carrier as he opened my door, and I collapsed into my seat, exhausted. He placed the carrier in my lap, and we were off.

"Pawsitively Pets," was all I said, between gasps.

In the parking lot of the pet store, I gave Harvey my remaining fifty bucks and a specific shopping list. He left the car running, and once he was inside, I pulled the top of the carrier open to find a puppy so ugly, he was cute.

If he had been taken care of properly, Goliath would have been flat-out adorable, but in his current matted, mangy, malnourished state, he was more on the dilapidated side.

Goliath backed into the farthest corner of the box and shivered, shaking the whole carrier. I stretched my hand, palm out, to him. He sniffed for a few minutes before running his tongue over the tips of my fingers.

"Okay, I had to get a different brand of dry food because the one you wanted was out of the puppy stuff," said Harvey as he opened his door.

Goliath jumped away from my fingers and back into his corner.

"You scared him."

Harvey tossed the bags into the backseat and rolled his eyes. "I think maybe you meant to say thank you."

I sighed. "Thanks."

I held my hand out for Goliath again, and Harvey leaned over me to get a good look at him. "All right, what's the final stop for this guy?"

"Back to my place."

"Alice, are you planning on keeping him?" What he didn't say was, *You're dying. Not really the most opportune time to acquire a new pet.*

"No, Harvey, I'm not, but Goliath needs a bath almost as much as you do, asshat." I smiled.

Harvey shifted the car into drive. The corner of his mouth lifted as he shook his head.

At home, I changed into a swimsuit from too many summers ago and pulled out an old tank top to cover the unfortunate sagging. I sat in my tub and waited patiently for the tap to run lukewarm. Harvey held Goliath tucked beneath one arm, like a football. When I gave him the okay, he handed him over.

Harvey knelt down next to the tub for damage control. All four and a half pounds of Goliath tensed with stress in anticipation of the running water, but once he felt the warmth hit him, his body melted entirely. I massaged the shampoo deep into his fur, and his neck drooped a bit as I loosened cakes of dirt that the shelter had missed. Harvey rinsed him down using a big plastic cup and then wrapped him in a fluffy towel straight from the dryer.

After toweling off Goliath and letting him loose on the bathroom floor, Harvey reached down with both hands and pulled me to my feet. My knees wobbled, and my feet slid beneath the soap suds, but he steadied me, holding me firmly in place. As I stepped over the tub, Harvey reached for another towel and draped it over my shoulders.

At that moment I wanted nothing more than to burrow myself into Harvey's chest. He wrapped his arms around my waist and dipped his head to my shoulder, where he rested his cheek. Goliath explored the bathroom floor and licked our feet experimentally.

Harvey held me tightly like I might slip away, and just once I tried to. I tried to fall out of his arms, but he pulled me back to him. I reached up, circling his neck with my arms, and played with the overgrown curls at his nape. He sighed quietly.

Harvey picked his head up from my shoulder and his brown eyes found mine, and then it occurred to me: nothing was private anymore, not between us.

He kissed me, a quick kiss at first, his lips sealed. I remembered that night at Lake Quasipi and then again at prom. If there was going to be another step, I would have to be the one to make it. I held the back of his neck and pulled him down to me. I expected him to be sweet and slow, but he wasn't. His hands ran over my sides and down the slope of my back as he kissed my shoulders. His fingers left a scorching trail over my skin, nothing like Luke's sweaty hands. Harvey's lips met mine. I felt the coppery taste of blood on my tongue. I didn't want to, but I pushed him back.

"My mouth," I said. "My gums have been hurting."

"I think I can find other things to kiss besides your mouth," he whispered.

A shiver of heat spread up my spine and through my belly as his lips fell on my cheekbones and my forehead and my eyelids and my neck. For a moment, I forgot about my droopy bathing suit, and my bleeding gums turned into a whisper as the pain in my joints eased.

My chest tightened. "Stop," I breathed.

He did, but held me up by my shoulders.

"I can't—I need to catch my breath."

He pulled me into his arms while Goliath licked my toes. In this moment, it wasn't fair, and I wanted to stay. I was scared and angry, but mostly angry, because I didn't want to die. I didn't want to die and leave Harvey and my parents and Natalie. I could have had this, but whatever lottery decided life and death chose differently. My whole life could have been this—Harvey and me standing as close as physics would allow. Panic began to knot in my chest. I would be gone. I would die and be nothing but remains and my memories would be lost forever, and that made me want to scream and claw at the universe, begging it to let me stay.

Harvey began to sway from side to side, with me still in his arms.

We stayed like that for a while, and I let his touch soothe me as we danced to a silent song only we could hear.

★ ★ ★

The next step I left up to Harvey. I told him to take Goliath next door along with the bag of food, treats, toys, and information from the shelter. Harvey had strict instructions to tie Goliath's leash to the light post in Miss Porter's front yard, ring the doorbell, and then haul ass out of there.

For a moment, I thought about keeping Goliath for myself. My parents wouldn't say no. Not right now. He'd looked so scared. But I couldn't. In a few months, I'd orphan the poor dog all over again.

I collapsed onto my bed and eyed the collection of prescription drugs on my nightstand until I found the painkillers that knocked me out like damn elephant tranquilizers. The good stuff, the stuff doctors doled out when they felt really bad for you.

The next few minutes were spent drifting in and out of consciousness. I heard a loud squeal of sheer delight, loud enough to penetrate the double pane of my bedroom window. Harvey cracked open my bedroom door, his face flushed red, his chest heaving. He had this enormous grin on his face, and before he could say anything, I beat him to the punch.

"Good deeds are tiring, and entirely overrated," I said, laughing a little. I was exhausted, but it had been worth it.

Harvey collapsed into the old wicker rocking chair in the far corner of my room. He said nothing, but his stupid smile said everything. I fell asleep to the sound of Goliath's nervous yelps echoing from next door and the rhythmic squeaking of the floorboards beneath the rocking chair.

Alice.

Now

Eric ran to the front of the café to pick up our steam-ing mugs of cider. He sat down in the chair opposite me and placed our drinks down on the round, wobbly table between us. Whenever either of us accidentally hit the table leg with our knee the cider sloshed around and splattered onto the surface.

It was a freakishly chilly night for the month of April, especially considering my half-packed suitcase at home full of shorts, tank tops, and swimsuits. Natalie had decided, for the first time ever, to close the studio for spring break. Tomorrow was a half day at school, and my parents, Nata-lie, Harvey, and I would all be driving to the beach on Sunday morning. My mom's boss had a house there on the water, and he was letting her use it for the week.

This all sounded great, perfect even. Except that Har-vey and I hadn't talked in over a month. My mom kept trying to pry me open and find out what was wrong, but when her attempts at cracking me had failed, she sent in backup—my dad, who had even worse luck.

I should have been relieved that Harvey had backed off. He'd started dating Dennis's twin sister. I'd seen them together in the hallways and suspected something, but it was my parents who officially broke the news to me. We all sat at the kitchen table, eating dinner, when my dad asked if I'd hung out with Harvey and his new girlfriend.

I swallowed my food and bit down on my lip.

My mom looked at me questioningly. "Yeah," she said. "Natalie said he's dating Dennis's twin sister. She's the blond one, right?"

I nodded.

"She's cute," said my mom.

That night, I barely slept. My entire body was on fire.

At school, I punished myself by watching them. They held hands. They kissed. They did . . . couple's shit. And, God, of all the people he could have picked, he chose Debora. Debora who was a snotty little overachiever, the type of girl who reminded the teacher that there had been a homework assignment due. She'd intruded on our trip to Lake Quasipi and now she was intruding on my life. She may have been cordial to me a handful of times, but now she was dating Harvey and that seemed to cancel everything else out.

Whenever I saw him walking her to class or searching for her hand with his as they shuffled down the hallways, I found myself plotting her demise. This wasn't okay. He couldn't be with someone, not so soon. I wanted to destroy her. But then I stopped myself, which surprised me. This little, minuscule spot of good inside of me told me that Harvey was happy, and anything I did to ruin her would ruin him. And that would be unforgiveable. Even if I did manage to ruin her and split the two of them up, what would I do then? I didn't know how to be with Harvey.

Going to the café with Eric had been one of the few times he and I had gone out in public together. Typically, our time together was limited to our little fort under the bleachers and sweaty makeout sessions in the back of his rusted Range Rover. Eric had avoided me for a couple days after the incident at my house with Harvey. I didn't go out of my way to track him down; I knew that in time Eric would find me.

He found me under the bleachers during third period. Plopping down next to me, he held out a mini sleeve of Oreo cookies from the vending machine. After the bell buzzed announcing the beginning of the period, Eric said, "So what's the real deal with you and that Harvey guy?"

"We were friends." I lay back on the gym floor. "Then he fell in love with me." It wasn't the whole truth, but it wasn't a whole lie either, and I thought that more than fair.

Not talking to Harvey meant that if I wasn't with Eric, I was alone, and when I was alone, Celeste always seemed to find me. It was more of the same empty threats and promises of revenge. *You might want to watch your back. Don't for a minute think you've gotten away with anything.* Nothing she said could scare me because I didn't have anything left to lose.

"Alice?" Eric said, snapping his fingers in front of my face. "Where are you, Allie Cat?" I hated that nickname. Eric blew on his mug of cider, gripping it with both hands.

"Sorry, what'd you say?"

"Are you going to be around for spring break?"

"No. Going to the beach with family."

Silence sank between us, and I wondered why we were here and not pressing our bodies together in the back of his car, but he'd insisted on going somewhere to talk.

"What about you?" I asked. "Plans for spring break?" Talking and not just playing Go Fish or making out turned out to be almost uncomfortable.

"Kind of," he said.

I'll admit I didn't know Eric very well. But I did know if he had something to say he always came right out and said it. "Kind of?"

"Yeah, we're, uh . . . moving."

I sat up straight, looking directly at him. "What do you mean you're moving?"

"My aunt's job transferred her again."

His aunt? It had never even occurred to me to ask Eric about himself. I didn't even know he lived with his aunt, which made me wonder where his parents were. I'd had plenty of opportunities to ask Eric about himself, but I hadn't. I thought he was like me, just running.

"We moved here in November, but her job shuffles us around a lot." He set his arms down on the table, rocking it, and pulled at some dead skin around his thumbnail.

"Oh. So, next week then?" I asked.

"I guess." He cleared his throat. "I probably won't see you after tomorrow."

"I guess not." We both stared holes through the little table separating us. "So you live with your aunt?" I didn't know why I even bothered. This wasn't exactly the opportune time to get to know Eric.

"Yeah, my parents were never really around."

"I didn't know," I said quietly.

"You never asked." Those three words drifted down between us like three feathers that would inevitably hit the ground, but took their time. Gravity at its finest.

"I've never moved" was the only thing I knew to say.

Without really thinking about it, I reached across the table and held his dry hand in mine. We sat there for a while having our own silent conversation until the bell above the door chimed, jolting us back to the little café. In walked Harvey with his hand on the small of Debora's back, guiding her to the counter. I watched them, and Eric watched me. They held hands loosely, the way people do when they've been together for a long time. All the animosity I felt for Debora rose up through my body like vitriol. I wanted to annihilate her. I wanted to dismantle her perfect little life piece by piece, leaving only Harvey intact.

Eric squeezed my hand, but I barely noticed. "You okay?"

My breath caught and the anger inside of me deflated. "Fine," I answered, still watching them over Eric's shoulder. As they left, Harvey's gaze paused momentarily on Eric and me. I so wished that he'd given me a hint of something— some kind of reaction—but he didn't. He just left.

I pulled my eyes from the door and smiled at Eric, but it felt sad on my lips. "I can't believe you're moving next week."

"Well, actually," said Eric, suddenly perking up, "my aunt's got a couple months left on her lease. She says I can finish out senior year if I really want to. What do you think I should do, Allie Cat?"

The nickname pricked at my nerves, reminding me of myself. This was the part of the conversation where I was supposed to tell him to stay.

"Do whatever you want, Eric. You're a big boy. I'm pretty sure you can make your own decisions."

His shoulders fell. "Well, I guess you'll find out what I decide next week," he said.

I was sad for Eric because he'd never known a home, not like I had. But I wasn't sad enough to give him one.

Harvey.

Then

"Harvey, do you even know what you're doing?"

"Yes, Alice, I do. I watched a video online."

"Give me that," she said, yanking the apple out of my hand.

I handed her the pen along with the knife. She fumbled with the utensils but didn't get very far.

Before she had the chance to cut our last good apple to bits, I swiped it from her.

"Hey!" She sat on the bench in a huff. We had already gone through eight apples, all victims of Alice's frustration.

I held the pen between my teeth and sat down next to her. After placing the apple on the picnic table, I carefully maneuvered the knife through the apple, trying to create a tubular shape. "I can't believe you put this on your list, Al. It's so stupid," I said through clenched teeth.

"Harvey, I can't even think of a single person who has graduated high school without smoking marijuana."

"I can think of plenty. And come to think of it—they're all really successful. Maybe they're on to something," I said. "And the fact that you refer to pot as marijuana shows how much of a non-pot-smoking kind of person you are."

She opened her mouth to speak, but before she could I cut her off. "And, Alice, you have cancer! Aren't people with cancer not supposed to smoke?"

"Harvey, I'm going to be biting it sooner rather than later. I don't think my future success is all that valid of a concern here, okay? It's not like I've got lung cancer. And I could probably get medicinal marijuana, you know, so it's not all that illegal."

In the last year, Alice's attitude toward mortality had turned from accepting to cavalier. But now she was to the point of being capricious. Whenever she said anything about dying or expiration dates, I wanted to slap my hand over her mouth, because I was scared that somehow Death would hear her taunting him and smite her for it.

"We're nearly done with the list," she continued. "Not doing this now would be half-assed. And I'm not going to this fund-raiser unless I'm stoned." The pothead terminology sounded so foreign coming from her.

"But won't everyone know you're high?"

"Blame it on the pain meds. What are they going to do? Kick me out of my own fund-raising event for trying to dull my pain?"

Alice didn't verbalize it much—that she was in pain. But it was everywhere, all over her. This weird part of me wanted to feel everything she felt, including the pain. It wasn't even that I wanted to carry her burden, but I was scared of her going somewhere I couldn't follow. "You can't play the cancer card forever, Alice."

"You're right, just until I'm dead. Then I dub you the

carrier of the card, which shall henceforth be known as the 'my friend died of cancer' card."

If it weren't so true, I would have laughed.

Things were getting worse. I overheard my mom talking to Bernie and Martin the other night. They said that they were going to focus on Alice being "comfortable." The thought made me numb. I didn't ever think it would come to this, that the sum of Alice's life would amount to her level of *comfort*. I always thought we would look back on this and I could say, "Hey, Alice, remember that time you had cancer?"

I worked diligently on the apple and came up with something manageable. I stood and pulled a little mini ziplock baggie from my pocket that screamed *illegal substances*. Alice's gaze followed the baggie, her pale blue eyes eager and only slightly apprehensive. "We can just say we did it, Al. I won't tell anyone."

She bit her lip in thought; she looked sweet. I blinked my eyes and sweet Alice was gone. "Stop being a pansy, Harvey."

I sighed loudly and stuffed the dry green flakes into the top of the apple where I had used a pocketknife to create a long cylinder that ran to the core. "Ready?" I asked, giving her one last chance to say no, but she stood up next to me and nodded once.

I handed her the apple, and she pressed her mouth to a horizontally running cylinder that cut straight through the bottom of the vertical cylinder. All of this was fancy talk for Apple Bong.

Alice looked at me expectantly. I took my little plastic

gas station lighter and held it to the top of the apple. "I've never done this before, but online it said to suck in, hold for a couple seconds, then blow out slowly. And in case you didn't get it by now, I think this is a horrible idea."

I lit the lighter, the leaves crackling, and then she sucked in like I told her to. She held the smoke in her lungs for a couple of seconds before trying to blow out smoothly, but instead unleashed a fury of coughing and wheezing. She held her hand to her chest as she tried to catch her breath and stumbled backward. I wrapped my arm around her waist and guided her back to the picnic bench.

We had decided that the best place to do this would be in a public park. Craven's Park was on the outskirts of town and had recently been partially redone, so we opted for its older, less-trafficked area. The leaves were beginning to change, most of them still clinging to their branches. At the moment, I was supposed to be working the after-school shift at Grocery Emporium, but I had called in sick last night.

"This is stupid, Alice."

I'm sure she would have had some snarky remark to bite back with if she wasn't trying to catch her breath. I patted her back, smoothing the nonexistent wrinkles in her paper-thin T-shirt. I tried my very best not to think of the outline of her bra beneath my fingers. Her shoulder blades stuck out, each vertebra of her spine visible through her shirt. "Alice, there are so many things wrong with this picture. I am officially the worst friend of all time for letting you do this."

She said nothing, but pulled the apple back to her lips. I lit it again, and this time the process went a little smoother. She inhaled twice more and passed the apple to me. I took one hit and passed it back to Alice again. We went like this for a while, just stopping to add more crumpled leaves to the top of the apple.

A breeze pushed through the park, leaves whispering as they fell to the ground.

"Harvey." It came out like a breath, like she needed my name to breathe. "Harvey," Alice repeated back to herself quickly. "Harvey, tell me why on earth Natalie gave you that name," she demanded with her eyes closed.

"You know why, Alice." My name had always been a little bit of a sore spot for me. I hated it; it sounded so old and . . . old. I always wondered what my life would have been like if I were a Nick or a Carson or an Asher.

"Tell me again."

"My mom wanted my name to sound American." My mom lost both her parents soon after graduating high school. The two of them were Romanian immigrants and neither of them spoke English. When she got pregnant with me, she dropped out of her touring ballet company and settled in the nearest town. I'd asked about my dad— *Was he part of the ballet? A local? A stagehand? Dead? Did she tell him about me? Is that why he left us?*—but no answers. My mom met Bernie at a student-run legal clinic where she sought custody advice. They'd been friends ever since. I rolled my head back a little, watching the clouds slide across the sky. "She saw my name on a list of popular American names in the back of a dictionary."

"Yeah, popular fifty years ago," mumbled Alice. "Harvey, there's a play about you; did you know that, Harvey?"

The air around us was gray. A bittersweet smell filled my nostrils, making me dizzy like the perfume section at Feldman's Department Store.

"Harvey," she said, and then looked at me expectantly. "The play is called *Harvey*, Harvey!" She was saying my name too many times and in too few sentences. I hoped it was because my name felt good on her lips.

Alice broke the silence with a shrill, high-pitched laugh. It sent a shiver up my spine. "I looked it up once," she said, still talking about the play. "I did a search on your name. I don't know why."

And I didn't know why either, but I was happy to know she thought of me when I wasn't around.

"That's funny, isn't it? I don't know." She was talking a lot and quickly, a sort of nervous chatter. It made me anxious. "It's about a man, Harvey. A man with an imaginary friend. Can you guess which one of them is named Harvey?" She didn't give me time to respond. "The friend is named Harvey!"

My mouth was dry and my brain couldn't form words. Alice was rambling. Alice, whose words were always so perfectly chosen to be the right amount of bitter and sweet, was talking nonsense. I shook my head. This was a bad idea.

"Harvey," she said abruptly, her voice completely sober.

She sat up and turned to me, scooting in closer and hiking one knee into her chest. "Harvey, you are my *Harvey*."

"Har-har, Alice."

"No, you're my imaginary friend," she said, like it was so obvious and should make complete sense. "You're my Harvey." She picked up my arm, draping it over her shoulder, then rested her cheek against my chest.

I wanted to ask her what she meant, but Alice thought she was high as a kite so maybe now wasn't the time. But was I invisible? Imaginary? Or maybe I was so crucial to her that she didn't care what other people thought when she talked to me, her "imaginary friend." Either way, there was one thing I knew for sure. Being an imaginary friend was a one-way street. If that's what I was to Alice, then maybe she only ever saw me when she needed me. I wondered what would happen when I needed her.

"Alice, come on!" I held Alice's elbow as she stumbled at my side through the church parking lot.

We didn't go to church, but Mrs. Barton, the head of the Parent Teacher Association and Mindi's mom, did. When word spread about Alice, the PTA moms armed themselves in preparation for extreme fund-raising.

At first, Bernie and Martin thanked them but declined. However, in recent months the hospital bills had multiplied, and slowly each "No, thank you" turned into a "Yes, please." So here we were, at Alice's third Breakfast for Dinner Fund-raiser. I'm not going to lie; last time the omelet bar was pretty solid and the pancake chef was equally legit. The caveat was the pricey tickets at forty bucks a person. Which was a lot of money, especially for a family with kids, but I'd quickly learned that people loved to give when the giving was public knowledge.

"Harvey, on a scale of one to ten, how good do I look right now?" asked Alice with her hands on her hips, striking a pose in front of the church.

She lost her balance, and I caught her just before she toppled. "Ten. Alice, let's go home. I'll call your dad and tell him you don't feel good."

"No." She wiggled out of my arms and stalked through the church entrance.

Mindi sat at the registration table with a little gray cashbox in front of her and twirled her gum around her finger. I was tempted to tell her how grossly unsanitary that was—especially while handling money—but I didn't.

"Hi, Alice," said Mindi, her voice rhythmically drab.

"Hey, bitch," said Alice. Sometimes girls call each other "bitch" in a friendly comrade type of way. That, however, was not the tone Alice was going for.

"Your hair looks nice," said Mindi, motioning to Alice's bare scalp. My jaw dropped. Who said that kind of shit? It was ruthless and cruel, but Mindi was totally mindless and always loyal to Celeste.

"Sorry I'm late," said Alice, and leaned over the table. "But better me than your period. Pregnancy scares are such a bitch, but you know what I mean, right, Mindi?"

Ouch.

Mindi's mouth fell open, her eyes watering instantly and her nostrils flaring.

Most people were nice to Alice, especially with the whole cancer thing. But I think Alice took pleasure in the fact that no matter how sick she was, Mindi and Celeste were still so brutal with her. And because of that, Alice fed the fire between them even more intensely than before she was sick.

"Hey, guys," called Bernie from across the church dining hall. She waved us over.

"I've already got you two a plate," said Martin. "Sit down; grub up!"

From where we sat, I saw my mom talking to Mrs. Barton near the buffet line. My mom wore her dance clothes and her usual bun, trying her best to inch away from the grease-saturated food as if it was a cold she might catch.

Alice pushed around some scrambled eggs with her fork and ate half a pancake. I devoured my plate and the remainder of hers. As I scooped up my last bite of ketchup-covered hash browns, Alice said, "Let's go get some more juice."

Looping her arm through mine, she pulled me along, and I trailed behind her, my feet dragging. A few feet away from the beverage table she came to an abrupt halt, with me tripping to a stop at her side.

"Celeste," she said sweetly, her eyes fluttering, as she swept her hand to her chest.

"Alice," said Celeste, biting each letter.

"You were just darling in *Oklahoma!* Harvey," she said,

turning back to me, "she was darling, wasn't she?"

Celeste stood there, her arms pressed to her sides, muscles twitching.

Alice paused and leaned forward, her hand cupped around her mouth like she might share a secret. "It was so nice of the costume department to, you know," she said, motioning up and down the length of Celeste's body, "accommodate you."

Celeste's cheeks flushed red.

I always knew Alice could be mean; there was nothing new there. But Celeste wasn't even fat. I guess she was bigger than most dancers, but Alice didn't say those things because they were true; she said those things to be hurtful. And for that moment, I didn't really want to be associated with her. I wanted to be walking next to the girl I'd sat in the spinning teacups with and the girl who had saved Goliath from the pound and who had humiliated Luke after he beat up Tyson and had danced with me outside of the prom. Not this girl.

She didn't notice when I took a step back.

"And how are you and Luke?" asked Alice. "How does he even keep his hands off you?"

Celeste leaned in close. "Oh, he doesn't. That's why you guys broke up, remember?"

I didn't hear what else she might have said. I was halfway to the exit before I even looked back to see Alice nose to nose with Celeste, her hands on her hips. From over Celeste's shoulder, Alice spotted me, and I walked faster.

I didn't want to be her other half to this. Not anymore.

I'd made it to my car door when I heard her call my name.

I looked up to see her walking across the parking lot as fast as her body would allow. "Wait!" she said. "Don't leave me in there with those assholes." She caught up to me, her chest heaving. "Why'd you leave me?"

I shook my head and opened the car door and closed it behind me without a word.

"What the hell, Harvey?" She stood right outside my window. "Talk to me."

She didn't get it. She really didn't get it.

I rolled down my window and breathed through my nose, trying to harness my anger so it wouldn't slip away, so that she couldn't make me forget why I was so pissed in the first place. "You can't talk like that to people."

She scoffed. "Oh, come on. Those girls are bitches and you know it."

I threw my hands up. "So let them be bitches. When you say shit like that, you only make it okay for them to act the way they do."

"Whatever. You don't get it. Someone needs to put them in their place. And, yeah, maybe I was meaner than usual, but it's not like I get high every day."

I reached across the car and opened the glove box. Next to my lighter and pocketknife sat a small baggie from this little head shop outside of town called Purple Dragon. I rolled down the window, my fist clenched around the bag. "No," I said, and threw the baggie at her feet. "Alice, you're not high. You're just mean."

According to the label on the baggie, what Alice and I had smoked had been completely legal pine-flavored tobacco. Honestly, I wouldn't even have known how to get real pot.

Alice picked it up and read the label.

I didn't wait to see the reaction on her face.

For the first time, I left Alice, and the joke was on her. I wanted to laugh, but nothing about it was funny.

Alice.

Then

After the pot incident, I gave Harvey a day before I tried to apologize, but he ignored my messages for the rest of the week before calling me back. I don't know what made me so quick to apologize. Maybe it was Harvey rubbing off on me. Or maybe it was the feeling of being holed up in my house, waiting for nothing. Every day, and especially the ones without Harvey, began to lack purpose. I'd always taken for granted the little things like studying for tests or quizzes and the anticipation of Fridays; but now, as I spent my days at home under the watchful eyes of one of my parents, I missed those small goals that gave purpose to everyday life.

I lay sprawled out on the couch with my laptop, hunting for the latest social-media-worthy school gossip. The juiciest bit I'd come across was the fact that Mindi was dating some senior named Mike Tule. This amused me to no end because Mike Tule looked like a total tool.

I got up for a glass of water to take my meds. As I settled back into the couch, my phone rang.

"Hey," said Harvey. He was at work. I could hear the voice on the intercom listing off the Daily Deals.

"Hi. I've, uh, been trying to call you."

"I'm on my break. I've only got, like, five minutes left." He sounded distant, like the type of boy who left a trail of confused girls in his wake.

"Oh," I said, stunned that he was still acting this way. "We can talk later."

"Well, what did you want?"

I couldn't believe he was still pissed at me. "Didn't you get my messages?"

"Yeah. Yeah, I did."

"I apologized." I sat up and breathed out through my nose, trying to scale back my irritation.

"Oh, come on, Al, I wouldn't really call—" He sighed into the phone. "Just, never mind."

"What?" I said, my temper climbing. "Don't be a punk. Just say it."

"You said you were sorry that I was pissed off. That's not how apologies work."

"I said I was sorry. Jesus."

"You can't apologize for my feelings and expect things to be better." He paused. "Especially not when you're the reason for them."

I knew what he was talking about, but that hadn't been what I meant. I didn't think. "Harvey—"

"No," he said. "An apology like that makes it sound like you had nothing to do with why I was mad when *you* were what got me all angry in the first place." His voice rose with each word. "That's not okay."

"I—I'm sorry. I didn't mean for it to sound that way."

I almost said it, that I was sorry for how I'd acted and what I did, but instead I said, "Do you want to write up your own apology and I can sign it? Would that work better for you?"

"I have to get back to work."

"Fine," I said. "I'll call you later."

"I'll be there in a sec," he called to someone on the other end. "Yeah, okay," he said to me, and hung up.

He was right and I knew it. My damn pride had gotten in the way. Again.

About an hour later I texted Harvey and asked him to come over after work. It took him another two hours to respond with a simple "K."

By the time his key turned the lock, my parents were getting ready for bed, but I waited.

We sat there, and I knew it was me who had to talk first.

"Hey, Harv," said my dad, peeking his head in from the hallway. "Leftovers in the fridge. And, Alice, don't stay up too late."

I nodded and waited for his door to click shut before turning to Harvey. "I'm sorry," I said.

He looked at me expectantly.

I chewed on my lip for a second. "I'm sorry for being an asshole and treating Celeste and Mindi the way I did. And for dragging you into it."

"I just like you the way you are when it's only us," he said, his lips pursed, "and I wish you could be that way all the time. And I don't want to be your imaginary friend. I want to be your friend."

I nodded. "I want that too." I felt my eyes watering. I couldn't handle him being mad. I couldn't risk dying that way.

The corner of his mouth lifted. It felt so good to see him almost smile. "Okay," he said.

The tension inside me unwound all at once, leaving me suddenly tired. "Okay, like we're good?"

"Yeah." His lips split into a smile. "Being mad at you sucked."

I liked that it was hard for him to be mad at me. Maybe I liked it a little too much.

Alice.

Then

I had no good reasons for wanting to learn how to drive except that I was sixteen years old and I felt the universe owed it to me. I would never go to college or have my own apartment, but I could drive. When I'd put it on my list, I'd envisioned myself on an open road, going ninety; but, admittedly, I wasn't so good at the whole driving thing, so this parking lot would be the closest I'd get to an open road. I asked Harvey to teach me a few weeks after our fight. He'd been stubborn at first, refusing to teach me in his precious little car. When he realized I wasn't going to stop asking, he obliged me, but only if we stuck to the old, abandoned SaveMart parking lot.

I wove up and down the empty lot with Harvey in the passenger seat. I'd skipped out on my usual breakfast of pain meds this morning so that I would be alert. Turning the wheel felt different than—

"Alice, brake!" screamed Harvey. "Now!"

I slammed my foot down on the left pedal, hoping that it was the brake and not the gas. Harvey's Geo came to a jarring halt. I sighed, but not loud enough for him to notice. The wheel felt different than I'd thought it would and I'd turned hard, expecting the car to feel heavy, and then all of a sudden we were about to hit a light pole.

"See?" I said. "We're fine."

"Fine?" He pushed the gearshift between us into park. "We were almost not so fine," he said, pointing to the light pole outside my window.

"It's not my fault your alignment's off," I said, crossing my arms over my chest.

"My *alignment* is fine, thank you very much. Besides, why couldn't you have your dad teach you this? I don't even get why—just, never mind."

He couldn't understand why I was even bothering to learn how to drive. That's what Harvey thought, but couldn't say out loud. I knew it.

Leaning over, he touched my leg. I let myself rest my head on his shoulder. His body sighed beneath me. This was good. Recently, we'd fallen into this rhythm where it was okay to hold hands and kiss. He wasn't my boyfriend. Whatever this was felt bigger than that. Normally, that would have freaked the shit out of me, but wherever I was going, I would go without regrets.

For Harvey, all this was probably cruel. But for me, it was the last meal—all the sweet things that were never meant for everyday consumption.

He kissed the top of my head. "Okay," he said. "Let's try this again. Put the car in reverse."

I sat up and pulled away from him like a cat, enjoying the way his touch hit every one of my nerve endings.

Looking over my shoulder, I put the car in reverse.

Harvey placed his hand on the wheel, helping me guide the car backward without hitting anything.

"Just make circles around the lot," he said.

So I did.

"I guess we're getting close to the end, right?" asked Harvey.

I took my foot off the brake, letting the car roll to a stop.

"Your list." He shook his head. "I meant your list. There's not much left on it, is there?"

"Oh," I said, and pressed my foot down on the pedal again. "Yeah. Yeah, I guess not."

"It's been almost a year." His voice was void of emotion. It'd been almost a year since I was diagnosed. I wanted to go back in time and examine every single decision I'd made to see what might alter my path.

There were a few more things to do before I could go from *is* to *was*, from *here* to *gone*. I'd figured out every little detail of the remains of my list, except for one thing. It was for Harvey. I wanted to give him something, something he could take with him and keep forever.

Part of me felt like I'd failed Harvey. When I made my list, I'd wanted to do something for him. I didn't know what. And I wasn't sure what would be big enough, important enough. But now I was running out of time—the one thing I'd never been able to control—and it seemed that my good deed for Harvey would be my one incomplete resolution. It was the thing that plagued me at night like a dripping faucet. But, in a way, I preferred to keep it like that because when the list was done, there would just be the waiting. Waiting for the moment when my body would say no more. I hoped that *this*—this whole year of us being together, whether we were planning or kissing or fighting—was good enough for him. I hoped he'd never forget this year of his life. No, our life. Because, thanks to Harvey, the year I died had become the year I lived.

I made another lap around the parking lot, my foot getting used to the gas and the brake. "What would be on your list, Harvey? If you knew you were going to die."

He reached over again and cupped his hand around the back of my neck. "You," he said. "Being with you."

I nodded, blinking for a second too long, trying to make his words last a moment longer.

"I don't know how, but I'd want to make sure my mom was okay. And your parents too. I'd quit my job too, like fuck-this-I'm-out-give-me-all-the-gourmet-cheese quit my job."

I laughed. We were so different. Harvey wanted good. He wanted to leave the ones he loved in a good place. I'd just wanted the last word. But I wouldn't be sorry for that now. It was too late for sorry.

"And, maybe," he said, "I'd want to find out what the deal was with my dad. Just so I could know once and for all."

I nodded. There had to be answers to his questions. But Harvey was never very good at getting what he wanted. Even when we were kids and he stumbled upon his mom's Christmas present hiding spot, I was the one to dig through the shopping bags and find the Rollerblades he'd asked for every year for the last three years.

Without warning, my mouth went dry and my head began to pound to the point of dizziness. I hit the brake and slid the car into park.

"You okay?" he asked.

I nodded. "Give me a sec." An echoing pain spread through my body. I concentrated on the dashboard to stop myself from bursting into tears as I breathed in and out through my nose.

Harvey came over to my side and opened the door. "Come on," he said. "Let me take you home. Maybe we'll start watching a few of those movies Dennis gave me."

He helped me out of the car and walked me to the passenger side.

"Thank you, Harvey," I said.

"For what?"

I sat down, taking a deep breath. "For always saying yes."

Harvey.

Now

The last day before spring break was always torture. It was even worse than the last day of school because teachers were still trying to teach. Thankfully, though, today was a half day. But that still didn't change the fact that I was fourteen minutes into second period and my ass was already falling asleep.

Last night, I'd gone to Debora's house to help get stuff ready for the senior luau put on by the student council every year before spring break. After making a few signs, we ran out for caffeine and that's when I saw Alice and Eric. I thought that having a girlfriend would soften the blow of Alice not choosing me, but it didn't work like that. Debora was great; she just wasn't Alice. Mr. Ramirez droned on about the meaning of "full faith and credit," putting all of us to sleep. I watched the door, ready for the bell to ring so I could escape. Dennis's head bobbed in the window. He motioned for me and mouthed, *Now.*

I shrugged my shoulders.

Not kidding, mouthed Dennis, his eyes wide and his face manic.

I raised my hand.

"Something to add to the conversation, Mr. Poppovicci?"

I hated my last name. "No, sir. I need to go to the restroom."

Ramirez thought for a moment, then held out the hall pass. "Make it quick."

I took my backpack and ducked out the door with the hall pass in hand.

Dennis waited for me a few feet down, out of breath.

I stuffed the hall pass into my back pocket. "Dennis, what's going on?"

"They—" He shook his head and waved his hands around, searching for words. "Outside the gym there's this— Damn it, just come with me."

I followed him and we cut through the auditorium to the other side of the school.

"I wish you would stop and tell me what you pulled me out of class for."

Dennis didn't slow down. "It's hard to explain." He was acting weird. Like, weird for Dennis.

"Well, try. Now," I said.

He rubbed his hands down his face and groaned. "They made some kind of shrine to Alice, like a memorial."

I froze. "Wait. What?"

"It's fucked up, man," he said, his nostrils flaring, his eyes wide.

I couldn't connect the dots. "What do you mean a memorial? Who's they?"

"Like the type of memorial they would have given if she *had*, you know, died. Candles and pictures. The kind of stuff you see on TV, but worse. And I don't know who *they* are, but I have three people in mind."

I stuffed my hands into my pockets to stop them from shaking. "Shit. What—"

"I couldn't find her," said Debora, bursting through the main entrance at the top of the aisle.

I turned to Dennis. "You sent *Debora* after Alice?" I whispered. "Do you have dementia?"

"I had to get you out of class. I saw her in the hallway. Game-time decision," he said, his hands held up in defense.

"Okay. Okay. Let's go." I turned to find Debora behind me. She nodded, her lips pressed in a thin line.

We ran out of the auditorium and into the athletics wing, trophy cases lining the walls. Dennis ran ahead, and I followed him to the farthest end of the hallway where all the old, dusty, sun-stained trophy cases sat untouched.

We stopped in front of the last case. Every surface was covered in cloth. Old, dying flowers had been thrown across the surface. There were candles; those idiots could have started a fire. And pictures of Alice. Her eyes had been crossed out and things like *bitch* or *whore* had been written across each print.

I shook my head. "No," I said. This was too cruel. And low. My stomach twisted. I was horrified by the possibility that anyone could even be capable of something like this. This was wrong. Even by Alice's standards.

Part of me wanted to let Alice see this and feel this, like maybe she needed to. But the other part of me—the bigger part of me—wanted to fix it all for her. And maybe if I fixed this, I could fix us.

"So sick." My voice peaked on the word *sick*. "It's just sick. I can't believe Luke and Celeste would do this. I mean, I can, b-but . . ." My voice trailed off. I might have been mad at Alice, but I couldn't let her see this. There was no question.

"Those assholes," gasped Debora.

I looked at her, a little shocked. I'd never heard her swear before. It sounded awkward, almost.

"I searched everywhere," she said, "but I couldn't find her."

"What do I do?" I asked. She would know what to do. She always knew what to do.

"Nothing. We get a teacher," she said, like it was so obvious.

"No," I said. "No. We can't do that. If we get a teacher, then the administration will find out, and they'll call Bernie and Martin, and then Alice would really freak out."

"Harvey, not only is getting a teacher the right thing to do, but I don't know how else we'd get this case cleaned out. It's locked."

Sometimes I had to remind myself that she was my girlfriend, and I don't think that's how it was supposed to be.

Dennis stood behind her, shaking his head.

In any other world, Debora would have been right, but things were tense enough between Alice and Bernie. This would be one more thing.

"Okay," said Debora. "We'll try it your way, but no promises. I'm going to go find the key to this case. Dennis, you stand guard here. Don't let any crowds congregate. We don't want to draw any attention to this. Harvey, you find Alice."

With her clipboard tucked beneath her arm, Debora speed-walked down the hallway.

"Wait," I said, and jogged to meet her. "What about your senior luau?"

She ran a hand over her normally smooth but currently frizzed hair. "It'll be fine. I've got a few freshmen helping."

"Thank you?" I didn't know what else to say.

She smiled for a second. "Find Alice."

I had no clue where Alice was, but I had to find her. A bad dream, this was a bad dream. The kind where your feet are stuck in quicksand and your throat is dry and you can't scream because if you could fucking scream it would all stop.

Alice.

Now

I didn't have it in me to go to first period. To my surprise, no one had confronted me about the classes I'd skipped since being back at school. But if they tried to, I'd tell them that I was puking my guts out in the bathroom and that I still felt weak.

It was true, though. There were still times when I felt just as sick as I had before. Dr. Meredith had told me I'd feel like that sometimes. The only difference was that I didn't get the awesome pain meds anymore. During my last appointment with Dr. Meredith, he confessed that he had yet to discover what triggered my remission. Since my recovery had been steady, and I had had such a negative response to that last round of chemo, he agreed to let me finish the rest of the school year before beginning my closely monitored intensification treatment. Everyone seemed confident that my stint with cancer was a thing of the past, but I didn't know where their absolute positivity came from. Because, for me, cancer would always be a shadow I lived in, an addiction that was never quite through with me.

Between first and second periods, I waited in the second-floor girls' bathroom for the first bell to ring. After the hallway cleared, I traced a path through each corridor, dragging my fingers along the walls—leaving invisible signs of life. I wondered where Eric was and if he'd even bothered to come to school today.

Shuffling through the music hall, I heard a teacher coming and slipped into an unused classroom. When the hallway was empty again, I opened the door, but saw Harvey and shut it immediately. I flipped the lights off in the classroom and squatted down, so I could still see him as he sprinted past me and turned the next corner. *Where was he going?*

I headed for the gym, where I usually met Eric beneath the bleachers. Maybe if he was here, I could at least say good-bye. I didn't know. All I knew was that I didn't want to be alone. When Eric left, he would take my distractions with him. And now here I was, with a whole week of family and Harvey ahead of me, and it seemed like the things I'd been running from all along might find me anyway.

Inside the gym, I glanced beneath the bleachers to check, but no Eric. The first-period girls' phys ed class played dodge-ball on one side of the gym while the student council set up for the senior luau on the other side. The game of dodgeball looked brutal. There were only six girls still standing and Celeste was one of them—of course. I watched from beneath the bleachers. Now it was four to two. Celeste's team held the two balls still left in play. Celeste pelted hers at one of the two girls, a chubby freshman. The ball bounced off the girl's hip and hit her shorter counterpart in the boob.

Coach Wolfen blew his whistle from where he sat in the volleyball perch and yelled, "Game!"

The girls filed into the locker room as I jogged across the court to see if maybe Eric went to the snack machines.

"Watch out!" yelled Celeste from where she stood by the locker room door. "Walking dead!"

I didn't stop, but just gave her my favorite finger.

"I don't know where you're supposed to be," called Coach Wolfen, his finger pointed at me, "but you'd better get there!"

Walking into the hallway, I found myself in a crowd of gasps. There was some laughter too. At the back of the crowd, I saw Mindi, her lips curved into a cold smile.

The door behind me opened. Celeste leaned forward and whispered, "I know how you love to be the center of attention."

Dennis shoved through the crowd. "Alice." He pulled me by my arm. "It's stupid. Don't waste your time. Harvey's looking for you."

"What are you talking about?" I glanced down at my arm. "Let go." All I felt were bodies huddled together and hushed whispers as everyone turned to me. It couldn't have been more than fifteen or twenty students, all seniors headed to the luau, but it felt like hundreds. And the weight of their eyes almost sank me all the way through the cracks in the linoleum floor.

Dennis gripped my arm a little tighter.

I pulled away from him. If I spoke, I didn't remember what I said.

I pressed through the crowd. It wasn't difficult. No one pushed back.

Fingers brushed my elbow and my eyes followed them

to Debora, reaching past two or three people, trying to grasp me. My brows furrowed, but I pulled back and continued moving forward.

I stepped into a small open space surrounding an old trophy case, and I swore my ears popped and all I heard was static. Black fabric covered the glass shelves. And wilted carnations. *I hated carnations.* There were a few mini arrangements of flowers too, like the ones you see at funerals on wire stands, but smaller. There were signs with things like IN MEMORY OF and REST IN PEACE. Where there weren't carnations, there were candles, mostly in those tall cylinder glasses like they used in Catholic churches. Some had decals with saints or Jesus or the Virgin Mary. Peppered between the flowers and candles were pictures.

Pictures of me. Pictures of me laughing and dancing.

There were a few school pictures too, going as far back as elementary school. Some were big, some were small, but every picture had one thing in common—my eyes had been crossed out with a black ballpoint pen, insults clouding my vision. Whoever had done this—and I knew who it was— had dug the pen so hard on the pictures that the glossy finish had been scratched off so all that remained was white paper. It looked angry and violent.

The only thing I could hear were my shallow breaths as it dawned on me. This was my memorial. In the late-night hours, I'd wondered—fantasized even—about what it might look like and who might be there. Would there be music? Tears?

Here it was, the proof of my life in a dusty old trophy case.

This was life's memory of me. Scratched-out eyes, wilted flowers, and melting candles. I touched the glass in wonder, like a child at an aquarium where a whole world lived behind the glass. And beyond this glass existed a whole world without me, where I'd died and left behind *this*. Because I knew who did this, I could close my eyes and see it all play out. This was Celeste's master plan. The key to the trophy case—that must have been Luke. He could have stolen it from Coach Wolfen's office without the coach even knowing. And Mindi had probably taken care of every little thing in between.

My eyes drifted to the bottom right corner of the case. Propped up against some sad-looking flowers was an old photo of me; I was no older than seven or eight. I sat on the floor of the studio with my hair smoothed into a bun, and Harvey sat across from me with his fists held out, hiding an object—probably a penny or something—in one of them. My eyes were scratched out, but I'm sure they'd been squinted, trying to discern which fist the penny was in. I took the smallest of steps back and saw the whole thing. Each picture was a milestone in my life. And here it was— my life—all gathered in one case for everyone to see, like a simple thing that could be explained.

The marvel of living through my own funeral slipped away as sheer horror swept through me. Tears spilled down my cheeks. I couldn't be here for this. I wasn't supposed to witness my own memorial.

That girl in the case was dead. And that girl in the case was me.

Harvey.

Now

The third bell for second period buzzed. I'd covered every inch of school property and no Alice. Her phone went straight to voice mail every time I called.

The hallway leading to the old trophy case was congested with students, many of them going in and out of the gym. I fought against the current of bodies. There were murmurings of *Messed-up shit* and *Was that the girl with cancer?* that made my feet move faster.

The crowd shrank slowly, like the show was over. The last warning bell buzzed. And then I saw her.

Alice was there, standing in front of the case, and all of a sudden I was drawing a blank. I knew I was supposed to find her, but I didn't know what I was supposed to say when that happened. And I didn't expect to find her here of all places.

I placed my hand on her shoulder to let her know— *I'm here.*

Her chin lifted as her gaze fell on my hand. When she recognized the hand as mine, she let out a shaky sigh. Standing next to her, I caught a glimpse of a few stray tears

245

still sliding down her cheeks. The shrine thing in front of us was hideous, with drying flowers and too many candles. It was garish, a cartoon version of a memorial.

Alice took three deep breaths and exhaled slowly, hiccuping a little.

We stood in silence for what felt like hours, waiting for an interruption.

Alice's eyes followed every detail as she stood with her arms crossed, holding herself together. She dropped her hands to her sides, and we stood so close that when her hand brushed past mine, I grabbed it and held on to it. You don't expect this. You don't expect to stand next to the girl you love at her own funeral.

"I couldn't find the key." It was Debora.

Alice's shoulders tensed at the sound of her voice. She pursed her lips together and dropped my hand. Silently, she walked off, past Dennis and Debora.

I almost called out for her to wait, but what would I tell her then? What magic words would I say that would fix us and this fucking mess?

"So sorry for your loss," Luke called out, laughing from where he stood in front of the gymnasium door.

Alice spun around and marched straight over to him. I had these moments when I wanted to protect her, but in this case she wasn't the one I was scared for.

Luke smirked. "I bet you didn't—"

There was no warning, just Alice's swinging fist connecting with Luke's nose. And then there was blood too.

Luke screamed, holding his hands over his face.

Debora clapped her hand over her mouth, gasping.

"Get out of here," I told Debora, and she ran inside the gym without a word.

Alice lifted her fist again, but Dennis pulled her back. Luke stood there laughing at them, and the anger that simmered inside of me boiled over.

Yanking the collar of his T-shirt with both hands, I pushed Luke up against the wall. "Give me those fucking keys to that case, or I swear to God I will break every one of your fingers and when those heal, I'll break them again!"

He spat in my face.

The gymnasium door swung open.

"In my office, all of you. Now," barked Coach Wolfen.

Coach Wolfen may have been the head of the athletic department and the coach of, like, six teams, but his office wasn't made to fit any more than three people.

Luke leaned on the edge of Coach Wolfen's desk, while Alice sat in a chair and Dennis and I stood behind her.

"You," said Coach Wolfen, motioning to Dennis. "Clean out that case. Now." He opened his desk and threw Dennis a key ring.

Dennis left, and Coach Wolfen pointed at Luke. "You said you needed those keys for some project the pep squad was working on. You lied to me, son. Your ass could get expelled over something like this."

Luke held up his hands. "It wasn't even my idea!"

Of course it wasn't.

"You and I are not done talking," he said to Luke. "You

two." He pointed to Alice and me. "Detention for a week, starting the Monday after spring break. Get out of here. And you," he said to Luke. "Have a seat."

I shut the door behind Alice and followed her out into the hallway.

Dennis stood in front of the case. He'd dragged a big black trash can right up next to him and was tossing everything. He looked at me, his eyebrows raised.

"A week of detention," I said.

I turned, expecting to see Alice behind me. But she was gone, walking down the hallway. I watched her go, her silhouette shrinking as she went.

Harvey.

Now

"I wouldn't have to work hard," sang Martin.

He couldn't sing, but I thought everyone had at least one song that was meant for them, one song that they *could* sing. "If I Were a Rich Man," from *Fiddler on the Roof,* was Martin's song—his one and only.

It was pouring outside, those big, fat raindrops so heavy they could crack your windshield. So far our spring break vacation was turning out to be pretty dreary. Bernie navigated from the front seat while Martin drove. Alice, my mom, and I were crammed into the backseat. Both Alice and my mom had been adamant about not sitting in the middle. I would have been adamant about that too, but I was the last to be adamant about it. Therefore, I was stuck with the bitch seat.

Alice wasn't talking to me. As we loaded the car this morning, she sat outside her house, on the porch, watching everyone else do the work. She seemed eerily calm, shell-shocked, almost. Like how people act when someone they know has died in a freak accident. I didn't even know how to talk about what had happened at school. How to ask her if she was okay. So, really, I wasn't sure who wasn't talking to whom. But the sum of it was that we weren't talking to each other.

Due to their time-consuming jobs, my mom and Alice's parents rarely took us on vacations. In my entire life, I had been on four vacations, and they had all been with Alice, Bernie, and Martin. We always went places that only took a few hours to get to by car, mainly because our time was limited and no one wanted to waste it traveling. Mom's Saturday classes went until three o'clock, so we did the four-hour drive to the beach on Sunday morning, giving us exactly one week of vacation.

Typically on road trips, people pass the time sleeping or reading, but this had always been a big no-no on our trips. For us, the only car rule was that if the driver couldn't do it, neither could you. We all took turns listening to our preferred tunes, starting with the driver (typically Martin, but never my mom). Martin's choices were usually lots of obscure eighties and nineties rock and the *Fiddler on the Roof* sound track. When the music silenced between tracks, he glanced at Alice and me through his rearview mirror.

Bernie followed his gaze and hit the Power button on the stereo. She turned around as best as she could with her seat belt fastened and said, "Out with it."

Alice watched scenery pass us by through her window, and I tried to stare a hole through the center console, but Bernie had one of those magnetic gazes that drew your eyes to her even when you were doing your best not to look.

"Harvey," said Bernie, dragging out the last syllable. She was such a lawyer.

I swallowed. "Yeah?"

My mom must have found this amusing because she crossed her arms and turned her body to face Alice and me.

"What's wrong?" asked Bernie.

"Nothing's wrong," I said. *Some assholes threw a mock memorial for your daughter, and the only faculty member who witnessed it would rather pretend he didn't.* "School's been stressful lately, right, Al?" I did my best to sound friendly, but her name sounded bitter and strained in my mouth. I was mad at her for not talking to me. And maybe that was shitty, but I'd just gotten a week of detention for her. I didn't need her to say thank-you or anything, but maybe a hello would be nice.

Alice tilted her chin. I think it was supposed to be a nod.

Bernie dug into us. "You two listen to me very carefully." She over-enunciated each word. "The three of us," she said, making a triangle with her finger, pointing from Martin, to herself, to my mom, "work extremely hard with very long hours. This may be your spring break, but this is our vacation. Understand me when I say: petty bullshit will not ruin our vacation." My mom bit her lip, trying not to steal Bernie's thunder by laughing. "Are we clear?"

"As mud," mumbled Alice.

"Yes," I replied, my voice rough.

Then she turned the stereo up all the way. The Who's "Baba O'Riley" pumped through the speakers. Martin caught Alice's eye in the rearview mirror and gave her a meaningful look, their eyes having some sort of conversation that I couldn't decipher. Alice sat back in her seat, her shoulders relaxing enough so that they rubbed against mine. Something had shifted in the car, and I think I had Martin to thank for that.

By the time Martin gave his encore of "If I Were a Rich Man" (because he never just sang it once), I was orchestrating the song with my bare fingers and Alice was shimmying her shoulders to the beat, but barely, and she always stopped when anyone looked at her.

Things had taken such a significant turn that when we got to the beach house, Alice didn't even complain about having to share a room with me. Granted we each had our own beds, but still I was surprised when she shrugged her shoulders without protest.

We were told the house had four bedrooms, but that turned out to mean four beds. My mom offered to sleep on the bunk bed with me, but Bernie said that she should enjoy her vacation as much as anyone, and sleeping in the same room with her son was not very vacation-worthy. I volunteered to sleep on the couch, but was told by Martin that it was silly to sleep on the couch when there was an open bed. The compromise was this: Alice and I would share the room with two bunk beds, but we'd have to keep the door open at all times. But Alice never did like to follow rules.

Alice.

Now

My dad gave me that look. That fucking look that said, *You owe us this*. And, okay, I did owe them this, but I also felt like the world was crumbling beneath my feet. Still, I tried to smooth my attitude around the edges just enough so that everyone could have a nice week. After the last year or so, my parents, Natalie, and Harvey deserved a week of peace. But peace, as it turned out, wasn't really my thing.

In every quiet moment, all I heard was the throbbing silence of Friday morning. Every inch of it—the flowers, the pictures, the candles—haunted me, and I knew that no matter how hard I tried to forget, I would die with those images. Maybe I should have let it be a good thing, and maybe I should have left all the horrible parts of me there in that hallway to be forgotten in that graveyard of memories, but I didn't know how to do that. I didn't know how to separate out the wrong parts of me while keeping everything else. It felt like the cancer—forever inside of me. I didn't think it worked like that, though. I didn't think I could cut out the pieces of me that no one liked. There would always be remains, and that version of me would always exist. On top of all that was this huge weight of devastation. The more time I had for all this to sink in, the worse it felt, like an untreated wound.

It rained all day Sunday, which was fine because everyone was exhausted. My mom failed to mention that the beach house, on loan from her boss, had only three bedrooms. When Natalie offered to share the bunk bed room with Harvey, I almost agreed with her, but my mom froze me with one of her signature glares and told Natalie she was being ridiculous. I shrugged, deciding it wasn't worth the effort.

I walked into our room on Sunday night and found Harvey in the process of putting his sheets on the top bunk. I threw my duffle bag on the floor and said, "I call top," and walked out of the room.

When I came back after brushing my teeth, Harvey lay on the bottom bunk flipping through an old *MAD* magazine he'd probably found in the closet. I closed the door behind me and twisted the thumb lock.

"We're supposed to leave the door open," he said, not looking up.

"I have to change."

It was dark out, but the white nighttime clouds brightened the blackness. I turned off the light and, with it, the buzzing ceiling fan. The slat blinds cast long lines across the dim room. Under the blanket of darkness, the room didn't look so bad. Everything always looked better in the dark, including me.

I strode over to my duffle bag on the floor, turned my

back to Harvey, and yanked at the button of my denim shorts. The sound of my zipper sliding down cracked the silence while the ceiling fan whirred to a stop.

Harvey's eyes slid down my back. I could feel them in the same way you could feel the sun on your face while you're sleeping. Every time I closed my eyes, I saw him. But now it was him and Debora. On Friday morning, Harvey had been there for me, like always. And I thought I was ready to be there for him until Debora showed up, reminding me that Harvey wasn't mine to be there for anymore. Right now, though, Debora wasn't here.

I wiggled out of my denim shorts and yanked off my T-shirt.

Harvey gasped, which he tried to disguise with a cough. I pulled my tank top on over my head and reached my hand up my back, beneath my tank, unhooking my bra with two fingers. *Teach my mom to let me sleep in the same room with a teenage boy, even if it was only Harvey.* I slid the straps off my shoulders, pulled my bra out from underneath my shirt, dropped it on the floor, and then pulled on my boxer shorts. I unlocked the door and climbed up to the top bunk. Slowly, my body was filling in again, and I could get used to this, this healthy body. But I knew it could be temporary, and that this time in remission might only be a short reprieve. I listened as Harvey turned over in his bed in a huff, the springs creaking against his weight.

And just like that, the Harvey/Alice balance had been restored to the universe.

★ ★ ★

Monday morning, I woke to the sound of rain splattering against the window. Harvey stood on the edge of the bottom bunk, his elbows looped through the wood slats, peering down at me.

"I'm kicking your ass at Sorry in five minutes," he said, pointing to the closet on the other side of the room, which was completely cleared out except for a tall stack of old board games.

"Huh?" My brain wasn't awake yet.

"The board game—Sorry."

I propped myself up on my elbows and said, "Oh, I think you're the one who's going to be sorry."

"Your ass is grass, Al."

It was like he woke up and decided that we were okay. We didn't have to talk about it or our feelings or whatever bullshit. We were okay. And I wanted to live in that state of blind happiness for as long as I could.

Tuesday was Operation. I couldn't hold my hand steady enough and got frustrated, so I sabotaged Harvey by punching him in the armpit. Wednesday was Monopoly. I won and foreclosed on every inch of Harvey's property. Thursday was Life. I was in charge of doling out the little peg figures and made the executive decision that all of Harvey's stick people would be pink and mine blue. I chose not to marry and sold all my children to an Eastern European Iron Curtain–era traveling circus. Harvey and his life partner, Rhonda, had nineteen children, which we caravanned in other cars using twisty ties found in the kitchen drawers. Friday was Clue. I killed everyone, using every weapon, every time. The end. (Actually, it was the maid.)

I took every chance I could to bend over with my ass in the air or to brush my boobs up against Harvey's arm. I felt pretty stupid, but I didn't know how else to stop him from forgetting. Because now that I couldn't have him, I knew that I would never get over him—at least not any time soon. It could've been because Eric was gone, but every time I thought about him with Debora, I felt like someone was ripping off my fingernails one by one.

But what if this worked? What if he couldn't resist me and he broke up with Debora? His happiness would depend on me, and that was a weight I didn't know if I could carry. I thought about all the ways I could give Harvey happiness, but everything I could do for him seemed to rely on my inability to be consistent and present—to be *always*. There was still that one thing on my list that I hadn't been able to complete. Something I could give to Harvey, a little piece of satisfaction that would be all for him and not at all for me. It was the thing I planned out in my head in those moments between asleep and awake when my brain was unable to tell the difference between dreams and reality.

After playing Clue with Harvey on Friday afternoon, I passed out on the couch. I woke to a darker, quieter house than what I'd fallen asleep to and a blanket tucked around my shoulders. Rain tapped against the windows as the smell of coffee wafted in from the kitchen. I followed it to find my dad sitting at the table with a half-empty mug of coffee, reading a bright green book about new wave music.

"Where is everybody?"

"Oh, hey," he said, sitting up a little straighter and pulling on his earlobe. "Picking up Chinese food. Should be back soon."

I sat down in the chair next to him. "How long was I asleep?"

He folded over the page he'd been reading and closed his book. "Only a few hours." He took a sip of his coffee.

I nodded and touched my fingers to my cheek, feeling the creases left by the couch. "Hey, Dad?"

"Yeah?" He looked at me and I couldn't hold his gaze, because I was scared he would see all the things I'd ever seen and know all the truths I'd never told him. Not telling him about Mom made my throat ache. I bit down hard on the inside of my cheek. "Did you ever meet Harvey's dad?"

He shook his head. "Never met the guy."

"You don't know anything about him?"

"Nope. Natalie only talked to your mom about that stuff." He leaned forward. "How come? Did Harvey say something?"

"No. No, I was—"

"We've got egg rolls!" called my mom from the front door.

Dad patted my arm. "Grab some plates, would you?"

"Okay."

We ate dinner and when we were done, we each plucked a fortune cookie from the bag full of leftover soy sauce packets. Mom made everyone read theirs out loud. Dad's was about taking a chance on a sudden business venture. Natalie's said something about patience making the world go 'round. Mom's told her to let compassion guide her decisions.

Harvey cleared his throat. "'Every road has a fork.'"

It was my turn; I cracked my cookie open, but it was empty.

Alice.

Now

"Alice. Alice, wake up." Harvey hovered over me. I rubbed my eyes with the heels of my palms, and stretched my muscles so hard they stung. "You just fell asleep, but—"

"No shit," I mumbled.

He stared down at me the way teachers always did. "Like I was saying, you just fell asleep, but look," he said, pointing to the window at the foot of our bed.

I pulled myself upright. It took a moment for my eyes to adjust to the lack of light. I twisted around and slid onto my stomach, facing the foot of the bed. Harvey stood on the ladder, watching me.

I stuck my neck out over the edge of the bed and immediately saw what he was referring to. *Stars.* Thousands, probably millions or trillions of stars hung against the black velvet sky. The rain had stopped and the clouds were gone.

"I can't wait to get in the ocean tomorrow," Harvey said. "I wish we could go in tonight."

Harvey had always loved to swim. I told myself that I didn't mind it, but the ocean always made me uneasy. It was so bottomless and unknown. That's why I surprised myself when I said, "Now. Let's go now."

Skipping the ladder, I jumped off the top bunk and rummaged through my duffle bag for a bikini top and bottom. I didn't even wait to find a matching set and found myself with a neon green bottom and navy-and-white-striped top. Harvey grabbed his trunks and went to the bathroom.

I met him on the deck. He held two towels and was wearing his trunks and a sweatshirt.

"It's a little cold," he said. "You okay?" He wrapped a big, fluffy towel around my shoulders in such a familiar way. *Maybe,* I thought, *maybe this thing between us isn't gone.*

I didn't answer and just ran right off the deck and down to the ocean. The beach house itself was a piece of shit, with this faint mildew smell, but the view was what counted. And when it wasn't raining, the view was worth it. Dropping my towel, I ran into the ocean.

But then I stopped when the water hit my knees. The shock of the cold ocean water sent a shot of terror up my spine. Harvey ran ahead of me, the water splashing around him. The moon soaked him with dim light. He had filled into his long, lean frame—even more so over the last few months. Slim muscles coated his bones, clearly visible beneath his skin. Not until he was in up to his waist did he turn around to see where I was.

"You want to go back?" he asked.

He turned, and the way Harvey looked at me, with the moonlight dancing shadows across his features, made me wonder if he had known all along that I was uncomfortable with the ocean. It made me feel weak, so I forced myself to ignore the crippling scream in my chest and ran to meet him.

His hand drifted through the water to find mine and I took it, my body easing with relief. Suddenly, my mom and Luke and Celeste mattered a little less.

As we went out farther, the ocean floor began to disappear from underneath us, and I gripped Harvey's hand a little tighter. I knew how to swim, but he pulled me along anyway. The ocean was quiet except for the sound of lazy waves lapping against jagged rocks. Finally, Harvey let go of my hand so he could float on his back. I wanted to cling to him, but I settled for treading water and staring at the moon. If I stared at the moon long enough, I could forget about the abyss beneath me.

"Question game," I said. "If the government was populating another planet and they asked you to go, would you?"

"Would you be there?" He moved upright and dipped his head beneath the water, his wavy curls springing when he resurfaced.

"Maybe."

"Then yes. If you had to eat one food for the rest of your life, what would it be?"

"Peanut butter." My guilty pleasure. Give me a ticking bomb slathered in peanut butter and I would gladly dig my own grave.

"What would you do if your mom got married?"

"That would be weird. I guess if he was an okay guy it wouldn't be bad. I've never really thought about it. I wouldn't, like, call him Dad or anything." His voice was a little lost, reminding me of the boy version of Harvey. I think he was genuinely considering this possibility for the first time ever. "It would be good, I think," he said, a little unsure of himself. "What about Eric Guy? How's that going?"

I smiled. "He's good." I didn't know why, but I didn't want to tell Harvey that Eric was moving. It felt like I would be losing some game.

"How's it going with Debora?"

Harvey blew bubbles in the water, which I found to be a little gross. "I like her. Dennis thinks it's weird. She's nice, though. And pretty brilliant."

"And pretty in general," I added. It was true. Even if I didn't want it to be. She was pretty in a first-day-of-school kind of way.

"Yeah," he concurred. "Yeah, she is."

Harvey swam out a little farther, but I couldn't make myself follow. I couldn't feel the ocean floor beneath me, but I knew the farther out I went the less the floor beneath me would exist. Something slid against my leg. *Seaweed, please be seaweed.*

"What do you want to do tomorrow, Harvey?" I asked, trying to distract myself.

"Actually, I wanted to talk to you about that." His voice echoed from somewhere ahead of me, but I couldn't spot the silhouette of his bobbing head because the moon had slid behind a cloud, blocking the light from our little world.

"Okay."

Silence.

"Harvey?"

Silence.

"Harvey?" I called again, the anxiety in my voice rising.

Silence.

"Harvey!"

The ocean was still.

I began to panic. "Harvey!" I screamed, my voice choking on sobs. My muscles tightened, but I couldn't make myself be still and float. There was a jackhammer in my chest, completely obliterating my attempts at breathing. The salty water was wet in my mouth. Then I realized my lungs were full, not with air but with salty ocean water, and my eyes stung. All four of my limbs thrashed, creating splashes at the surface. I looked up to see the moon creeping out from behind the cloud; it looked wavy and distorted from beneath the water. My limbs wouldn't push me forward. A pane of glass sat above my head, keeping me from the surface.

Something torpedoed past me, grabbing me underneath my arms as it did. Water spilled from my mouth as I broke through the surface. My eyes were blurry, and I choked on the rush of oxygen. Harvey held me tight. I wrapped my legs around his waist, leaning my head against him. I was freezing, but his body warmed me. He treaded water for the both of us.

"Hey! Al, it's all right. Are you okay?"

I nodded against his chest.

After I caught my breath, Harvey swam back to the beach with me still clinging to him. It was slow going, but every muscle in my body felt useless. When the sea-floor returned to us and we were able to walk, Harvey pulled me in front of him with my back to his chest and his arms wrapped tightly around my waist, squeezing me like I might disappear.

On the beach, my legs wobbled, my muscles having forgotten the laws of gravity. Harvey held my hand and spotted me as I stumbled through the wet, cool sand. If I hadn't been in complete shock, I would have relished the feeling of it sliding through my toes. I stood in the moon-light, shivering violently. We reached the pile of clothes and towels, and carefully he surveyed my body for damage before pulling his sweatshirt over my head and guiding my limp arms through the sleeves. I stared over his shoulder at the ocean, the unknown, the answers to questions I didn't want to ask. Then he wrapped one towel around my waist and the other around my shoulders. I tore my eyes from the ocean, turning my focus to him.

Then I kissed Harvey. I stood on my toes and kissed him on his salty lips. He didn't say anything or push me away. He stood still, not kissing me back. His jaw twitched, but then that was it. My mouth went dry as my lips slipped into a wordless *Oh*. I didn't know what I expected to hap-pen. But I did not expect for him to place his hand around my shoulder and walk me back to the beach house in silence, which was exactly what he did. Was it Debora? Was she why he wouldn't kiss me? Harvey didn't say no to me. Even when he said he would or even when he wanted to, he didn't. My breath quickened, and I walked past him and back into the house.

Inside our room, he said, "You've got to change out of that bathing suit, Al. You're shaking. I think you went into shock or something." Then he left, giving me some privacy. I dried off and stripped out of my soaking mismatched bikini in favor of fresh underwear, boxer shorts, and his sweatshirt. I slid onto the bottom bunk bed, Harvey's bed, and rolled over on my side, curling into the wall.

I heard the door open. Harvey climbed up the ladder and pulled the blanket off the top bunk, and then he pulled both his blanket and my blanket over my body, tucking me in. He wasn't going to sleep next to me. Completely disappointed, my eyes stung with the threat of tears. I'd lost him, and this time he wasn't coming back.

But then his weight sank into the mattress as he climbed under the blankets behind me. His hand slid up my bare back beneath the sweatshirt, and he began to trace letters of the alphabet on my back, like Natalie used to do to us when we were little.

"Q," I said. My muscles eased beneath his light touch, despite my racing heart.

He tried again.

"W. Harvey, where did you go?" I asked in a small voice that I had never heard myself use before.

"I thought I felt the key to the beach house fall out of my trunks while we were swimming."

"Oh. B."

"Then I remembered I left it on the towel, back on the beach."

He continued to trace letters and some numbers too, even after I stopped guessing.

"Al, it's okay to be scared."

I swallowed. My mouth was dry and wordless. Just images of the water rushing around me, as I created my own panic. A nonexistent storm that had only been real in my head. My cheeks flushed.

"Huh," mused Harvey.

"What?"

"Did you notice the plastic stars on the ceiling?" Harvey stopped tracing on my back, the absence of his touch jolting me.

I rolled over and leaned past him to look up at the ceiling. "Like the ones in your room," I said. "Let's sleep on the top bunk." I crawled over him, the heat of his body pressing against mine for a moment, and climbed the ladder before he could object. He followed me up the ladder with both blankets thrown over his shoulder, but not before opening the window next to the bed.

"It feels so good outside," he explained. "But I'll make sure you stay warm." I didn't say anything, because that's exactly what I wanted, for him to keep me warm.

We lay down flat on our backs, side by side, our bodies barely fitting in the twin-size bed, beneath the glow-in-the-dark stars, the secrets between us thinning.

"Someday," I said, "when we're married to different

people, we won't ever be able to talk to each other." Turning on my side, I draped an arm over his chest.

"I know," whispered Harvey, running his fingertips along my arms.

I slid in closer to him. "I couldn't be happy for you, you know."

I'd always heard that when you truly love someone, you're happy for them as long they're happy. But that's a lie. That's higher-road bullshit. If you love someone so much, why the hell would you be happy to see them with anyone else? I didn't want the easy kind of love. I wanted the crazy love, the kind of love that created and destroyed all at the same time.

But Harvey had moved on, and all we had was whatever was left of our spring break. Here, tonight, Harvey felt easy and right, but tomorrow the light of day would melt the simplicity of night to reveal what we really were—a complicated, confused mess.

He squeezed my hand once. "Me too," he confessed. "It would feel wrong."

He turned into me and did that thing that always crushed me—he kissed my cheeks and my eyelids, saving my lips for last. His mouth was salty, but it didn't make me thirsty. My hands drifted along the waistband of his shorts and up the back of his T-shirt. My body kept moving, even as I could feel the ground slipping out from beneath me, like in the ocean. His hands did the same, sliding up the sweatshirt I wore and up the length of my back and around to the front of my chest. I exhaled in his mouth.

And then he pulled back and sighed. For a second, my lips continued to move, confused by the absence of his. The echo of his hands on my skin left a searing heat in my chest.

I laid my head against him and he wound his arm around my shoulder. "What's going to happen to us, Harvey?"

He pressed his lips to my head and said, "It's a surprise, I think."

Harvey.

Then

Hello?" I called. "Al?" The house was quiet, which had become the norm now that Alice spent more time sleeping than not. I hated to think of her so still like that. Instead, I thought of how I'd taught her to drive a few weeks ago in the SaveMart parking lot and of the way that my fingers had brushed against hers as I'd helped her maneuver the steering wheel.

After locking the front door behind me, I trudged down the hallway to her bedroom. Bernie had been invited to a client dinner with her firm. It was an attempt to include her, despite her dying daughter. A Good Samaritan act.

Months ago, Bernie had cut back to half days at the office. Her five half days turned into two or three half days, and then those turned into mere hours a week. She tried to do most of her work from home, but a lot of the cases she worked on were handled by groups of attorneys, so it wasn't an easy job to do solo. Originally, Bernie had declined the dinner invitation, but Alice had insisted that Bernie and Martin go. After much deliberation, they decided to attend only if I came over and stayed with Alice. Typically, Alice would guffaw at this, but she called me herself and explained the situation. She was completely reasonable and not at all bothered by asking me to babysit her.

She was up to something.

I knocked lightly on her door. "Alice?" No answer. "Alice?"

"You can come in now, Harvey."

When I opened the door, Alice stood there with a small bath towel wrapped around her paper-thin body, water dripping off her and pooling at the carpet. Her legs were so much thinner than I remembered, making her kneecaps seem big and bulbous. Her body swayed a little, like she was bracing herself against a strong gust of wind that only she could feel.

"Oh, sorry," I said. "I didn't realize you had just gotten out of the shower. I'll be on the couch."

"Come here."

"Is everything okay?"

"Come here."

She could have said "Light your car on fire," and I would have done it. I stepped forward a few steps.

"Closer," she said, and I spanned the last couple steps between us. "Closer, Harvey."

The space between us was nearly nonexistent, but I filled what little there was, pressing our bodies against each other. We were in a little bubble, and outside of that bubble I could hear the entire world spinning on its axis ten times its normal speed.

Alice held her arms wrapped around her chest, keeping her towel in place. She looked up, her bottomless eyes steadying me, taking away my dizziness. Everything felt stable and solid again while she held my eyes with hers.

Then Alice dropped her arms. Her towel fell to the floor, bunched up in a heap around her ankles.

"What are you doing?" I breathed. She wrapped her arms around my waist and held herself against me, my clothing separating our bare skin.

"I want to do this, Harvey," she whispered into my T-shirt, walking backward, with her arms still circling my waist, pulling me with her.

"You—you're sick, Al." She looked so fragile, like a feather could break her.

"It's a good day, Harvey. I can't say that very often," she said softly. And then, in her sharp, familiar voice, "Do not ruin this." She tilted her face to mine, and I dipped my chin to meet her.

Our lips touched. It wasn't our first kiss, but in that moment, I knew the meaning of it all. I knew every word in the dictionary, every color in the rainbow. For a moment, cancer was cured and the world had halted to a stop in an eerie state of perfection.

With our lips still joined Alice reached for the bed behind her, and leaned backward. I wrapped my arms around her, bending my body to the curve of hers as she pulled away the blankets. I laid her down on the cool sheets, gently, like she might break. Then I stood back and really looked at her.

There was no denying that Alice had always been the driving force behind my hormones. But what I saw was wrong, not what I had always dreamed (yes, *dreamed*) Alice would look like. She was completely bare, and I saw everything the baggy T-shirts had been hiding for months. Her waist dipped in dramatically, her rib cage moving slightly with each breath. A mean-shaped bruise wrapped across her hip, purple at the center and yellowing at the edges, fading into her lighter-than-ivory skin. She bruised so easily now, and I wondered what small infraction was the cause of this one. The sharp ridges of her sternum jutted out, her collarbone draped with ashen skin. Tiny red dots splattered across her thighs and shoulders, broken blood vessels. I had only ever seen them a few at a time, but here with nothing to hide behind, they were an epidemic. Her lack of hair didn't shock me. That, I had grown used to.

She bit her bottom lip and used her arms to cover her bare chest. I was a horrible person, but I didn't want to remember her like this. I didn't want to remember that this shell containing Alice was withering away. I closed my eyes tightly, with my arms at my sides, my fists curled tightly.

"Harvey?"

But I wanted to do this.

I opened my eyes and Sick Alice was gone, her wavy brown hair fanned out around her on her pillow, framing her face and shoulders. Her cheeks were full and her curves filled out. The rosy tint teasing beneath her ivory skin had been restored.

I didn't care what Alice looked like. I never had. I just wanted her to be alive. I hovered above her, knowing that what we were about to do could never be undone. Her fingers played at the hem of my T-shirt as she slipped it over my head. My lips met her neck and spread small kisses to her ear and back as she turned her head to the side, her lips parting and her eyes closed.

She twisted over to her bedside table, opened a drawer, and retrieved a condom, holding it between two fingers.

I stood and slipped out of my remaining articles of clothing. What if I didn't do this right? What if I *couldn't* do this?

"Harvey," Alice said, her voice slipping through my insecurities. "Harvey, I need you to be in this moment with me because you're the only one I'd ever want to share it with."

Her words swept away my doubt. I lay down next to her, propping myself up on my side with my elbow.

It was true. I didn't know how long we would have after this. It could be five days or five years, but no matter how short or long our time was, I could no longer spend it as friends. I didn't need a label to own her with. I needed to know that we were *more*, that she would belong to me just as much as I had always belonged to her.

"Is this . . . have you done this before?" I asked.

She shook her head no.

A little bit of the tension inside of me settled. Not that I wanted her to be a virgin or anything. I wasn't like that. It was that this would be as new to her as it was to me. "I can't be just friends after this, Alice."

"I know," she said.

"You're okay with that?"

She nodded. Her eyes told me she loved me. Tonight, she loved me. Even if she could never say it. Does love still exist if you can't say it? If you can't admit it? I wasn't sure, but her eyes had told me enough. I took her face in my hands and pressed my lips to hers. She tasted like Chapstick, waxy and sweet.

And I found out sex wasn't this perfect, airbrushed, mind-blowing thing. It was quiet and sweaty and personal. But it felt good. And I'd get better at it. I wished I could get better at it with Alice.

I had loved her for so long. I didn't think it was possible for me to feel any more for her, like she had already maxed out all my feelings. But that wasn't how it worked. That night Alice swallowed up a whole piece of me I never knew existed. She ruined me that night.

When you'd loved the same girl for your entire life, it was hard to believe that there might be anything after that. When you've loved one person so wholly, do they take that love with them? Was that how it worked? If so, I was okay with that. I loved every bit of Alice, even the horrible, ugly parts of her that made other people cringe. If this was all the love I could ever give, then my love had been well spent. When Alice was gone, she would take all my love with her. Whether she was floating through some heaven or decomposing six feet under, that part of me would always go with Alice.

Alice.

Now

I woke up to blinding sunlight and the blankets pushed down around my feet. The humidity from outside filled the room. I reached for Harvey, but he wasn't there. I blinked my eyes into focus and saw him, kneeling in front of his duffle bag.

"Good morning," I said.

"Morning. Smells like hash browns." We were still okay. The goodness between us hadn't disappeared.

"I closed the door so you could sleep a little later," he said, pointing to the door. "Bernie was in such a good mood she didn't even notice."

I inhaled the aroma and realized I was starving. I skipped down the ladder and grabbed a pair of denim shorts to change into.

"I put your swimsuit in the bathtub to dry," said Harvey, his hand on the doorknob.

"Right, thanks," I said, yawning. "Close the window, Harvey. It's freaking hot in here."

"Can I talk to you after breakfast?"

I shrugged. "Sure."

He left, and I changed quickly into my shorts.

It seemed that starving was a common theme at the breakfast table. My dad made hash browns and waffles. Every crumb disappeared in minutes. The much more beach-appropriate weather had lifted everyone's spirits. Harvey volunteered us for cleaning duty while my parents and Natalie sipped coffee.

I scooped up a handful of soapsuds and blew them into Harvey's face. Unfortunately for him, his mouth was open, and he coughed so hard I was surprised he didn't hack up a lung.

With Harvey still coughing and our parents deep in conversation, the doorbell rang. I ran to answer the door with a greasy iron skillet still in my hand.

"Alice! Hey, Alice, let me get that!" yelled Harvey, his voice raspy, as he chased me down the hallway with his hands covered in soapsuds.

I ignored him and swung the door open to find Debora. Debora with a small overnight bag on her shoulder. *No.* I held my breath, hoping that she wasn't here to be with my Harvey, even though I knew she was.

"Alice." I turned around to find Harvey with his eyes on Debora but my name on his lips. This was a mistake. This was a *family* vacation. Debora was smart, nice, and cute, but she was not family.

Natalie rushed down the hallway with my parents at her heels. "Oh, Debora! I'm so glad you were able to make it."

I whipped back around to Debora on the doorstep, eyes wide as Natalie gave her a quick hug. Behind her, a silver Toyota Camry was parked in the driveway. Again, I turned around to face Harvey, hoping for some kind of explanation.

He stood with his mouth open.

But then it slid over me like wax. He'd invited her here. And they all knew. My mom, my dad, Natalie. All of them had known she would be here. And Harvey, he let me put myself out there last night. I pushed air in and out of my nose, forcing myself to remember to breath. I wanted to crush him.

"What. The. Hell. Harvey," I growled, my voice low and angry.

"I tried to tell you. Last night, remember?"

In the water, before he thought he had lost the key. We were talking about today, and he wanted to talk to me about something, I remembered. This morning, in our room. "No. I don't remember." Each word clipped.

The narrow hallway was too small for all of us. Debora still stood at the door, unsure of what to do with herself. I wanted to rip out her goddamn hair. That's what I wanted to do. I pushed through Harvey, Natalie, and my parents, weaseling out of each of their attempts to grab me. The iron skillet was still in my hand, swinging at my side. My mom chased after me into the living room as I walked through the sliding glass door and onto the patio.

"What the hell has gotten into you?" she demanded, sliding the door shut behind her.

"Go away."

"Alice." Her voice wasn't kind or gentle. Everything in me was withering, and she chose now to yell at me. I closed my eyes and saw the pictures. The flowers. The candles.

Rest in Peace. No matter how fast Harvey and Dennis had managed to take down that display, it would always exist. I would always see it. I would never forget.

"I *said* go the fuck away." It wasn't the words themselves but the way I said them that would create a big wave with my mom. Heat from my ears spread down my neck and across my chest.

She grabbed my wrist (the one not connected to the skillet) and squeezed hard. My hand began to turn white, and I could already feel her fingerprints branding my skin. "I don't know when you turned into such a little bitch, but things are going to change in a big way."

Most mothers don't talk to their daughters like that, but my mom and I had never been most mothers and daughters. I remembered reading about wolf packs when I was younger. Each wolf pack could only have one alpha, one chief. This was the very unfortunate truth of my mother and me. We were two alphas who could never coexist in peace. The only time we had was when she thought I was dying.

I was angry. Boiling. Last night I chose Harvey. This morning Harvey chose Debora. And now this: my mom was finally biting back at me, like I'd been waiting for. She had changed so much when I was sick, so much to the point that I doubted she was even the same person anymore. Everything beneath my skin felt like it was on fire. I wiggled my wrist out of her grip. With the skillet still in my hand, I swung my arm. Then I let go, sending the iron skillet straight through the sliding glass door and into the living room of the beach house.

My mom's jaw dropped. Very few things could shock my mother, but *this* had. Hell, it shocked me too. At the sound of shattering glass, Natalie, my dad, Harvey, and Debora all flooded the living room, the glass crunching beneath their feet.

"I saw you," I whispered, my voice escalating with each breath. "I saw you with a man that wasn't Dad. I waited for you to tell me." And now I was sobbing, screaming and sobbing. "For you to be *honest* with me because *we always tell the truth, even when we think it does more harm than good*," I said, reciting her own words back to her. "You should've left us then. Ripped the Band-Aid off. Because the lies are destroying us," I said, my voice catching on every syllable. "You ruined me. You made me this way. This." I motioned to myself, my chest heaving now. "Is your fault. And now it's too late to fix it."

Then I ran, as fast as I could, as far away as I could.

I couldn't look at my dad. I couldn't bear to see what this truth did to him. But it was out now. I didn't know who I'd been lying for, who I'd been keeping Mom's secrets for. But now there were no more secrets between them, and it was up to my parents to decide what they would do with that truth. As for me, I was done with it.

When the beach house was only a speck on the horizon, I collapsed on the sand. I didn't know how long I sat there before Harvey plopped down next to me.

"Leave, Harvey."

"Not until I explain."

"No," I said, "let *me* explain."

"Alice, I—"

"You are in love with me, and you always have been. But this is the *truth,* Harvey: I don't love you. Not at all. Not you, not anyone, not anything." And because that wasn't enough, because I hadn't done enough damage, I said, "You're sad and pathetic. You have no spine, and the fact that you think someone like me could ever love someone like you only proves my point."

"Stop it."

"I used you. You know it. I know it. Everyone fucking knows it." Each word built one on top of the other like a brick wall. Harvey didn't want me, but I couldn't let him be the one to close this door. I couldn't. "Everything you thought was real is a lie. Don't pretend like you don't know that. You were a means to an end, Harvey. There's nothing else you can do for me, so leave. I don't need you. I don't want you."

He sat there for a moment.

"Leave."

"This is it, Alice. This is really it. When I leave, I'm not coming back to you. I'm not saving your ass. I'm not going to be your partner in crime. I'm not going to be that guy for you anymore. You never seem to be done with me, but trust me when I say, I am done with you."

Then he left, and with him he took the sun, the moon, the stars, and anything inside of me that might have been good.

Harvey.

Now

Every little thing between us had led to this moment. I should have known Alice would tell me to leave. I think, maybe, part of me did know. Everything about it felt desperate yet inevitable, and no matter which way we went, this was the end of our story. But still, standing out there on the edge of the beach, I expected something to happen. Even though she rarely ever gave me any reason to think she might be anyone other than herself.

I was so angry. *You were a means to an end, Harvey. There's nothing else you can do for me, so leave. I don't need you. I don't want you.* She couldn't say those things to me. She couldn't. I should have told her about Debora, and that was my fault. But it didn't feel like that mattered anymore. The world around us had exploded, and there was no determining what blame belonged to whom.

I trudged back up the beach to where my mom, Bernie, Martin, and Debora all waited on the back porch. The wind whipped around me, sand burning my legs as I began to jog toward them and away from Alice.

Last night was an anomaly, one last night of good. But now that was gone, and with it so were we. I couldn't go back to her again. Because if I did, I'd never be able to look at myself, and she would always know that when it came to us, she called all the shots. I loved her—but it didn't make me happy anymore. Not even a little bit.

Even though I didn't want to care, I kept hearing what she'd said to Bernie, about another man. I wanted to ignore it. My mom hadn't seemed shocked and neither had Martin. I didn't have the balls to ask them what was going on, not with what had happened. There was something going on, though, and maybe Alice didn't have the whole story, but she had more than I did. I was the only kid at the kids' table.

I popped my knuckles before shoving my fists into my pockets. Even though neither Bernie nor Martin were my parents, I couldn't ever picture it being true—that she'd cheated on him. Marriage didn't ever really work, but it worked for them. They'd always been the exception to the rule.

I took the steps to the beach house two by two. Bernie stood there waiting for me, still in her robe. "Where is she?"

"Is she okay?" asked Martin.

My mom stood behind them, staring over my shoulder at the little dot on the horizon that I assumed was Alice, while Debora bit her lip nervously, her eyes darting from me to the wood-planked floor.

"She wants to be alone." *Forever.* "She'll be back later."

Martin clapped his hands together. "All right, gang, let's enjoy our best vacation weather yet! Debora, let me help you with your bag." He guided Bernie by the elbow with Debora at their heels. "Watch for the glass," he said.

The three of them went inside, leaving my mom and me.

She approached me slowly, like you would a wounded animal. "You okay?"

I mashed my lips together, the way you do when you're trying to smile but your body's telling you to cry or scream or something.

"Hey, talk to me."

A tear spilled from the corner of my eye, and I pushed the tips of my fingers into my tear ducts as hard as I could. When the tears came anyway, I gave up and raked my fingers through my hair. My mom stood right where she was, letting me have my moment.

When we were kids, this boy at school shoved me into the mud after I accidentally cut in line at the monkey bars. When Alice saw what he'd done, she pushed him to the ground and straddled him, getting in one good punch before the teacher supervising recess pulled her off him. Our parents were called, and my mom ended up coming to get us both and taking us to the ballet studio to get cleaned up before her next class. After she bandaged me up, I sat on the office floor reading a book while she fixed Alice's hair into a fresh bun. She had run out of bobby pins and was crouched down in front of this box she used to keep safety pins, needle and thread, and hair stuff in. She sighed and shook her head. "She'll break his porcelain heart." She said it so quietly her lips barely moved. I didn't know what it meant then. I didn't realize loving Alice would be a curse.

My tears stopped and the salty winds dried my cheeks.

Mom took a step toward me and held both my hands with hers.

"You can't save the world."

I nodded. "I know that, but why can't I at least save her?"

She stepped even closer to me, so that we were nearly nose to nose. I expected her to say something, to answer my question because that's what moms did. But she didn't; she wrapped her arms around me, her fingertips barely touching as her arms circled my shoulders. I should have felt stupid, slipping into my mom's arms like a little kid, but it felt okay.

"Let's have a good day today, okay?"

I couldn't talk, because I didn't know what sounds might come out, so I nodded into her shoulder and agreed.

Alice.

Now

It was well past one in the morning before I got back to the beach house, and thankfully my parents had left the porch light on.

"Shh . . ." I pressed my finger to Brian's lips after he tripped over a pile of flip-flops at the door. We'd met that afternoon on the boardwalk. "Watch your step, Brian."

"My name's Trevor."

"Right, Trevor. I'll call you Trevor and you can call me Ashley," I said, and rolled my eyes as we stumbled through the dark living room of the beach house. A pile of a person slept on the couch, their shadow breathing in and out. The person, I assumed, was Harvey. I swallowed the lump in my throat. I thought about telling Brian to leave, but the image of Harvey's eyes on Debora as she stood there on the doorstep wouldn't let me.

"No, really, my name is Trevor."

"Whatever."

After Harvey left me on the beach, I spent the day walking around the boardwalk, which was really a sad tourist trap. Most of the stores were poorly stocked. A couple even had OUT TO LUNCH signs up for more hours than they had actually been open. The shops were half-assing it because spring break was just their warm-up for the long summer season.

That's where I met Brian or Trevor, whatever his name was.

He was close to my height and a little muscular, but at least a year younger. Freckles sprinkled his nose and cheeks. His rusty brown hair flopped with every step. I couldn't recall the color of his eyes. That information seemed to fall into the same abandoned mental folder as his name.

When I first saw him there on the boardwalk, he looked like a candy striper in white shorts and a red-and-white-striped polyester polo shirt. It all looked very uncomfortable. "Smile!" he said, holding up the camera around his neck.

I crossed my arms over my chest and said, "Get me out of here."

"Did you say something?" he asked as he pulled the camera away from his face. He tore an orange ticket from a ring of tickets hanging around his wrist.

I squinted. "When's your shift over?"

"Uh . . ." He looked at his watch. "Thirty minutes. Your picture will be ready in an hour. What's your name?"

"Alice." I think he was waiting for me to ask his name, but I didn't. "Any townie stuff going on tonight?"

"Well, yeah, I guess. Nothing big, but yeah. You want to come?"

I held out my palm to him. "Address."

He fumbled for a pen and finally found one in a cargo pocket of his hideous white shorts. He was cute in a second-string kind of way. When he finished scribbling on my palm, I pulled my hand back to study the address.

"Thanks," I said, and began to walk in the direction of the beach house.

"I could pick you up!"

"I'd rather you didn't," I called, not turning around.

I walked back to the beach house. Thankfully, everyone was out for dinner. I hadn't showered last night and still smelled like the ocean, but worst of all I still wore Harvey's sweatshirt. I was quick to shower and let my hair air-dry, which was still very short and had only recently grown into something manageable—a sort of sun-kissed, messy, golden brown coif. I'd begun to work my way back into some of my old clothes too. Over a white two-piece I wore a blue-and-white seersucker spaghetti-strap dress. I looked whole, but I didn't feel it.

Before leaving, I left a note for my parents saying I'd be back later. When I showed up at the address (which was within walking distance from our beach house), I found mostly locals and mostly guys. The few girls present gave me dirty skank looks for intruding on their territory.

Brian/Trevor instantly attached himself to me, fetching me drinks and introducing me to anyone who would listen. Most of the guys at the party were the type of people who pronounced "bro" as "bra," and I had the sneaking suspicion that Brian/Trevor was someone's little brother. When the party began to disperse, I sweetly asked him if he could give me a ride home. In the driveway, I invited him inside. He hesitated for a moment, but then followed me through the front door.

We squeezed down the narrow hallway and I waved him into my bedroom.

"You have a bunk bed?" he asked.

"Come on." I climbed the ladder to the top bunk.

"Wait, top bunk? Why don't we use the—" He ducked down to take a look at the bottom bunk. "There's someone down there!" he whispered, pointing frantically at the bed below me.

He continued to stare, dumbfounded, at the bottom bunk. I unzipped my dress and pulled it over my head, standing there in my white swimsuit. "Brian, are you coming or not?"

His eyes widened. He climbed up to the top bunk in two steps, skipping rungs.

I pulled him down to me, wrapping my legs around his waist. Our lips collided roughly, our pace mismatched and wrong. I moved fast, my kisses harsh. He tried to be slow and gentle, giving soft pecks. His hands slid down my shoulders, so I did him the favor of moving them to my chest. He gasped. I wanted to smash his body against mine until I became just as much of a stranger as he was.

"Wait, Alice." I tried to silence him with my lips. "Alice," he murmured. "I think you're a great girl." A great girl? Who was this guy? "And you're beautiful; God, you are so beautiful."

"Yeah, you're okay too."

He rolled off me and rested on his side between me and the wall. "Alice, I have a girlfriend." He went quiet. It took me a second to realize that he expected me to react and that his confession was supposed to be shocking, like a big reveal or something.

From below us came a quiet sigh. Debora.

"Oh. Okay," I whispered. "Let's just have tonight."

His eyes lit up, like he'd won the hormonal jackpot. "You're okay with that?"

"I'm great with that, Brian."

"My name is—"

I pulled his face to mine and made our lips move together. It didn't matter to me what his name was or whether or not he had a girlfriend. I only cared that he could make my life melt away for however long he could last. All I wanted was for him to do this to me and take away the raw misery I felt. My heart throbbed, reminding me that I was alive, even though all I felt was everything but.

We rolled over so that I was straddling him. This time he got the point and his hands roamed my body more aggressively. He pulled the string that stretched across my back, holding my swimsuit top in place. I leaned down closer to him and a moan fell from his lips. I felt myself disappearing.

A sharp memory of my body pressed against Harvey's on this very mattress last night. His kisses on my eyelids and my cheeks and— I froze, completely paralyzed. The whole situation came into focus. This stranger. In my bed. Debora on the bottom bunk. Harvey in the living room.

I grasped for the strings of my bikini, trying to hold my

swimsuit top in place as I scrambled off his lap and into the corner of the twin bed farthest from him.

"Get out. Go." I felt disgusting. This was wrong. Maybe I had lost Harvey, but I couldn't lose myself, especially not when I had a choice.

"But you said—"

"I said get out. *Now*."

He practically fell from the top bunk, then gathered his shoes and combed the carpet for his car keys, tripping his way to the door. I closed my eyes tight with my knees pulled to my chest. The bedroom door clicked shut behind him. I felt like I was drowning again, like last night. And again, it was all my fault.

When I heard the front door shut, I climbed down the ladder to lock the dead bolt. On my way back, I heard the buzz of the kitchen light and tried to tiptoe past Harvey, who was standing there with half a piece of cold pizza in his hand.

Too late. He had already spotted me, pinning me in place with his eyes. He dumped the rest of the pizza in the trash. I watched him as he stood there, his chest bare, wearing only blue plaid boxer shorts. His hair was disheveled and his face lined with pillow creases.

Humiliation crept up my chest to my cheeks; I crossed my arms. Not in defiance but in defense.

Then he spoke to me, which I never expected to happen again. His voice was detached and cold. "He didn't know how much to leave for you. I told him first one's on the house. Isn't that right, Al?"

The worst part was that he called me Al. It felt familiar, but really it was a knife in my ribs. My chest tightened, and my eyes burned, holding back tears. I didn't say anything.

He didn't mean it, I told myself. He only said it to get back at me because I had hurt him.

In my bedroom I found Debora sitting upright on the bottom bunk, with the blankets lying neatly across her lap. She reached for her glasses on the nightstand and unfolded them carefully before pushing them up the bridge of her nose, her eyes relaxing as her world fell into place. The little lamp on the bedside table let out a small pool of light.

I wanted her to disappear. I wanted her to dissolve.

"Get out, Debora." Maybe if I told enough people to get out they finally would.

"No." She clasped her hands in her lap. She wore pink-and-white-striped pajamas, the type of PJs that button up the front and look like they should be ironed. Each of her even blond hairs sat uniformly in place.

"Leave."

"You are hollow on the inside, Alice; did you know that?" she asked. "Rotten too. And no one cares. No one cares because you make it so difficult to. I should tell you to go on being rotten on the inside, but I can't because Harvey is so invested in you. Here's the sad truth: Harvey cares for you. He more than cares for you, and he still would even if you were as ugly on the outside as you are on the inside. Harvey, the one you string along mercilessly. Not some slob who wants you as arm candy, but Harvey.

He loves you, and for whatever reason, this transcendental devotion he has for you defies the laws of science and love."

Tucking her hair behind her ear, she said all of this in a calm, even tone, like she was reading from a history book. Regardless of her tone, her words hit me and drilled into my chest, burrowing deep and deeper. I *was* rotten on the inside, and I didn't know if that had happened over time or if it had always been so. For a moment, I felt bad for Debora. Here she was telling me how much her boyfriend loved me. The worst part of it was that she was more deserving of Harvey than I was and she knew it.

I sat down next to her on the bottom bunk, and the tears that I had swallowed back in the kitchen with Harvey poured down my face. My shoulders shook as sob after sob broke through my chest.

I loved him too, but it wasn't that happy-ending bullshit. It was disfigured and crushing. "What do I do?"

"About Harvey?"

"No, well, yes, but no. What do I do—" I stopped, letting my tears eat up my words. "About what's wrong with me."

"I don't really know, Alice. I think it's different for everybody. But maybe you should figure that out on your own, before dragging Harvey through it."

Wiping my nose with the back of my hand, I nodded.

"I know what happened last Friday with the memorial stuff must have been hard. I still can't believe someone would even do that. I don't know what to say except that I'm sorry that had to happen to you."

"Thanks."

"Listen," she said, "I can't tell you what to do. I mean, *you* of all people, obviously. You don't listen to anyone. But don't destroy Harvey. Because you can. You have that power. Love's different for him. For Harvey—"

"Do you like him?"

She didn't answer.

"You should tell him," I said.

"I don't think there's room in his heart for me or anyone else, not when you live inside of it."

More tears. I felt an awkward hand on my back, patting me.

"Stop," I said, not at all comforted by the touch.

"Thank you." She sighed.

I smiled.

I knew the first step to filling the black hole inside of me, and it started with an apology. The most difficult things usually did.

Harvey.

Now

I'd only been asleep for about forty-five minutes when that asshole stumbled out of Alice's room last night. I'm not a violent person, and I'm not the type of guy who's going to beat up some dude because he looked at the girl I liked the wrong way. But when I saw that guy's silhouette moving through the living room, I wanted to kill him.

This time yesterday morning, I'd woken up next to Alice with our bodies huddled together, our foreheads touching, and our skin warm with early-morning sun. I wanted so badly for that to be my every morning. I'd made a point of being the first person in the house to wake up. Considering Bernie's requirement to keep our door open, I didn't think she would have appreciated us sharing a twin bed.

I meant to tell Alice about Debora joining all of us for the last two days of our trip, but every time I had the opportunity, the moment was too good to ruin. Especially yesterday morning when it was the five of us in the kitchen. It was all too easy to forget Debora. I'd held back that night when Alice first kissed me. But, later, as she and I lay in bed, I left the memory of any girl that wasn't her on the beach.

A few weeks ago, when I'd asked my mom if Debora could come, she raised an eyebrow and nodded. Bernie and Martin knew too. Everyone but Alice knew. And all of that was my fault, but this went so much deeper than me dating someone else.

"Hey, Harvey." Debora stood in the doorway of the sliding glass door, which was actually useless now, thanks to Alice and her iron-skillet pitching skills. I had to admit, that had impressed me.

"Hey, Debora." I pulled my legs in and patted the length of lawn chair in front of me. She dropped her duffle bag and sat down in front of me. "So I guess you're checking out of this mess early, huh?"

"I should go home."

"Yeah," I said. "Thanks for driving out for the night. I'm sorry it was like this."

She nodded, her hair grazing her chin. "Harvey, I want to be with you. But I can't." Her finger traced a pattern between us. "You two are too . . . intense. I don't think I can be in the middle of that, not while trying to stay sane."

I knew this was coming. I lay awake all night thinking about it—and well, Alice too. Debora didn't need to get caught up between me and Alice. Even Dennis had said so.

"Dennis is freaked out about us anyway." I squinted my eyes at the beach behind her. "You can tell him if you want. Or I can," I said, staring into the sun, letting my eyes ache.

"I'll do it."

I squeezed my eyes shut for a second. "Need help taking your bags out to the car?"

"No. I've just got the one."

Debora was as put together as ever in a khaki skirt and polo, but she looked tired, less perky than normal. Sometimes you don't know how wrong your life is until you imagine it from an outsider's point of view. Debora must have thought we were crazy. And we were, too.

"Debora?"

"Yeah?"

"It wasn't bad. Being your boyfriend."

"I was thinking that maybe if someday you decide—"

I kissed her. Her lips felt full and soft. My hand drifted to her face and I held her cheek lightly, my hand almost hovering. I parted her lips, just barely. She leaned into me once and then pulled back. It felt . . . good.

"Well, I'll see you at school." She stood and smoothed invisible wrinkles out of her khaki skirt, avoiding eye contact with me. I could be happy with Debora. We would be good for each other.

"I'm sorry for all of this." I thought about telling her that I'd kissed Alice, but it didn't seem like it would make a difference. It was probably wrong of me not to say anything, but I didn't want to hurt Debora any more than I already had.

"No," she said. "I think I wanted to fool myself into believing that you were ready for something that you're not."

"Yeah." I was an ass. I knew from the moment I'd asked Debora out that I wasn't over Alice. I was too selfish to even bother wondering how this might end.

"This isn't my story; this is all Alice. But you know where to find me. Be smart, Harvey."

Alice towered over me, eclipsing the sun, with her hands shoved deep into her pockets. "Hi."

"Hi."

She sat down on the edge of the lawn chair, exactly where Debora had been. After she left, I had drifted off to sleep beneath the early-morning sun. "What time is it?" I yawned.

"Eight thirty."

"Our parents still asleep?"

She nodded.

"What is it?" I asked.

"We need to talk, Harvey." Her voice was soft and so unlike her.

She pulled her knees to her chest, concentrating on a point past my shoulder. I turned, my eyes following her gaze to the shattered sliding glass door. "Harvey, there's something wrong with me."

She paused, and I waited. Whatever she had to say wasn't going to come out easy.

"I'm sorry for everything. I've used you and manipulated you, and I don't know how I'll ever fix it. And us, I've ruined us completely. But you—" She paused again. "You freak the shit out of me, Harvey. I don't get it— how you can feel like there are no consequences for living with your feelings on your sleeve. Because there are, you know. There are consequences so horrible, and I wish I could ignore them like you can—the feelings and their consequences. I wish it didn't matter to me." She stopped, pushing her fingers through her hair. "I don't know how you love me. I really don't."

"I wish I didn't." I almost took it back, until I remembered what she'd said to me yesterday on the beach.

Her lip trembled. "I know I can't fix us, but please let me try."

I wanted to reach for her. But I couldn't. I didn't want to be her pathetic Harvey anymore.

When I didn't respond, she took a deep breath. "I need you to know—" She stopped, twisting a piece of thread hanging from the bottom of her denim shorts. "I need you to know that I really care about you. You make me crazy. Angry and happy and terrified."

That was it. After everything—our childhood, the cancer, her list—that was all she could say. "You *care* for me?" My jaw twitched. "Alice, I—I care about our principal, and my boss, and the lady at the donut shop who gives me extra donut holes. But I love *you*," I spat. "And you know what that feels like? It's like a fucking cheese grater against my heart."

Her face scrunched up like she was about to cry. "I'm sorry." She let out a shaky sigh, but it wasn't enough to stop her tears. "I wish I could be better." Her voice shook. "I want you to have everything you deserve. But I can't give you that."

I leaned toward her, our faces only inches away. "Say it. That's all you have to do." I tried to hide the desperation in my voice. "Say you love me." I needed to hear her say it out loud.

She turned her head to the side, facing away from me, and knotted her fingers in her hair as her shoulders began to shake.

It wasn't supposed to end like this. Rubbing my hand up and down the back of my neck, I asked. "Why? Why can't you say that to me?"

She shook her head and bit down on her thumbnail.

She couldn't even give me a reason—a fistful of words that would explain to me how it could be that she didn't love me. It didn't matter, though. She wouldn't say it. I was done. Saying good-bye to her would hurt, but nothing could ever hurt worse than this.

"Alice," I said, forcing myself to look at her even if she wouldn't look at me. "All I ever wanted was to be proud of myself and to be with you, but I can't be both at the same time. And now we're too far gone. There's no going back from here. I won't do this anymore."

Silently, she cried, her whole body trembling, but I couldn't comfort her. Not anymore.

After a few minutes, she stood and walked to the doorway.

"Hey," I said, my voice barely working. "What did that mean yesterday?" I had to know, and I knew my mom would never give me the whole story. "About your mom and another guy?"

Her face stayed blank and unmoving as she said, "She's

been cheating on my dad. I saw her. Before I had cancer. Luke did too."

I opened my mouth.

"He told Celeste."

A puzzle of memories slipped into place. "Is your mom still, you know . . . ?"

She shrugged and walked inside, little pieces of glass that Bernie had missed with the broom in her wake.

Alice.

Now

It'd been about a week and a half since spring break and about two and a half since The Day I Died. I started calling it that in my head: The Day I Died. Our detention had been served, and now the only proof of my faux memorial was my memory of it. And it seemed to be there every time I closed my eyes. Candles, dying flowers, and tears. The tears that made me cringe with embarrassment. The tears that made me want to lash out and retaliate against Celeste and Luke.

I felt out of place in this room. Although they'd never made me uncomfortable in the past, the mirrored walls made me too aware of myself. I'd only turned on half the lights in the studio and was grateful for the minimal lighting. The black leotard I'd found in my closet was loose, so I'd taken a safety pin to the straps, making an X across my shoulder blades. Behind my ear was a small bald spot where my hair hadn't grown in yet.

The cool wood floors bled through my tights, a familiar relief against my skin. Inside the stereo, I'd found an unlabeled CD with a mix of popular warm-up songs. Starting out with some sit-ups seemed like a good idea. When I lifted my upper body, my abdomen whined in protest. I was so out of practice I swore I could hear my body creaking and groaning.

After a few labored repetitions, I sat upright and spread my legs so far apart I was almost in the splits. The muscles that stretched along the insides of my legs burned. I reached forward and laid my cheek flat on the cool floor in front of me—difficult, but still possible. Sweat began pooling at my hairline. I tried rolling through the splits and onto my stomach, but my hips felt like they were stuck in mud. I sat, frustrated, with my cheek still pressed against the floor. I inhaled a great big gulp of air and tried again. With little grace, I rolled through the splits and onto my stomach.

"Aw, is this the comeback part of your story?"

Celeste.

I'd barely seen her or Luke since returning from spring break. So much had happened since their little prank that I'd forgotten to be angry with them.

She stood in the doorway, light flooding in behind her silhouette, with her hands on her hips. "Don't stop on my account."

I didn't.

She shifted her weight, leaning up against the door frame.

"I guess you didn't hear," she said after a moment.

Still on my stomach, I studied myself in the mirror, panting, tired from a simple exercise.

"Luke and I broke up."

Took long enough. "Who did the breaking?"

A few seconds passed before she said, "He did, actually. Said he didn't want to start college with a girlfriend."

Or maybe he didn't want a girlfriend in general. "He probably would have cheated on you anyway. If he hadn't already."

"I guess you would know from experience." Each word felt like it was meant to sting, but only fell short one right after the other. She inspected her manicure and ran a fingertip along the edge of each of her nails. "You know," she said, her voice quiet, "I have some ideas for Luke. In case maybe you're interested."

I sat up, still watching her in the mirror. She was right. Together, we could destroy Luke. And she didn't even know about the picture of him stowed away in my room. But the idea of revenge no longer gave me the satisfaction it once had. In a way, part of me felt strangely empty, but it was a good kind of empty. Spring-cleaning empty. The kind that left room for better things.

I would never like Celeste, but I could see now that we were only the result of my own making. I didn't care anymore about who'd started what. I only cared that I was the one to say no more. I could make this second chance at life whatever I wanted it to be, and I didn't want to waste any more time on Luke, Celeste, or Mindi. Shaking my head, I said, "Thanks for the offer, but I'm out on all the games."

"Huh." She studied me for another long moment. "Surprising." Then she turned and walked away.

For me to have surprised someone—especially Celeste, who always expected the absolute worst of me—meant that I was doing *something* right.

I slid on my worn ballet flats and moved to the barre to start on the basics. I swooped down low, reaching to the floor, and then stood upright, my muscles beginning to warm with each movement. I concentrated on my breathing, counting through each motion.

"Shoulders back. Posture's all off."

Natalie walked up behind me and placed one hand on my back, the other on my stomach, and pressed in. Beneath her touch my entire body fell into place, my core aligning. "There."

I nodded.

She sat on the floor with the soles of her feet touching and her legs in a butterfly stretch. She pushed down on her knees and sat up alarmingly straight. Besides asking her for the studio space, we hadn't spoken since spring break. Natalie had never held anything against me—not even when I quit ballet—but I'd crossed a line, and I didn't know if she could just let it go this time.

"What prompted this?" she asked.

"Excuse me?" I asked, my feet in fourth position and my arm extended in front of me.

"Lift your arm a little, parallel with the center of your breastbone," she said pointedly. "Why are you here?"

"Dr. Meredith said I should be staying active." I'd had an appointment with him the Tuesday after spring break, and he said my body would adjust quicker if I was somehow more active. My dad nagged me for a few days before I called Natalie about some studio time.

"This studio space is available from seven thirty to nine

o'clock on Tuesdays and Thursdays." She stood from her spot on the floor in one graceful movement. "I'm closing up soon after nine. I'll give you a ride home then."

"Okay." It sounded more like a question.

She left, and I continued working through each position over and over again. The empty room left me nothing but my thoughts, and those always seemed to drift toward Harvey. I had walked out onto the deck of the beach house fully prepared to tell him that I loved him. But when the time came, the words stuck to the roof of my mouth like peanut butter. It was the last piece that I didn't know how to let go of. All I could think of was all the ways that love had failed. Standing in front of a mirror, in my room by myself, I could say it. I could say I loved Harvey. But when it was *to* him, the words sat trapped inside of me because we were in high school and we wouldn't last, and because nothing—not even my parents—ever seemed to last, and because when someone loved you, you had power over them, and because love made people do really dumb shit. And that was why I couldn't say it.

The few times I'd seen Harvey since spring break had been at school and he avoided me every time. I'd walked past him in the halls a few times, my hand lifting involuntarily, about to wave, before remembering he had no reason to wave back. Dennis and Debora were always there with him too. And of the three of them, Debora was the only one who ever acknowledged me with a wave or a nod, like we shared some kind of secret. And the weird thing was that we sort of did. She and Harvey had stopped holding hands. I didn't want to take pleasure in that, but I did. I so did.

Since both Harvey and Eric were noticeably absent from my life, I spent most of my time at home. My mom didn't really talk to me, only my dad. When we got home from our trip, I went straight to my room and only left it for food until I went back to school the next morning. Almost all communication had gone through my dad since the pan-meets-glass incident.

After my mom got home from work that first Monday night after spring break, she came into my room without knocking and said, "I'm angry. And I don't think we should talk while either one of us still feels this way, but your father and I worked out our issues after you were diagnosed. I just needed you to know. And that little fit you threw was way out of line." She stopped and took a deep breath, reining herself in. "As soon as you're well enough to get a part-time job, you'll be paying us back for that glass door. That's all I'm going to say for now."

Beyond a few yeses and noes, we hadn't spoken since then.

At the end of my studio time, I felt like cooked spaghetti—completely limp. It didn't hurt so much while I was moving, but the minute my body had time to catch up, my muscles were sorely displeased. As promised, Natalie drove me home.

"School's done in six weeks," she said as we pulled out of the parking lot.

"Yeah. Six weeks too long."

"Your mom said you'll be doing more treatments over the summer."

I nodded, twisting the strap of my dance bag in my hands.

"Maybe you'll want to work for me part-time when all that's over." Her voice was quiet, but not at all tentative.

"That would be good," I said. I'd always said that I'd rather not dance than have to teach. Especially in a small-town studio like Natalie's where most people only signed their kids up for the tutus and not the ballet, but being inside a studio had made me feel a little more like the me I wanted to be.

When we pulled into my driveway, she put the car in park and said, "When you're ready to go back on pointe, there's a rosin box in the far corner of that studio you were in tonight."

I nodded. "I remember." I loved rosin boxes. The way they smelled. The way the powder from the rosin crystals left a trail behind me, giving my toes traction on the slippery wood floor.

We said good night and she waited for my dad to answer the door before reversing out into the street.

Alice.

Now

I watched the clock as the minute hand fell on the two. *Four thirty-two.*

My mom would be home by five. She rarely used her home office except to store important papers. My dad had left for the grocery store forty-five minutes before, and I'd already been hunting through files for the past half hour. Nothing had pointed me in the right direction.

The silence between me and my mom was going on three weeks.

Since I'd sworn off the scheming and manipulating, life had been quiet and lonely. And not at all rewarding. So now I was scheming in a new way. Scheming for redemption. And this scheme required a great deal of snooping, which I'd been doing for the last week.

The front door creaked open. I whirled around and fell into my mom's chair, in front of her computer. My mom shuffled through the mail, with her phone cradled in the bend of her shoulder. "What?" She sighed. "No, we're going to have to file an appeal." She looked up and saw me there at her desk.

"Paper due tomorrow," I lied. "My laptop was moving slow."

She nodded. "I'll have your dad take a look." She turned and left me with the sound of her bedroom door opening and closing. I went upstairs to get ready for ballet.

Natalie was sick. She never got sick. Even her immune system knew better than to fail her.

Simone, the jazz teacher, had subbed all of her evening classes, and because Natalie was not here and it was a Thursday night, I had no ride home.

I called home and left a message on the voice mail. Now it was just a toss-up between who would pick me up. My bet was on Dad, seeing as my mom had relegated everything involving me to him. She was still pissed about the whole iron-skillet thing.

At two minutes to nine my mom's car pulled into the parking lot.

I sat down in the passenger seat and pulled the seat belt across my chest. It was completely quiet—no radio, just the low hum of the engine. She sat there with her arms crossed and her lips pressed together in a straight line.

I knew that eventually one of us would have to crack and break this silence, but I never expected it to be me. "Mom?"

She put the car in park and took her foot off the brake, then rolled down her window. "Your dad asked me to pick you up."

"Oh. Was he not home?"

"Oh, no. Your father was home."

More silence.

Her eyes seemed to be focused on the rain-slick pavement in front of us. "He said that we need to talk."

I wasn't surprised to learn that my dad had finally lost his patience. "So, what now?"

She shrugged.

Her indifference pushed me from annoyed to infuriated. "Fine, Mom. Let's pretend. Let's pretend that I didn't see you with some man and that this friction between us is nothing but a little mother-daughter tension. Is that what you want? If this remission is the real deal, then it'll only be one more year and then I'll be off at school or wherever. We can pretend for one year, right? And then you can leave him and everything will be broken, but at least we'll have been honest. Because that's what counts."

Then she did something I rarely saw my mother do. She cried. Laying her head against the steering wheel, her whole body curved into a hunch.

No matter how angry I was with my mother, I didn't know how to watch her cry. So I said what people always say when someone cries. "It's okay, Mom."

"It didn't last for long," she said through her tears. "He was an old law school professor. I told your dad about it right after you were diagnosed." My diagnosis. It would always be a landmark in our lives. There would always be before and after. "I wanted to be honest with you, Alice. But then you got sick. I couldn't do that to you. I couldn't tell you that truth and expect you to deal with my lies on top of every-thing else."

"He knew? This whole time Dad knew?"

She nodded.

Maybe I should have been mad, but I was relieved to know that my dad already knew and it wasn't because he had heard it from me. Still, that day had been this domino in my life, and she wanted to brush it aside because for her it had been over this whole time. Finished business. But I'd lived with this and carried it like my own secret. I wondered what life would have looked like if I'd stayed at school that day or if my mom had left five minutes earlier.

"Why?" I asked. "Why'd you do it?"

"Getting old is a bitch." She laughed a little. "Life starts happening, and you begin to realize that every decision in your life only eats away at the control you have over everything else until there's nothing left. You get married; decision made. That chapter of your life is closed. Kids, college, jobs. It's easy to let all those decisions take away the unpredictability and excitement even when they don't. Choosing to—" She paused. "Choosing to be with someone else gave me some of the control back." Her tears splattered down her face. "And then you got sick, and I realized life was going to do whatever the hell it wanted and the control we think we have is a facade." She paused again. "In the last year, life stopped being about what and started being about how. I'm proud of my choices—you, your dad, the law—and now I want to be proud of how I live those choices." She took a second to catch her breath. "I'm sorry. I am so sorry. I'm not going anywhere. I love your dad. And I love you," she said, wiping her face even though there were no more tears. "I want to work on us."

"I don't know how to talk about this," I said. And it was true. "But I don't think either of us is in the habit of talking about our feelings." Telling Harvey how I felt that morning hadn't been easy, but I did it. With my mom, this felt different. I didn't know how to tell her that I understood. That when it came to me making commitments, I felt cornered too.

"I'm going to make an effort to change that, Al."

What really bothered me about our argument at the beach house was that as soon as I had my mom's undivided attention, I ended up saying all the wrong things. Maybe this would be my opportunity to say the right ones. "Mom, I'm sorry too. I'm sorry for what happened at the beach house." I sucked in a breath. "And for everything before that. I've been so shitty to all you guys for a while now. I'm sorry." I didn't think I could live like this with my mom anymore. I couldn't see us changing; we were both so stubborn. But we had to try because living without each other sounded pretty miserable too.

We sat in the parking lot and talked for a long time. It wasn't easy at all. It was strained and uneven. But it was a start. A beginning.

When we got back home, my dad was waiting for us on the front porch. "All better?"

"We're on our way there," said my mom.

My dad turned to me and hugged me, really hugged

me. "I love you, Alice Elizabeth," he whispered. Over his shoulder, I saw my mom, her lips curved into a faint smile.

The sweetness of it all made my teeth hurt, but it was true.

Harvey.

Finals had wrapped last week. It was officially summer. I didn't make As or anything, but I'd passed eleventh grade, so I called it an academic success.

Miss P's yearly recital was in a week, and now that school was out, my mom asked me to come in and play for the classes whenever I had time so the students could practice with a live accompaniment. When I got off work at five, I drove straight to my mom's studio.

By the time I arrived, the intermediate class was almost through their warm-up. I had a few minutes so I waved to my mom, pointed to the bathroom, and jogged down the hallway.

All the other classrooms were dark except for a small echo of light coming from the last studio. Passing the bathroom door, I walked to the end of the hallway. A piece from *The Sleeping Beauty* played loud enough for me to hear when I stood close. It was one of my mom's favorite ballets.

Alice sat on the floor next to the rosin box in a black long-sleeve leotard with a low scooping back and light pink tights. Using white cloth tape, she taped her toes quickly, like the routine of it had come back to her without any trouble. My mom had told me about this. That Alice was dancing again. I tried to feel indifferent about that.

After sliding her feet into her shoes and tying her ribbons—Alice never did use any toe cushions—she stood and tapped the box of her shoe in the rosin box, dust flying up around her.

Without waiting for a break in the music, Alice began to dance, like she was trying to pick up where she'd left off. Every joint in her body all the way down to her fingers communicated back and forth, her movements falling into a rhythm. But this time when she danced, I didn't have that same feeling as when we were younger. That feeling that said she was too good for me and that I would never speak her language. I'd always *known* Alice, but in the last year and a half I'd seen every piece of her under a magnifying glass. Her flaws, her strengths, her vulnerabilities. She spun, spotting herself in the mirror, as she kicked her leg out and gained momentum with each turn. I loved her because I didn't know how to stop, but she wasn't on this pedestal anymore.

And then she fell, her legs slipping out from beneath her.

When I finished playing for my mom's class, I found Alice sitting on the floor of the lobby with her legs stretched out and piles of papers in front of her.

I turned my back to her and tried walking past her without being noticed.

"Hey." Her voice was soft, but I knew she was talking to me.

Only a few feet from the door, I turned. "Oh. Hi." It was one thing to see her, but to have to talk to her and pretend like all that I felt for her had disappeared wasn't something I was capable of.

She pulled all her papers into one big stack. "I'm waiting for your mom to finish so she can take me home."

I nodded, taking a step toward the door.

"Unless you can drop me off?"

It would have been easy to say yes, but I couldn't go back now. I shook my head. "I'm supposed to go to Dennis's," I lied.

"Oh, okay." Her lips curled into a sad smile. "Have a good night."

I walked out before she could say another word. I didn't know if my will could take it.

Harvey.

Now

Except for a few slips and falls, my mom's yearly recital was a success. I dropped the last box of props into the back of my car and let out a sigh. I'd had to wear a suit that was two years too small, and my ass hurt from spending my entire Sunday afternoon on a piano bench. Alice had been backstage the whole time, helping the younger classes get lined up while I was in the orchestra pit by myself.

Checking my pockets to make sure I had my keys, I reached up and slammed the hatchback door shut.

"This is for you."

I turned to find Alice standing in front of me, holding out a stack of folded-up pieces of paper wrapped in twine. She wore a black leotard with a little black dance skirt—the kind you could see through—and black tights.

When I didn't take them, she pressed the stack into my hand. "What are you doing tomorrow night?"

"Working," I said, weighing the papers. Each page looked to have been unevenly ripped out of a notebook. The only marking I could see was the number one written with pencil on the first paper.

"Call in sick. You know Dennis will cover for you if you ask him to."

I shook my head, my nostrils flaring. "You've got to be shitting me. I'm not doing this anymore, Al. I told you. This isn't happen—"

"Harvey," she said, reaching up and cupping my face in her hands like she'd done so many times before.

The feel of her skin against mine silenced me.

"I haven't given you any reason to, but trust me. Trust me this one last time and expect better of me than I deserve. Last time, I swear."

I opened my mouth. I felt myself slipping away and without anything to hold on to.

"Tomorrow," she said, "wait until late afternoon. Like, three. The pages are numbered. Read them in order and don't read the next one until you've completed the task before it."

Falling into this pattern—her telling me what, when, and how—felt sickeningly familiar. "Do you need me to pick you up?"

She shook her head. "No. This is for you to do alone."

Harvey.

Now

I almost tore apart the whole stack of papers the second I got home, but I stopped myself. I wouldn't let myself get excited, and if I didn't open the notes early, I could convince myself that this didn't matter to me. Sleep felt impossible and when it came it was short-lived. When I woke, the stack of papers taunted me.

By noon, I nearly gave in. I slid the first note out from the pile.

No. I couldn't do it. I'd waited this long. I could stand a few more hours.

Like Alice had told me to, I called in sick to work. I watched the clock and prayed for three p.m. When that didn't work, I watched a few hours of daytime television. Which was embarrassingly enjoyable.

Three o'clock finally came.

I unfolded the first paper, nearly ripping it in half.

Harvey,
Follow these directions to Alton. Once you reach your destination, unfold the next paper.
—Al

Directions without reasons. Of course.

Alton was about forty-five minutes north of us. I stopped for gas and drove. My mind was too busy for the radio, so I rolled the windows down and soaked in the early-summer heat. Maybe Alice would be meeting me in Alton. I couldn't figure out how she would get there without me to drive her.

My foot weighed a little heavier on the gas pedal, but I didn't care. I was too anxious.

When I arrived in Alton, I found it was much like Hughley. Small businesses, a few big chain stores on the outskirts of town, and mostly two-lane roads. I'd never been here, but knew that our teams played their teams all the time and that Bernie always said they had the best shopping. But, really, there was nothing special about Alton, so for Alice to have wanted me to come here made no sense.

I followed her handwritten directions to a small parking lot full of empty storefronts. At the end of the strip mall was a narrow little place called Oscar's. The windows were heavily tinted and there was no OPEN sign. Above the door were decals that spelled out SUITE 667. I checked Alice's directions, and cut across the parking lot, sliding into a spot right up front. My Geo was one of three cars.

After turning off the ignition, I opened the piece of paper labeled with the number two and held my breath.

Go inside.

Exhaling, I crumpled the piece of paper and threw it into the backseat. I shoved the rest of the notes in my pocket and went in, hoping there wouldn't be anyone checking IDs.

Inside, a haze of smoke hung to the ceiling, and it took me a moment for my eyes to adjust to the dim lighting. The only employee seemed to be an old lady behind the bar with a name tag that read BETH. Diamond-patterned hunter-green wallpaper covered the walls, peeling at the corners. The bar where Beth stood was at the back of the room. Lining the walls were high-back booths the same color as the wallpaper. Tables and chairs peppered what little floor was left.

Before deciding where to sit, I reached for the next note.

Welcome to Oscar's. Sit down at the bar and order a drink. Supposedly they have really good gin and tonics. TRUST ME.

I sat at the bar, in the stool farthest from Beth with her big red hair and white roots. My hands were sweating. I was going to get arrested. I was totally going to get arrested for underage drinking or, like, *attempting* to drink while underage.

Beth slid a coaster to me and strolled down the length of the bar.

Okay, so Beth had these nails. Not fake nails. *Real nails.* Long nails coated in chipped red nail polish. Everything about her smelled of smoke, like she was the source of the smoky haze. She was one of those ladies who could have been fifty-two or ninety-four and you'd never know. Her jeans were high-waisted and too tight and her boobs spilled out of her yellow V-neck shirt. Beth, with her boobs and her nails and her fake red hair, scared the shit out of me.

"What can I get ya, sweetcheeks?"

I twisted my hands together in my lap. "I, uh." I cleared my throat. "Gin and tonic."

She made this nasally noise like a buzzer going off. "Try again."

"Uh, I'll have a Sprite."

"One Sprite!" she called to no one in particular.

I opened the next note.

SUCKER!

Rolling my eyes, I reached for the fourth note.

I got you good. It should be almost four. Sit tight and enjoy your nonalcoholic beverage. Open the next note when the music starts.

When the music starts? Where was Alice? The anxiety twisting in my chest had faded and now I just wanted to see her. Beth brought me my drink and left me alone after that. I was surprised when she didn't ask any questions about me or what I was doing here. But this struck me as the type of place where people didn't ask questions.

The customers were mostly men, although there were

a few women. Every one of them was over the age of forty and looked like they hadn't slept in years. A lady with a cat sweatshirt on and purple pants. A man with a fedora and a tracksuit. A balding man with a holey T-shirt and jeans with a cigarette box imprint in his back pocket, but no cigarettes. The only person who seemed out of place was an old man wearing tan slacks, a cream polo shirt, and a maroon sweater vest. He carried a well-used leather portfolio and wore an old baseball cap with a mesh back, but took it off when he came inside to reveal a thinning head of white hair. Age spots covered his face, and on his feet were spotless white orthopedic sneakers. This guy was someone's grandfather who'd probably gotten lost on the way to the pharmacy.

When he walked past the bar, Beth called to him, "Evenin', Porter. Usual?"

He nodded and gave her a faraway smile. Him I felt bad for most of all. Because, of everyone in this bar, he seemed to be the one who had lost the most.

I checked the time on my phone. Four thirty-five. I shoved my hand in my pocket and pulled out the rest of the notes. Frustrated and sure that Alice had sent me on a fool's errand, I held number five in my hand ready to open. This was bullshit. I didn't know what kind of kick Alice was getting out of this, but it made no sense. She was probably off with some guy while I was sitting here like a total jackass. I stood up to leave and slid my wallet out from my back pocket.

Then the music began. I sat down. I didn't know the

song, but it sounded familiar. It wasn't typical ballet music, of course, but it felt like I should've known it. My eyes followed every note to the sad piano in the corner of the room. It wasn't a grand piano, just a plain, old, light-wood piano. I never paid much attention to piano makes. I only played whatever was put in front of me. If I really thought about it, though, I always felt most comfortable with the piano at my mom's studio—a 1973 Baldwin Concert Grand.

Behind the piano was the old man with the sweater vest. I listened as each note fit together seamlessly, like he'd played this song a thousand times. If I closed my eyes, I could feel the touch of ivory beneath my fingers.

Porter's eyes crinkled a little as he focused in on Beth. She mouthed something for him to lip-read. *Out of gin.* He leaned forward and she moved her lips once more. Porter nodded and returned his attention to the keys.

My lips twitched, thinking about that day before freshman year, when Alice had mouthed to me to meet her in the front yard.

The note. Shit, I almost forgot about the notes.

Harvey, when I found out I was sick, I decided I wanted to give you something. A thing that would outlive me and all your memories of us. But I didn't get it done in time. I wasted my time with things and people that didn't matter. I'm sorry. I don't think I'll ever stop being sorry. Since I got a second chance at this whole life thing, I wanted to do something that should have been at the top of my list and finally give you the puzzle piece you deserve. Listen

*to a few songs. On the phone, Beth said Porter was really
good, but I don't know, she sounded kind of crazy too.
Whatever. Order another drink.*

If this was some kind of fantasy, this would be the
moment when Alice sauntered in and explained herself,
but not before kissing me. That didn't happen though.
I took her advice, ordered another Sprite, and listened to a
few more songs.

I was about to open the next note when Porter stood up
from the piano for a break. Stretching his back and popping
his knuckles, he walked over to the bar. "Beth," he said,
"you're slacking on me. I can't play for free without some
gin to wash it down."

"Oh, hush," she said. "You make your tips."

He chuckled. "If I was doing this for tips, Oscar's
wouldn't be my venue of choice."

They both laughed, like the whole thing was some kind
of inside joke.

I took a big gulp of soda and looked around, trying to
make it look like I hadn't been staring.

"I'll have what he's having," said Porter, and pointed at me.

"Oh, I don't think you want any of that," she said.

Coughing, I said, "It's soda."

"What?" asked Porter, motioning to the hearing aid in
his ear.

"Soda," I said. "Just soda. No kick."

"Ah," he said, and took the seat next to me. "Then the

boy will have whatever I'm having and I'm having a Jack and Coke."

Beth raised her eyebrows. "No can do. I already refused him once."

Porter leaned forward on the bar and smiled.

"Oh, fine, but if anything happens to him, that's on you."

Porter nodded once.

Beth made two Jack and Cokes and set a coaster down in front of me.

I reached for the glass.

"Just the one," she said.

Porter laughed a great big belly laugh and turned back for the piano.

He played another song and I drank my drink too fast, my vision going a little soft on the edges.

After a few more songs I turned back to the bar and opened the next note.

I wanted to find your dad. Isn't that so stupid of me that I thought I could even do that? Well, Porter's not your dad. He's too old. And that would be kind of gross. Open the next note when you're ready.

Blood rushed to my head like I'd been hanging upside down. My dad? Alice wanted to find my dad? I couldn't figure out how she would know to do that for me. She was right, though. Porter was way too old to be my dad. Maybe he'd just known him or something. I squeezed my eyes shut and ran my hands down my face.

I asked Beth for a glass of water. I downed the whole thing, cooling my liquor-warmed chest, and drank two more glasses. Porter finished another song. What did he have to do with this?

I started digging. I looked everywhere. Finally, I found all your emergency contact information from when we were kids in my mom's closet in an old accordion folder. I knew she would have something in case anything happened to your mom. Take a bathroom break or get another drink or something, because the next note—the last note—is the big one.

For once, I ignored Alice and went for the last note. Whatever she'd found out was folded up inside that little piece of paper.

I set the note back on the counter.

I didn't want to know.

I picked the note back up.

I had to know.

The clock on my phone said *6:15*. With the note in my hand, I took one last deep breath.

Harvey, this is my gift to you. And who knows, maybe it's not anything you want. But before you let your eyes skip forward, read this: my weird-shaped-doesn't-fit-into-a-box-sometimes-angry heart loves you, and whatever comes next, I want to be there. On whatever terms you decide. It's okay if you don't want to know what I have

to say. It's okay. But if you want to know, skip to the
bottom of the page.

I fished a piece of ice out of the bottom of my glass and chewed on it. She loved me. And it didn't feel like a condolence prize. This time it was a promise, and the only thing that would make it better was to hear her say it out loud. I touched my fingers to the page, letting my skin absorb each letter.

Okay.
William Joseph Porter is your grandfather. I don't know who or where your dad is, but Porter was the only family I could find. But he's YOUR family. It doesn't have to be now or this week or whatever, but he comes here every Monday, Wednesday, and Friday around 4 if you decide you want to know him.

I stood up and shoved the note into my pocket. I had a *grandfather.* A living grandfather. A laugh slipped out of my lips, and I slapped a hand over my mouth. I took a step toward the piano, then doubled back. I didn't know what to say to him or what I expected us to be. And my mom. I had to talk to my mom. I couldn't go behind her back on this. All of these possibilities and it had been Alice who had given them to me.

I wasn't ready to know Porter. I didn't know when I would be. But thanks to Alice, I knew where to find him. I needed to talk to someone, and there was one person who I wanted that to be.

★ ★ ★

If possible, the ride back felt even longer than the ride to Alton. The summer sun fell in the sky, flirting with the horizon.

My grandfather. I had a grandfather.

I didn't know what to do, but I knew where to go.

Alice's house added about ten minutes to the drive.

I sat at the last light before her house, waiting forever for it to turn green. I swear to God, the lights skipped right over my street. Rolling out to the middle of the intersection, I looked both ways and floored it.

When I got to her house, I parked and turned off the car all in one motion. I fumbled with the seat belt, remembering the day I came here after she'd found out she was in remission. She'd watched me through a window, like a ghost, as her dad told me *It's gone.*

I shaded my eyes with my hand and ran up the driveway, and this time she was there, waiting for me. Alice sat on the steps of the porch with her knees pulled into her chest.

I stopped less than a foot away. I couldn't find words, but it didn't matter. They wouldn't have done me any good. The sun dipped down behind her house, bringing her into focus.

Alice stood, closing the gap between us, and whispered in my ear.

Acknowledgments

I'm going to give thanks, I swear. But first, I want to tell you—whoever you are—that I barely graduated high school and completely bombed the SAT. I am telling you this because I want you to know that the path of dreams is flawed, and it is the beauty of flaws that makes you.

As promised, I would like to offer my deepest gratitude to:

Alessandra Balzer, my editor, for her incredible guidance in shaping these words into a book and for seeing potential in such raw form. And to everyone at Balzer + Bray, but especially to Sara Sargent for every little bit of help and for all the wonderful mail.

My agent and friend, Molly Jaffa, whose faith in my work has changed the course of my life. I will never be done saying thank you. And to the entire team at Folio, your enthusiasm and tireless effort pushes me forward every day. (Hi, Molly's mom!)

Annemieke Beemster Leverenz and Alison Klapthor, for this exquisite cover.

Jessica Taylor, who has read every wretched word I've ever written and whose talent amazes me.

Andrea Walkup and Valerie Cole, for all their encouragement and feedback when I was at my ripest and needed it most.

Kristin Trevino, who has always read first and cheered loudest. Ashly Ferguson and Allison Jenkins, whose kind support has been constant.

Corey Whaley, for listening to and challenging me. I want to see all the movies with you. Even the bad ones. (You're my friend, kind of.)

Jenny Martin (my betrothed), who is strong where I am weak.

Natalie C Parker, who is my surest compass.

My mom, dad, and sister, who are my foundation and who have encouraged me in this and every other thing.

Thank you to all my family, blood and otherwise: the Murphys, Komaromis, Buzwells, Werthmans, Pearces, (both of the) Trevinos, Pierces, and Richardsons.

My friends, who were there before, but especially to: Ashley Meredith (my dearest friend always), John Stickney, Hayley Harris, Veronica Trevino, Asher Richardson, Matt Meredith, and Nathan McCoy.

This community—every inch of it—has taken me by surprise. Each writer, librarian, blogger, reader, and publishing professional. Thank you all. And a special dose of love to the Lone Star community. Y'all are my home.

Many thanks to the following friends for their encouragement and love: Adam Silvera, the incredible women of the Fourteenery, Sarah Combs, Siobhan Vivian, Jennifer Echols, Margot Wood, Jeramey Kraatz, Stacy Vandever

Wells, Jen Bigheart, Kari Olson (for sharing her medical knowledge), Caron Ervin, Britney Cossey, and my Texas Wesleyan family, specifically: Dr. Salih, Professor Payne, Joie Arn, and Ann Smith.

Tiffanie DeBartolo, thank you for writing *God-Shaped Hole*.

My greatest thanks to all who have been affected by cancer and have been brave enough to share their stories. Every single blog post, interview, and eulogy that I've read has come to shape this book.

Ian, my buster, thank you. I'll eat you up—I love you so.

Turn the page for a sneak peek at
Julie Murphy's new novel, DUMPLIN'.

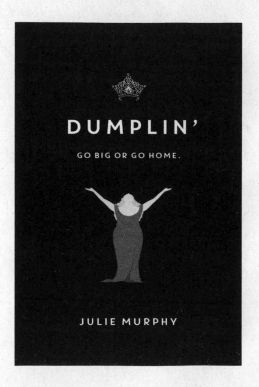

ONE

All the best things in my life have started with a Dolly Parton song. Including my friendship with Ellen Dryver.

The song that sealed the deal was "Dumb Blonde" from her 1967 debut album, *Hello, I'm Dolly*. During the summer before first grade, my aunt Lucy bonded with Mrs. Dryver over their mutual devotion to Dolly. While they sipped sweet tea in the dining room, Ellen and I would sit on the couch watching cartoons, unsure what to make of each other. But then one afternoon that song came on over Mrs. Dryver's stereo. Ellen tapped her foot as I hummed along, and before Dolly had even hit the chorus, we were spinning in circles and singing at the top of our lungs. Thankfully, our love for each other and Dolly ended up running deeper than one song.

I wait for Ellen in front of her boyfriend's Jeep as the sun pushes my feet further into the hot blacktop of the school parking lot. Trying not to cringe, I watch as she skips through the exit, weaving in and out of after-school traffic.

El is everything I am not. Tall, blond, and with this

impossible goofy yet sexy paradox going on that only seems to exist in romantic comedies. She's always been at home in her own skin.

I can't see Tim, her boyfriend, but I have no doubt that he's a few steps behind her with his nose in his cell phone as he catches up on all the games he's missed during school.

The first thing I ever noticed about Tim was that he was at least three inches shorter than El, but she never gave a shit. When I mentioned their vertical differential, she smiled, the blush in her cheeks spreading to her neck, and said, "Yeah, it's kinda cute, isn't it?"

El skids to a stop in front of me, panting. "You're working tonight, right?"

I clear my throat. "Yeah."

"It's never too late to find a summer job working at the mall, Will." She leans against the Jeep, and nudges me with her shoulder. "With me."

I shake my head. "I like it at Harpy's."

A huge truck on lifts speeds down the lane in front of us toward the exit.

"Tim!" yells Ellen.

He stops in his tracks and waves at us as the truck brushes right past him, only inches from flattening him into roadkill.

"I swear to God!" says El, only loud enough for me to hear.

I think they were made for each other.

"Thanks for the heads-up," he calls.

We could be in the midst of an alien invasion and Tim would be like, "Cool."

After he's made it across the parking lot, he drops his phone into his back pocket and kisses her. It's not some gross open-mouth kiss, but more like a hello-I-missed-you-you're-as-pretty-as-you-were-on-our-first-date kiss.

A slow sigh slips from me. If I could avert my eyes from all the kissing people ever, I'm positive that my life would be at least 2 percent more fulfilling.

It's not that I'm jealous of Ellen and Tim or that Tim steals Ellen away from me or even that I want Tim for myself. But I want what they have. I want a person to kiss hello.

I squint past them to the track surrounding the football field. "What are all those girls doing out there?" Trotting around the track are a handful of girls in pink shorts and matching tank tops.

"Pageant boot camp," says Ellen. "It lasts all summer. One of the girls from work is doing it."

I don't even try not to roll my eyes. Clover City isn't known for much. Every few years our football team is decent enough for play-offs and every once in a while someone even makes it out of here and does the kind of thing worth recognizing. But the one thing that puts our little town on the map is that we're home of the oldest beauty pageant in Texas. The Miss Teen Blue Bonnet Pageant started back in the 1930s and has only gotten bigger and more ridiculous with every passing year. I should know since my mom has led the planning committee for the last fifteen years.

Ellen slides Tim's keys from the front pocket of his shorts before pulling me in for a side hug. "Have a good day at work. Don't let the grease splash you or whatever." She goes to unlock the driver's-side door and calls over to Tim on the other side, "Tim, tell Will to have a good day."

He pops his head up for a brief moment and I see that smile Ellen loves so much. "Will." Tim may have his face in his phone most the time, but when he does actually talk—well, it's the kind of thing that makes a girl like El stick around. "I hope you have a good day." He bows at the waist.

El rolls her eyes, settles in behind the wheel, and pops a fresh piece of gum in her mouth.

I wave good-bye and am almost halfway to my car when the two speed past me as Ellen yells good-bye once more over Dolly Parton's "Why'd You Come in Here Lookin' Like That" blasting through the speakers.

As I'm digging through my bag, looking for my keys, I notice Millie Michalchuk waddling down the sidewalk and through the parking lot.

I see it before it even happens. Leaning against her parents' minivan is Patrick Thomas, who is maybe the biggest douche of all time. He has this super ability to give someone a nickname and make it stick. Sometimes they're cool nicknames, but more often they're things like *Haaaaaaaa-nah*, pronounced like a neighing horse because the girl's mouth looks like it's full of . . . well, horse teeth. Clever, I know.

Millie is that girl, the one I am ashamed to admit that I've spent my whole life looking at and thinking, *Things could be worse.* I'm fat, but Millie's the type of fat that requires elastic waist pants because they don't make pants with buttons and zippers in her size. Her eyes are too close together and her nose pinches up at the end. She wears shirts with puppies and kittens and not in an ironic way.

Patrick blocks the driver's-side door, him and his rowdy group of friends already oinking like pigs. Millie started driving a few weeks ago, and the way she zips around in that minivan, you'd think it was a Camaro.

She's about to turn the corner and find all these jerks piled up around her van, when I yell, "Millie! Over here!"

Pulling down on the straps of her backpack, she changes her course of direction and heads straight for me with her smile pushing her rosy cheeks so high they almost touch the tops of her eyelids. "Hiya, Will!"

I smile. "Hey." I hadn't actually thought about what I might say to her once she was here, standing in front of me. "Congratulations on getting your license," I say.

"Oh, thanks." She smiles again. "That's really sweet of you."

I watch Patrick Thomas from over her shoulder as he pushes his finger to his nose to make it look like a pig's snout.

I listen as Millie tells me all about changing her mom's radio presets and pumping gas for the first time. Patrick zeroes in on me. He's the kind of guy you hope never notices you, but there's really no use in me trying to be invisible to him. There's no hiding an elephant.

Millie talks for a few minutes before Patrick and his friends give up and walk off. She waves her hands around, motioning at the van behind her. "I mean, they don't teach you how to pump gas in driver's ed and they really—"

"Hey," I tell her. "I'm so sorry, but I'm going to be late for work."

She nods.

"But congratulations again."

I watch as she walks to her car. She adjusts all of her mirrors before reversing out of her parking space in the middle of the near-empty lot.

I park behind Harpy's Burgers & Dogs, cut across the drive-thru, and ring the freight doorbell. When no one answers, I ring again. The Texas sun pounds down on the crown of my head.

I wait as a creepy-looking man wearing a fishing hat and a dirty undershirt rolls through the drive-thru and recites his painfully specific order down to the exact number of pickles he'd like on his burger. The voice on the speaker gives him his total. The man eyes me, tilting down his orange-tinted sunglasses, and says, "Hey there, sweetcheeks."

I whirl around, holding my dress tight around my thighs and punch the doorbell four times. My stomach is squirming with discomfort.

I don't *have to* wear a dress to work. There's a pants option, too. But the elastic waist on the polyester pants wasn't quite elastic enough to fit over my hips. I say the pants are to blame. I don't like to think of my hips as a nuisance, but more of an asset. I mean, if this were, like, 1642, my wide birthing hips would be worth many cows or something.

The door cracks open and all I hear is Bo's voice. "I heard you the first three times."

My bones tingle. I don't see him until he opens the door a little wider to let me in. Natural light grazes his face. New stubble peppers his chin and cheeks. A sign of freedom. Bo's school—his fancy Catholic school with its strict dress code—let out earlier this week.

The car behind me at the drive-thru backfires, and I rush inside. My eyes take a second to adjust to the dim light. "Sorry I'm late, Bo," I say. Bo. The syllable bounces around in my chest and I like it. I like the finality of a name so short. It's the type of name that says, *Yes, I'm sure.*

A heat burns inside of me as it rises all the way up through my cheeks. I run my fingers along the line of my jaw as my feet sink into the concrete like quicksand.

The Truth: I've had this hideous crush on Bo since the first time we met. His unstyled brown hair swirls into a perfect mess at the top of his head. And he looks ridiculous in his red and white uniform. Like a bear in a tutu. Polyester sleeves strain over his arms, and I think maybe his biceps and my hips have a lot in common. Except the ability to bench-press. A thin silver chain peeks out from the collar of his undershirt and his lips are red with artificial dye, thanks to his endless supply of red suckers.

7

He stretches an arm out toward me, like he might hug me.

I drag in a deep breath.

And then exhale as he stretches past me to flip the lock on the delivery door. "Ron's out sick, so it's just me, you, Marcus, and Lydia. I guess she got stuck working a double today, so ya know, heads up."

"Thanks. School's out for you, I guess?"

"Yep. No more classes," he says.

"I like that you say classes and not school. It's like you're in college and only go to class a couple times a day in between sleeping on couches or"—I catch myself—"I'm gonna go put my stuff up."

He presses his lips together, holding them in an almost smile. "Sure."

I split off into the break room and stuff my purse in my locker.

It's not like I've ever been extra eloquent or anything, but what comes out of my mouth in front of Bo Larson doesn't even qualify as verbal diarrhea. It's more like the verbal runs, which is gross.

The first time we met, when he was still a new hire, I held my hand out and introduced myself. "Willowdean," I said. "Cashier, Dolly Parton enthusiast, and resident fat girl." I waited for his response, but he said nothing. "I mean, I am other things, too. But—"

"Bo." His voice was dry, but his lips curled into a smile. "My name's Bo." He took my hand and a flash of memories I'd never made jolted through my head. Us holding hands in a movie. Or walking down the street. Or in a car.

Then he let go.

That night when I replayed our introductions over and over in my head, I realized that he didn't flinch when I called myself fat.

And I liked that.

The word *fat* makes people uncomfortable. But when you see me, the first thing you notice is my body. And my body is fat. It's like how I notice some girls have big boobs or shiny hair or knobby knees. Those things are okay to say. But the word *fat*, the one that best describes me, makes lips frown and cheeks lose their color.

But that's me. I'm fat. It's not a cuss word. It's not an insult. At least it's not when I say it. So I always figure why not get it out of the way?